BREAKING BOUNDARIES

Teresa J. Reasor

Breaking Boundaries

Contact Information: teresareasor@msn.com

Cover Art by Tracy Stewart
Edited by Faith Freewoman

Teresa J. Reasor
PO Box 124
Corbin, KY 40702

Publishing History: First Edition 2015

ISBN-13: 978-1-940047-06-5
ISBN-10: 1-940047-06-4
Print Edition

DEDICATION

For all the competition and good-natured (for the most part) rivalry between the branches of military service, when the chips or down, or men's lives are at stake, Marine, Army, Air Force, and Navy personnel band together to support one another.

This is for them.

And to the many programs that support our wounded warriors, a heartfelt *thank you.*

TABLE OF CONTENTS

PROLOGUE

Afghanistan

THE SQUEAK AND rattle of the vehicle's chassis as they hit another pothole in the dirt-clotted road acted as a minor irritant compared to the hundred and twenty-degree heat inside. Corporal Cal Crowes, the driver, twisted the wheel to the right in an attempt to miss a hole big enough to bury a wheel and grunted in satisfaction when he straddled the pit.

"Fuck me!" Private Jasper Holland exclaimed. "Ollie Gunter deserves a fast trip to hell with a short poker."

Cal started to laugh at the comment and decided he didn't have the extra energy. The rolling oven they were traveling in, better known as a Humvee, slowly baked the moisture from his body like a sauna. The two privates trapped inside with him weren't fairing any better. The only one in their foursome getting any relief was Private first class Neil Carter, who was on the roof, riding in the gun shield.

The dusty road stretched ahead as they worked their way toward the northern mountains.

Jasper continued his grumbling, "Why couldn't he fix our damn air conditioning before this patrol? He had twelve fucking hours."

Though Cal had similar feelings about the mechanic, he need-

1

ed to pull rank and head off the bitchfest. "Griping about it doesn't change anything, Jazz. I'll deal with it as soon as we return to base."

"After eight hours in this fucking kiln, we'll be so dehydrated none of us will feel like taking on that shit brick," Private Mitchell Ellison said in a deadpan voice.

Cal tracked movement as they passed a cart being pulled by a young boy heading in the opposite direction. His jaw tightened. Sweat rolled down his sides beneath his shirt, but it did nothing to cool the sensation of being baked inside his body armor. The window next to him beckoned with the promise of some small relief, but the likelihood of having a grenade tossed into the vehicle or a lucky shot from a sniper, they didn't dare risk opening the window even a crack. "I'll deal with Ollie."

In the rearview mirror Cal caught Ellison's quick movement as he tossed a look behind them at the small convoy of vehicles following theirs. "I bet if we were SEALs Gunter would have fixed our vehicle," Ellison grumbled. "Those guys can get things done when they need it."

The Special Ops eight-man team, riding four to a vehicle in the convoy behind them, had looked well-armed and focused. Flash Carney, the team sniper, and Greenback Shaker had accompanied Cal's Marine squad on more than one patrol to clear buildings suspected of harboring insurgents. They were the only two Cal knew.

Those guys probably fixed their own damn vehicle issues when they had to. Maybe if his squad was able to do the same they wouldn't be steaming inside the armored Humvee with nothing but the faintest of breezes from above. The situation fed his anger, and there was an edge to his voice when he said, "I put in the order. Gunter didn't do the work, and I had no control over that. I'll have control over what happens when we get back, though. Now stow this shit and keep your eyes o—."

A shallow depression, suspicious and threatening, led up to the next pothole. Cal stomped on the brakes and swung the wheel sharply to the left to avoid it.

Sound roared through the vehicle, pounding his eardrums, his brain. The front of the Humvee heaved upward. The steering wheel clipped his chin and snapped his head back. His vision went white, then gray fading to black.

He woke to a harsh ringing in his ears and the smell of smoke. He threw out a searching hand. Who was beside him? Jazz? He gripped the mesh on the man's body armor.

Smoke billowed from the front of the vehicle. They'd been hit. They had to get out of the Humvee. He forced his eyes to stay open. Blood gushed from Jazz's mouth to run down his chin onto his BDUs. The car's engine sat in his lap, pinning him to the seat.

God. "Ja—." Cal's jaw hung numb and useless. His mouth was full of marbles. He used his tongue to work them out. Bits of his own broken teeth hung off his chin.

The door beside him was jerked open. The rattle of machine gun fire sounded muffled as it burst from a few yards to the right. He reached for his sidearm and drew it. He had to protect himself, his men.

He focused in relief on the camouflage uniform directly in front of him. Thick red hair stuck out from under a boonie hat. Dark green eyes, stony with purpose, scanned his face. A rust-colored beard covered the lower half of the guy's face. He reached in and dragged Cal free.

Cal's head pounded like his skull was being beaten to dust by a jackhammer. The world tilted and the sky, burning bright blue, blistered his eyes, and he closed them as pain knifed through his brain.

"My men," he tried to say and it ended up sounding like "M-mn."

"Where's that chopper?"

The words were still muffled, but he could hear them.

"Fifteen minutes out."

Bullets rattled and pinged off the smoldering remains of the Humvee's chassis. Red threw himself over Cal to cover him, his body curved to hold his weight off of him as much as possible. An explosion sounded from close by and the shots ceased. Red pried

3

Cal's sidearm out of his desperate grip. "You won't need this. You're covered."

"Bowie." Red flipped a length of stretchy rubber and a tongue depressor at the soldier beside him. "Get a tourniquet on that leg."

Cal barely felt the needle he jabbed into the bend of his arm. Red hooked up an IV.

Whose leg? Was it one of the guys'? When Bowie knelt at his side, Cal realized it was his leg they were talking about. Where were his men? Jazz? Neil? Ellison?

Cal tried to turn his head in the direction of the vehicle but the red-headed guy gripped his face. He nearly screamed as the pain shot to the top of his head.

"Don't move your head. You have a broken jaw and maybe a broken neck."

His body felt numb, but he could still move his arms and legs. "Mn."

Red stopped what he was doing to lean over him. "Focus on getting through the next minute, Corporal, then the next five. Keep breathing. You're going to make it."

By not saying anything about the others, he was saying they were dead. Ellison with his dry wit. Jazz with his soft Tennessee twang who tried his patience. Neil, the quiet boy from Oklahoma. They were gone.

The pain of it crushed his lungs and brought every injury he had roaring to life. He couldn't grit his teeth against the pain because his jaw didn't work. Both his legs burned with agony. He choked out a groan while Red cut away his pants and applied pressure dressings around different parts of his legs.

When they lifted him onto a stretcher he yelped, every muscle in his body spasming against the pain. His vision went white, then gray again.

"Stay with me, Corporal." The SEAL medic wrapped an ace bandage around the stretcher and his forehead, ensuring his head remained stationary. "I can't give you any morphine because you have a head injury. They'll assess you at the hospital and give you something for the pain then. You just have to hold on a little while longer."

Five minutes seemed like an hour when the numbness receded and his injuries began to scream. His whole face ached and his eyes watered. His legs were on fire. Red crunched a chemical ice pack and put it to his face. The coolness eased the pain a tiny bit. He gripped the man's wrist in gratitude.

A Black Hawk chopper came in low, spun around and landed in the desert a hundred feet from their location. The SEALs lifted the stretcher and carried him over.

The rotor blades whirled above, pounding him with air and jerking at his clothing. Three black body bags next to him rustled. He was flying back with *his* men, the men he'd begun the patrol with. Their faces, their voices, rushed back to him in a kaleidoscope of anguish. He'd swerved the Humvee too late to avoid the IED. The world had gone to hell. Tears streamed down his temples.

The medic on board the chopper reached across him and grabbed the IV bag from Red.

Flash, the SEAL sniper he'd worked with, leaned over him and gave his arm a squeeze. "You're going to make it, Cal. Believe it."

With the dead bodies of his men lying beside him, it was hard to believe in anything.

CHAPTER 1

San Diego, California

K ATHLEEN O'CONNOR BRACED her feet against the wind's intermittent tug. From the twentieth floor of the new high-rise, she looked out across the open expanse of blue sky, dark gray-blue ocean, and the plethora of multi-level buildings around her. The extraordinary view would certainly be a draw once the structure was finished. At four hundred fifty feet high, it wasn't the tallest building in San Diego, but it came close. She'd seen the plans and the scale model the team designed, and knew the exterior design for the complex would make it one of the most striking profiles in the city.

With her shiny new master's degree from MIT mounted in her new, square office space, she dreamed of seeing some of her own designs constructed. But first she had to take the baby steps of settling into a team and pushing for her ideas to be accepted. She knew a lot about working as a team. Her professors had insisted on it in college.

She'd believed she had teamwork down pat in her personal life as well, until Lee demonstrated to her that nothing she had to offer was enough.

She quashed the thought and its inevitable accompanying bitterness. She wasn't going to allow him to steal her joy. She was moving on with her life. She was going to be the most successful architect on the planet, have her own firm, and build structures that would be included in art history texts for generations to come.

Gee, was she setting the bar too high? The beginnings of a smile quirked the corners of her mouth.

"What do you think?" Paul Warren, project manager for Wiley Design and Construction, asked from behind her.

"It's going to be amazing once it's done."

"The crown jewel of the company."

"Thus far," she added.

Warren laughed. In his early thirties, he had already begun to gray at the temples. With his olive skin and hazel eyes, he was an attractive man. Luckily he did nothing for her.

Her life was going to be about her work from now on. She wasn't interested in an office romance. She doubted he was either. The vibes she was picking up were probably a knee-jerk reaction to the new kid on the block. She knew what she looked like in spite of her concealing dark blue jeans and gray MIT sweatshirt. Her hips were wide, though her stomach was flat. The sweatshirt strained against her breasts even though her waist was small. Her figure wasn't fashionable, but it was what her Irish-American genes had decreed. She was through trying to fight it. Besides, fat lot of good the struggle to change her curves had done back in Boston.

She held the yellow hard hat in place. She hadn't yet gotten the hang of adjusting the straps so it would fit properly. Her dark hair whipped across her face, blinding her. She removed the helmet, tucked it between her knees, gripped the long strands, and secured them with the rubber band she kept around her wrist specifically for that purpose.

The wind was picking up. It pushed against her with such force she swayed, her sweatshirt only partially holding off the biting chill.

"We always encourage a little competition in the company."

Good. "With eight brothers, I come from a family of competitors."

"Wow. Eight?"

She smiled at the shock in his expression. "My mom was determined to have a girl." Bet that scared him off.

She grinned when he abruptly changed the topic and said, "We have a few more sites to hit before we go back to the office."

"I'm eager to see them."

A shout came from down the platform. She turned in that direction. From twenty feet away a man lay on the concrete belly-down, his upper body hanging over the edge. "Someone's in trouble." She broke into a jog across the concrete slab and knelt on the concrete next to the prone figure. Jerking the aggravating hard hat off, she dropped it on the floor before peering over the edge.

Held only by the single-handed grip the man beside her had on one of his arms, a man dangled below. The man's eyes were wide with fear, his face pale, making the dark olive of his skin look gray. "Jesus, God, Cal, don't let me fall," he screamed.

The man called Cal grimaced and Kathleen could tell he was pushing against the concrete, probably to keep from being dragged over the edge by the other man's weight.

They needed a counterbalance.

"Grab my legs," Kathleen yelled at Warren while she flattened her body on the concrete. Warren gripped the waistband of her jeans and she ignored the uncomfortable familiarity of male fingers against her skin. She stretched both arms down. "Grab onto me," Kathleen yelled against the wind. Just beyond the man's shoulder, and twenty stories below, the ground rushed up to meet her as vertigo hit her and she experienced the falling sensation that went with it. Her stomach twisted. She closed her eyes against the sickening reaction and reached down blindly to grip the man's flailing arm.

His fingers found her wrist and bit into it while she gripped whatever she could with her other hand. Warren's shout was followed by the sound of running feet. The blare of an emergency buzzer attacked her ears. She flinched.

More hands gripped her legs and heaved back. Her fellow

rescuer's hard hat toppled off and went sailing over the edge as he was tugged back, too. The man being rescued was dragged onto the platform belly first. His face was stiff, and his eyes glittered wide with shock.

For several moments all of them just lay facedown on the cold concrete, their chests heaving. Someone killed the alarm, though for seconds it continued to reverberate in Kathleen's ears. Her wrist ached as the man's grip eased and he released her. She sat up.

Cal sat up, rolled his shoulders, and extended and retracted his arms a few times, as though easing overworked muscles. "You okay, Julio?" He gripped the man's shoulder.

Julio sat up, his face wet with tears, and he wiped them away with the torn sleeve of his shirt. "Thanks to you, man. You saved my life. I saw the ground rising up to meet me and you—you just jerked me out of the air."

He embraced his savior and pounded him on the back several times. Then he turned to Kathleen to grip her hand, and she noticed could barely feel the ache where his fingers had dug into her wrist. It was blessedly numb.

"Señorita." A stream of Spanish followed that she only understood because of his expression and the fervent kiss he pressed on the back of her hand. She offered him a shaky smile. "I'm glad you're all right."

More men pushed forward to see what was happening. Surrounded by steel toe boots and long legs, Kathleen was hit by a wave of claustrophobia and moved to rise. Numerous hands gripped her arms and helped set her on her feet. Someone handed over her hard hat. Others patted her shoulders, her back. Two men rested hands on Julio's shoulders in support.

"What the hell happened here?" Warren barked.

Julio raised his head. "The wind caught me, and I lost my footing and fell. Cal grabbed my arm, and I almost dragged him over the side, too. He saved my life." Julio's eyes flashed to her. "They both saved my life."

"It was a team effort, Julio," Cal said, his voice just audible above the force of the wind. He tilted his head up, and his startling blue eyes settled on her face. He gave her a nod of acknowledgement.

"It was you holding onto me, Bro, until help arrived."

Warren's expression morphed into stony, and Kathleen studied the project manager. Why would he be angry? Accidents happened. It was a miracle both men hadn't been killed.

"Are you injured, Julio?" he asked.

"No, just shook up." His dark skin remained pasty, and he was shaking visibly.

She was, too, now the danger had passed. She gripped the hard hat for something to focus on, and braced her feet as her legs went from stable to cooked spaghetti. Maybe she shouldn't have stood up so soon.

Tom Hill, the project foreman she'd met earlier, threaded his way through the crowd. "What happened?"

Warren quickly explained the situation.

Tom squatted on the balls of his feet next to Julio, and they spoke for a couple of minutes. "Hector," Tom looked up at one of the men standing close by. "Give him a ride home."

Tom straightened. "Crowes."

Kathleen stepped back, surprised by Cal's size as he climbed to his feet. Lying flat on the concrete, he'd appeared lean and long. Standing to his full height, he was transformed into powerful as he worked his wide shoulders and muscular arms, as though shaking off the strain. How long had he sustained the guy's weight before she arrived to relieve him of some of it? Even a few minutes would have been beyond difficult.

With his high cheekbones and intense eyes, he projected the air of a warrior. Kathleen recognized the stance, so similar to that of her father, a Boston policeman. And not just her father. Her brother Michael had followed in his footsteps. Her brother Mark served as a first sergeant in the Marines, Jason a sergeant major in the Army, and Zach a Navy SEAL. They all seemed to place their feet exactly the same way, shift their weight, and scan their environment as though facing off against a threat, even when they were at ease. This man had to be ex-military.

Tom extended a hand to Crowes and they shook briefly. "I'm glad you were around. Good work. Do you need to take the rest of the day?"

"No, sir. I'm ready to go back to work, but the wind is getting dangerous up here. I'd suggest we run more safety netting."

"Maybe we should put Cal in charge of that," Warren said.

Kathleen frowned and glanced at Warren. Why put a man in charge of running safety netting who'd just spent minutes—that had probably seemed like hours—hanging over the edge of a platform twenty stories above the ground? It seemed...insensitive and cruel.

She caught Hill's quick frown.

Cal studied Warren for several moments, his gaze narrowed. He nodded. "Roger that." He offered Julio a hand up. The slighter built man seemed calmer, and he'd regained some of his color. Cal bent and said something to him, then strode across the platform to the large service elevator they were using to transport materials to each floor. The crowd started breaking up.

Kathleen followed Warren and Tom Hill to the personnel lift. Julio and the other worker, Hector, got on with them for the trip to ground level. The solid metal cage blocked most of the stiff breeze, but the wire openings on each side allowed it to filter through, a good thing; otherwise the lift would have been airless and claustrophobic. As it was, Kathleen braced a hand on the metal support behind her and held on while it trundled down the vertical track to ground level.

The wind ceased as they reached the bottom of the structure. Hector pulled up the metal panel door, folding it back, and then parted the wire doors, and he and Julio departed.

Cal and the two other men who'd ridden down in the service elevators were already lifting the rolls of security net. Warren stopped, blocking Kathleen from exiting the lift. "Hey Crowes, did you find your hard hat?"

"One of the crew did." He held it up. A large crack marred one side. He shoved it on despite the damage and jogged to Julio to hand him his.

"You need to come in and write up an accident report, Cal," Tom said.

"Will do."

"Julio, you'll need to fill yours out before you go home."

"Yes, sir."

The three men moved off toward the foreman's trailer.

When Cal ran back to the other two men working with him, Kathleen frowned. She saw a limp she hadn't noticed before.

He and the two other crew members began to load the bright orange security netting onto the freight elevator.

"He'll wear that damn cracked hard hat to remind everyone what a hero he is," Warren murmured next to her.

Kathleen's breath caught. Quick anger followed, but she couldn't afford to speak her mind. She'd been an employee less than twenty-four hours. Being paired with Warren for the afternoon was giving her a real insight into the man, however. He'd first tried to put the move on her, and now he was being an ass. And not once had he asked her if she was okay.

"I need to have a word with Tom before we leave. Go sit in the truck while I talk to him."

"All right." Gladly. She needed a few moments away from him to restore her patience. Plus, her wrist was beginning to throb a little.

She stepped down out of the elevator and paused to allow a large concrete truck to roll by before jogging across the tracks it left.

Midway across the yard, she cut away from her path and strode purposefully toward the three men loading the safety net. "Hey, Crowes."

He straightened at her approach. Kathleen extended her hard hat. "It's too big for me since I haven't adjusted it yet, and you're more in need of it than I am."

Crowes' piercing gaze settled on her. She had thought his eyes were blue, but they were a deep blue-green, almost teal.

With his wide cheekbones and strong jaw projecting such intense masculinity, the woman in her cringed, regretting her barely-there makeup, her hastily confined hair, and how a few strands hung, stringy and tangled, on either side of her cheeks. The professional in her was determined he would accept the hard hat.

"That's all right. I can make do until I get a new one from the foreman's trailer." His slow, husky drawl sent a delicious chill through her.

"You still have several hours' work to complete, and I only have a couple of fifteen minute stops. Take the hat."

Crowes reached for her hard hat, a frown working across his brow. He switched the cracked hard hat for the new one and extended the damaged one to her. "Thanks."

She accepted it. "I noticed you were limping just a little. If you've hurt your leg, you need to get checked out at the hospital so the company can cover the injury."

His features went still. "It's an old injury; there's nothing can be done about it."

"Oh." Embarrassed, she cleared her throat. "I'm sorry. Take care." She nodded and walked away from him, and with every step was suddenly hyper-aware of how wide her butt looked in jeans. She cringed inwardly as she proceeded slowly to the truck.

"Miss."

Kathleen turned to find he'd followed her.

"What's your name?" he asked.

"Kathleen, Kathleen O'Connor. I'm one of the architects who works for Wiley Design." She extended her hand automatically and barely controlled the flinch, as her wrist twinged, more from the movement than from his firm grip.

"Cal Crowes. Nice to meet you. That was a hell of a thing you did up there. I appreciated the help." His unusual teal eyes swept her face. "You're new to the job?"

"Yes, I just started today."

"Congratulations. Hell of a first day."

Kathleen smiled. "Yeah, something to tell my family about. You didn't do too badly yourself."

"Why did you give me your hard hat?" he asked.

Because Paul Warren was being an asshole and something in his attitude toward Cal struck her as unfair. "Because yours is damaged, and it's a safety violation for you to wear it."

He glanced back at the foreman's trailer and seemed about to say something else, then shook his head. "I appreciate it."

"I'm sorry Mr. Warren suggested that you set up the safety netting."

"It's all right. Heights don't bother me." His smile was brief, but changed his intensity to amusement.

"I think they'd bother me if I'd just stared down twenty stories and held on to a coworker for what seemed like an hour."

He dropped his gaze to his feet and shifted his weight, as though the reference embarrassed him. "Not an hour, but it seemed a while for us both." He shrugged. "You got to get back on the horse sometime, and it might as well be now."

His attitude about the whole ordeal and his modesty despite rescuing his coworker made her admire him even more.

The wind buffeted them, kicking up the dry dirt. Cal shifted, blocking the stiff breeze and the dust, but not before a loose strands of dark hair whisked across her face. She reached up to remove them, but his finger was already there, looping them behind her ear.

Kathleen's breath caught and her stomach went into a free fall. They both froze. Cal continued to gaze at her for several seconds, his fingertips resting against her skin. When he finally dropped his hand, it broke the spell.

How could such an innocuous gesture seem so intimate? And how could she feel like her bones were melting from just a look?

She glimpsed movement when Warren opened the door to the foreman's trailer. He paused in the doorway, momentarily distracted as Tom Hill joined him there. She didn't want to cause Cal Crowes any more trouble, and she guessed there would be more if Warren caught him talking to her.

"Mr. Warren is coming back." Kathleen tilted her head to look up to the top floor. "Be careful up there."

"Roger that." He touched the narrow peak of the hard hat and strode away.

Warren cast a look in Cal's direction as he walked across the construction site yard. "What was Crowes doing?" he demanded.

"Nothing. I gave him my hard hat, and he thanked me. That's all."

Warren scowled. "Why would you do that?"

She shrugged. "He has several hours work ahead of him. It would have been a safety issue for him to continue wearing a cracked helmet."

He nodded to the damaged helmet she held in one hand. "But now you'll be wearing it."

"Only for a short time. And I won't be working on the sites. My brothers bought me a bright red one for a graduation gift. I'll wear that one from now on." They got into the truck and Kathleen reached for her seat belt.

Warren remained silent.

"If you don't want me on the other sites, I'll stay in the truck while you go up."

"That won't be necessary."

He sounded pissy. Which suited her just fine; she was getting a little pissed off herself. And disappointed. The excitement she'd felt about being invited to view the current construction sites had been wrenched away by Warren's attitude, and his dislike of Cal Crowes. What the hell was going on between the two men?

Warren focused on her. "Are you okay?"

"Yeah. I'm fine." She'd rather eat dirt than admit her wrist was throbbing to the beat of her heart. She pulled her sweatshirt sleeve down over it.

"What you did up there was admirable, but from now on, no matter what happens, let the crew take care of it. They deal with emergency situations—not all the time, luckily they're rare—but when it's needed."

"Crowes couldn't sustain Julio's weight without help. He needed a counterbalance to keep from being dragged over the edge. We were there, and the other men weren't."

Warren nodded. "Don't let what he did make him into some

kind of hero. Crowes has a prosthetic leg below the knee on the right side. He's a liability to the company and poses a danger to his coworkers on the site."

Shock held her still for a second then two. From what she'd seen, he was a productive worker, and had saved both Julio and Wiley Design's bacon. Anger brought heat to her face. "That liability just saved you from a lawsuit, Mr. Warren."

Warren's face reddened. "If he makes a mistake or has an accident, and it's caused by his disability, the company will be liable."

Kathleen struggled to keep her voice even and dispassionate. "If you fire him because of his disability, or show any form of prejudice against him because of it, you'll have every equal rights group out there on your ass, and it will come down on Wiley Construction like a ton of bricks. That may prove more of a liability than having a man with a prosthetic working for the company. I'd tread very carefully."

Warren glanced in her direction. "I didn't know you had a law degree to go along with your master's." There was a hint of sarcasm in his tone.

Kathleen breathed through the rage threatening to engulf her. "Employment regulations and rights are part of the curriculum. It's just good business. If your foreman hired him, he trusts Crowes can do the job. I'd stay away from it."

Warren remained silent, but his taut jaw and compressed lips gave her pause. If she'd said too much, it could come back on her as well as Cal Crowes. Oh, well, it was too late now.

CHAPTER 2

KATHLEEN MARCHED INTO the office she shared with three other architects—Hillary, Ed, and Dave. It was a relief to escape the truck and Paul Warren. If ever he invited her anywhere again, her answer would be a resounding *no*.

The office closed around her, quiet and creative. She loved the space. Each architect had a quadrant of the room. Large banks of tinted windows let in soft exterior light. Each of the other workers had personalized their space with books and pictures of family and the projects they'd worked on. She couldn't wait to do the same.

She already had pictures of her family on the counter that ran along one wall. She could put up pictures of some of the projects she'd done during her undergraduate and graduate programs. She'd worked with an architectural firm during summers and during her semester of co-op to complete some of the requirements for her licensing.

Above the desks hung a row of cubbies for storing work materials, books, and other things. Hers were empty, but they wouldn't be for long.

She settled into her computer chair and rested a plastic bag full of ice cubes on her wrist. It was a little swollen and bruised, but she could rotate it without much pain. She was certain it wasn't really injured.

"You got some sun today," Hillary Bryant, the other female

architect in the office, said from behind her.

Kathleen swiveled to look over her shoulder. The woman was tall, but rail-thin with a cap of light brown hair and brown eyes. "I think it was more wind than sun."

Hillary nodded. "It looks good on you."

Kathleen smiled. "Thanks." The woman had been welcoming thus far. Kathleen hoped for a good working relationship.

"How was the tour?"

"Eventful. One of the workers was blown off the tower project. One of his coworkers grabbed him just in time."

"Wow." Hillary gripped the only other chair in her section and sat down her long legs going on forever. "Tell me about it."

"It was on the twentieth floor. The wind had gotten pretty fierce, and they hadn't put up the safety netting yet." She shivered at the reminder of the twenty-story drop that had seemed to reach for her from over Julio's shoulder, and the vertigo following it.

"We've been very lucky. I've worked here nearly six years and I can only remember two accidents." She eyed Kathleen's wrist. "What happened?"

"I got too close to the action and bruised my wrist. It's nothing." She changed the subject. "From what I saw today, safety is stressed at all the sites. More than at some of the others I've been on."

"And how did you get along with Paul?"

"Okay." That was safer than saying they'd had an argument and she thought he was an A-1 asshole.

Hillary's brows rose. "You told him no when he asked you out?"

"Well, no. He didn't ask." *And I wouldn't have gone out with him anyway.* Now she was thinking back over their discussion, she hoped she hadn't burned any professional bridges by arguing with him. And if she had—Her stomach began to ache. "Is it standard practice for women to go out with him when they're first hired here?"

Hillary gave her a friendly grimace. "It usually happens." She leaned forward in her chair. "What happened?"

Kathleen grimaced. "We agreed to disagree on something...non-dating-related."

Hillary's lips twitched. "And you won the argument?"

"Let's just say my points were more persuasive than his. But I don't think I changed his mind." Kathleen swiveled her desk chair around to face Hillary a little more.

"Are you going to tell me what you argued about?"

"I had hoped not to stir the office pot until I've at least gotten to settle in a little. It isn't my style to make waves."

Hillary's brows rose and a look of quick interest lit her face. She held up a finger. "Hold that thought for a moment, and maybe by the time I'm finished, you'll decide to trust me with whatever it is."

She rose and went first to Dave Barker, the oldest of the architects in the pod, then Edward Reynolds. When she returned, she held up forty dollars. She offered a twenty to Kathleen.

"What's it for?"

"I had a bet going with those two that you'd turn Paul down. I thought you'd be too smart to fall for his special brand of charm."

Kathleen laughed. "So If I had agreed to go out with him...?"

"I'd have been forty dollars down. I'm splitting my winnings with you." Her smile widened with mischief.

Kathleen shook her head. "Keep the twenty and buy me a beer one day after work."

"Deal. Are you going to tell me what put you off of Paul?"

Kathleen sighed. "He was an insensitive ass to one of the workers."

"Men rarely realize when they're being insensitive."

Kathleen felt her anger rising again. "He realized." She described the accident, leaving her part of it out. "Crowes was the man whose head and shoulders were hanging off the platform. His workers dragged him back onto the platform, and he pulled the other man up to safety. I don't know how long he'd been holding onto him, but you could tell they were both exhausted and shaken up. Then Mr. Warren suggested Crowes needed to be the one to put up the safety netting."

The playfulness died from Hillary's expression.

"In the struggle, Crowes lost his hard hat, and it was damaged. Warren made the remark that Crowes would wear the thing to remind the rest of the crew what a hero he was. So I waited until Warren went into the foreman's trailer, and I approached Crowes and gave him my hard hat. When Warren came back to the truck and found out what I'd done he got angry. He said the man was a liability on the site because he was an amputee."

"An amputee?"

"His lower right leg. The foreman hired him, and Warren wants him gone." As her anger rose again, Kathleen pressed her hands to her cheeks hoping to cool them. "We got into an argument about disability rights and what a PR nightmare it would be if he fired Crowes without cause. Especially since Crowes had just saved the company from a potential lawsuit."

"And I guess that went over like a fart in a space suit."

Hillary's attempt to lighten the conversation did trigger a smile. "I guess you could say that."

Hillary laid a hand on her arm. "Wow, a really big first day for you, huh?"

Kathleen felt the anger drain out of her, leaving behind a disheartened tiredness. "Yeah. I hope I haven't made an enemy."

"I doubt it. Paul will be his normal charming self tomorrow, and it will be water under the bridge. But I wouldn't repeat what you've just told me to anyone else. You're part of the creative team, and that means you're expected to guard Wiley Construction's back."

"I thought that's what I was doing." She didn't plan to tell anyone else. Except maybe her brother Zach. Zach was a vault. She'd avoid Warren for as long as possible and hope things died down.

Hillary rose. "It's five o'clock. How 'bout that beer?"

Kathleen sighed and attempted to release the negativity and worry with it. "I'd love one." But now she had one more concern. Had she confided in the wrong person?

CAL LAID THE hard hat on his dresser, shucked his safety vest, and hung it on his bedroom doorknob. Catching a whiff of his own sour sweat, he worked the buttons of his sweat-stained blue work shirt and tugged it free, balling the garment up and shooting it like a basketball into the overflowing hamper to one side of the closet. He needed to do laundry. Later, after a meal.

He slouched on the end of the bed, pulled off his heavy work boots and socks, then paused to study his prosthetic foot for wear or damage. After an eight-hour shift, he needed a break from the device. His pulled down his jeans so he could reach the pressure valve on the side of the socket. He pushed it in and air entered the form cupping his stump. It broke the vacuum holding it in place, and he pulled his stump free. His jeans soon joined the overflowing work clothes in the hamper, and he sighed.

Next he removed his sock and liner to allow the limb to breathe. He'd have to wash his liner and leave it to dry after his shower, one of the daily chores he attended to faithfully. By doing it, he made certain he didn't develop any kind of skin infection.

He'd grown used to seeing the barren end of his leg, and the scar where the skin and tissue had been stitched over the end of the bone. It was another thing to bare it to someone else. Any girl he was drawn to, before he ever asked her out, he worried whether she'd be able to handle the sight of his lower leg and foot being—gone.

The military psychologist he saw on occasion said he made his amputation more difficult to accept by acting as though it was something to hide. But the guy didn't realize how gut-wrenching it was to see the revulsion on a woman's face when she saw it for the first time. His fiancée Stacy hadn't stuck around for long after the unveiling at the hospital. And he'd been grateful. He had enough on his plate to deal with at the time, without having to shore up a reluctant girlfriend whose first instinct was to bail when shit hit the fan.

The thought sent his mind straight to Kathleen O'Connor.

She hadn't bailed. She'd gotten right down on the platform and offered Julio a hand. Would a woman like her flinch from a little thing like a missing limb and some scars?

She was new to her job, but still upper management, or as good as. She would be out of reach even if he had the inclination to call and ask her out. There were steel-girded lines of demarcation between manual laborers and upper management. It was just an accepted thing. But the fact that she had helped save Julio's life and attempted to run interference for him with asshole Warren said something about her character.

And what the fuck was up with Warren? Every time the asshole was around, Cal felt like he had a bull's-eye painted on his back. It didn't take a mental giant to figure out that the guy wanted rid of him. He'd made light of being asked to put up the safety netting, but he'd been well aware of the head game Warren was playing when he ordered him to do it. There was something calculating and cruel about the bastard.

Cal lay back on the bed and threw his arm over his eyes. Not surprisingly, his shoulder protested, and he rubbed at the joint. Julio weighed more than he looked. Cal wouldn't allow himself to dwell on how close a call it had been. It was over. The whole thing had ended well. Julio was still alive and kicking.

His thoughts cycled back to Kathleen. Even though being looked upon as a hero embarrassed him, he hadn't minded that it had impressed Kathleen O'Connor. He'd been pretty impressed by her, too.

She kept her professional distance, but he'd noticed how soft color touched her cheeks when he looked directly at her. Everything about her was lush. Her lips, her breasts, her hips. With her thick dark brown hair and flawless skin, even in jeans and a sweatshirt she'd reminded him of an old time movie star. Ava Gardner maybe. Except she had green eyes. Not light green but true green.

Would she be open to going out with a construction worker?

A worker missing part of a leg?

Did he want to take a chance?

Probably not.

Cal sat up. His crutches stood propped against the wall close to the bed. He maneuvered around the mattress until they were within reach and levered himself to his feet. He'd take a shower, eat a meal, wash his liner. And there was always the laundry. Routine kept him moving forward.

His cell phone rang and relief relaxed the taut muscles of his back and shoulders. Saved from self-pity by the bell. He swung forward on his crutches and reached for it as it rang again. Julio's voice on the other end of the phone ratcheted up his tension again.

"Come over for dinner Thursday night, man. We're celebrating."

"What are you celebrating?" Cal asked.

"Life, man. Jessica just told me she's—"

Cal heard a feminine voice say something.

"*We're* having another baby. It's a good day, man."

"Yeah. It is." Whatever it was kismet, karma, luck, or a miracle, he was doubly glad he'd reached for Julio in time. "Congratulations, Julio. And yeah, I'd be glad to come. On one condition."

"What's that?"

"We don't talk about what happened today."

"Done. I don't want to either." His voice had the weighted certainty to it Cal recognized. "Jessica wants to thank you, though."

"Put her on the phone now, and we'll get it behind us."

Julio chuckled.

"Thank you for saving my husband's life, Cal." Her voice cracked when she reached the word husband.

"You're welcome. I wasn't alone in the effort. And Julio would do the same for me." The men who worked the job looked out for each other, much like his Marine Corps unit in Afghanistan. "Congratulations on the baby."

"Thank you." She cleared her throat. "Bring a date. There will be plenty of food."

"I'll see what I can do. Do I need to bring anything?" He had a short repertoire of edible dishes.

"No. Just bring yourself and a date. It will keep the crowd of women in Julio's family from hitting on you."

He stifled a bark of laughter. "I'll do my best."

"And the woman who helped save Julio's life, do you know her name?"

"Yes, her name is Kathleen O'Connor. She's an architect and works in the head office."

"Do you think you could get in touch with her for me and invite her to the barbecue?"

"I can call the head office and speak to her."

"I'd like for her to come so I can thank her as well."

"I'll see what I can do." It had been months since he'd attempted to ask anyone out. What would it hurt to try?

After a few more words with Julio, he hung up. If he hadn't been in that spot, at that exact moment, he wouldn't have been able to save Julio. His wife would be a widow, his children fatherless. Was that why he'd been spared in Afghanistan?

It was as good a reason as any.

CHAPTER 3

ZACH'S ALARM WOKE her at three-fifteen, and Kathleen rolled out of bed to start breakfast. She didn't have to do it, but part of rooming with her brother was about doing things for him more often than the one time a year when she normally had the opportunity.

For all the no-nonsense, Navy SEAL, tough-guy persona he projected, he loved to be fussed over. Until now she hadn't had a chance to cosset him because he'd been training off and on ever since she first arrived.

Making him breakfast was just a small way to show him how much she appreciated and loved him. She didn't know how many guys were coming to pick him up, but she fried two pounds of bacon. If there was any left, she'd make a sandwich for lunch. Next she scrambled a dozen eggs and made eight slices of oven toast.

When Zach came into the kitchen, his hair still wet from his shower and curling around his ears and neck, he sniffed the air like a bird dog. He hadn't bothered to shave, and his beard looked like rust against his skin. "What are you doing awake and up, Kathleen?"

"Feeding you and whoever's coming by to pick you up. They say breakfast is the most important meal of the day."

"They do say that." He grabbed a piece of bacon off the plate and bit it in half just as his phone went off. He left the kitchen to go into the living room and answer it. "Yeah. Kathleen cooked."

Five seconds later a quick knock sounded at the door. Since Zach was filling a plate, Kathleen went to answer it.

"Hey, sweetheart," Bowie greeted her and buffed her cheek with a kiss. With his smooth caramel skin and beautiful dimples, he was easily one of the handsomest men she'd ever met. He came home with Zach one Christmas after they earned their trident and had made himself as much a part of the family as the rest of her brothers. He did the scenting thing just like her brother. "Smells good in here."

Bowie pointed a thumb toward the door, clearing the way for the man behind him. "This is Bullet."

Kathleen studied the young African-American man. He had close-cropped hair and stood at least six two. With his wide shoulders and narrow waist, he looked like a sprinter and in as good shape as the rest of Zach's team. She found his smile engaging. "You don't have a pointy head at all," Kathleen commented.

Bullet grinned and offered her a hand. "Seaman Jeff Sizemore." He introduced himself. "And you don't look a thing like your brother."

Kathleen shook his hand. "Good thing, huh?"

"I heard that," Zach said from the kitchen.

"Go ahead and help yourself. There's hot coffee and orange juice."

"Thanks."

Kathleen left them to it and reclined on the couch to wait for them to finish so she could clean up. After they ate and left, she might be able to get in two more hours of sleep before she had to go to work.

"Your sister's beautiful and she can cook," Sizemore enthused.

"Don't get any ideas, Bullet," Zach mumbled a warning.

"Because I'm black."

"What the fuck does that have to do with anything? Because

you're male."

"Oh, is she a lesbian?"

A chair scraped across the floor.

"You okay, Bowie?" Bullet asked.

"Shit. No, I just snorted hot coffee out my nose.

Kathleen clapped a hand over her mouth to keep from laughing.

"No, she's not a lesbian. A fellow SEAL doesn't put the move on another SEAL's sister."

"Gee, I guess someone should have told Hawk before he married Zoe."

"Brett was in a coma and unable to make the rule clear. I'm wide awake and I'm watching you," There was a bear growl warning in Zach's voice that had Kathleen shaking her head. The teammates were constantly razzing each other. Constantly competing.

Zach's tone grew morose and genuinely angry. "All joking aside, she just broke her engagement to an unfaithful, hound-dogging cocksucker. She's not even close to being over that whole experience yet. So unless it's love at first sight and you're ready to proclaim your undying faithfulness and devotion right now..."

"Understood." Bullet's tone was much more subdued.

Kathleen tiptoed down the hall to her bedroom and closed the door.

Twenty minutes later, when Zach eased the door open, she'd regained her composure and thought about pretending she was asleep, but opened her eyes when she heard him place something on her nightstand.

"I'm okay, Zach. You don't have to worry about me. It hardly hurts at all anymore."

He knelt by her bed and smoothed back her hair. The light from the hall glowed from behind him, making it difficult for her to read his expression. "We both know different, honey." When he kissed her forehead he brought with him the smell of bacon and coffee. "It does get better. You never forget the hurt, but it dulls and you move on." He rose to his feet. "We're not all faithless assholes."

"I know." Or did she? Her whole belief system had been shaken, as much from the loss of her best friend as her fiancé.

"Thanks for feeding us."

"You're welcome. Tell Bowie I've decided to hold out for him. In another ten years and he'll have sown enough wild oats to be ready to settle down. He's already a member of the family, and we can make it official then."

"God forbid." He shook his head. "Love you, Thorn."

"You, too. Be careful."

"Always."

They both knew different. But there was no way she could control that any more than she could the past.

She reached for the object Zach laid on her nightstand. It was a small paper rose fashioned from a piece of copy paper. Zach had made them for her off and on during times of joy and sorrow. It was her brother's special way of showing he cared. The gesture brought quick tears to her eyes, but also a smile. He was more sensitive than he'd ever admit.

For some reason that thought brought Cal Crowes to mind. The way he'd played down what he did on the site reminded her of her brothers. She drifted back to sleep cupping the rose in her hand and thinking about her five-minute encounter with him after he'd saved Julio's life.

FOREMAN TOM HILL held a mechanical pencil and ran it back and forth between his fingers. "I don't know why Paul Warren has this burr up his ass about you, but you could make my life and yours easier if you keep a low profile around him."

Just when he thought the whole thing had died down, a news report pushed the issue front and center again. Cal focused on breathing through his anger, his face heated with effort. Fuck Paul Warren. He was an asshole. "I didn't save Julio to get attention. It isn't my fault someone released a video of the accident to the news stations. I didn't even know about it until I got here this morning, and those reporters were already here trying to get an interview."

"You didn't give them one, did you?" Tom asked.

"No! Like I said before, I *don't want* the added attention."

Tom tossed the pencil onto the stack of paperwork before him. "Dammit." He reached for the cup of coffee at his elbow, took a swig, then grimaced.

"All I want is to be able to work just like every other man on this shift. What the hell do you want me to do? And why exactly is it my fault the guy has an attitude about amputees?" Cal asked.

"It isn't your fault. But he's gunning for you. And I'm giving you a heads-up and telling you to be careful around him. If he tries to push you, don't lose your temper or do anything stupid."

"I won't. I've dealt with people like him before."

Tom's brows rose, his craggy jaw taut. "What do you mean?"

"Some people have the attitude that if you've lost a limb and can draw a disability check, why are you taking the job someone with two good legs can do?"

"That's—" Tom seemed at a loss.

Why was it he had to fight for the right to be independent and make a living? "Warren believes if something happens to me on-site, I'm going to sue the company. But even if I was a worker with two normal legs, that would still be a possibility. Julio's two good legs didn't keep him from going over the side. And it wouldn't have stopped his wife from filing a claim against Wiley because the safety netting wasn't up."

"I'm not sure that's what his problem is, Cal. I haven't been able to pinpoint exactly why he's so determined to get you off the site. All I know is every time he comes by here and sees you, he gets angry."

"Then that's his problem, not mine. I've never met the guy before. And I've never done anything to him."

Tom waved a hand as though in surrender. "I didn't call you in here to argue with you over this. I called you in just to ask you to avoid him if you can. You see him coming, take a break and walk away. I don't want any reason for him to contrive an issue again. And try to avoid those damn reporters out there, too. The head office is about to shit concrete over the video. We didn't have the safety netting up, and they're scared shitless Julio's going to file a lawsuit."

"Julio won't sue. That would jeopardize his job prospects if the company had to pay. What kind of issue did Warren start?"

"Nothing I can't handle."

"I've worked construction big and small since I was sixteen, Tom. You know I can do the job. My leg is not an issue."

"I know it's not. I've got your back, Cal."

Then why the hell had he called him in here? Why wasn't he going to the head office with this bullshit? If he lost his job over this guy—He wasn't going to go there until it happened. Waste of time to worry about something he couldn't control. But he was going to be watching his every step and making certain Warren had no grounds to give him trouble.

Cal drew a deep breath and tried to wrestle back the rage. He would not be made a victim over some guy's prejudice. He left the trailer before his temper was tried any further.

He looked toward the front entrance of the site, past the turnstile security box positioned for workers to come into the site. The news vans parked there all morning were finally gone. He breathed a sigh of relief.

He spotted Hector sitting on his truck, eating. Retrieving lunch from his own vehicle, Cal hiked himself up on the hood of Hector's beat-up Ford and leaned back against the windshield beside him.

"Everything okay?" Hector asked.

"Yeah. Now the news vans are gone." There was no reason to start a bitchfest with Hector. There was nothing he or the others could do about Warren.

"They're at Julio's house. He said he was sort of tricked into answering some questions."

"Shit! I hope he left me out of it." Cal studied his ham and cheese sandwich without appetite. He tilted his head back to study the misalignment of the steel beam the ironworkers were working into place topside.

There were some days you were constantly trying to fit a square peg into a round hole. The workers above him seemed to be experts at that. And they were daredevils. They had to be to do what they did. Out of all the different jobs on a site, theirs was definitely the most dangerous. Though heights didn't bother him, he'd never had any desire to do that particular job.

As he watched, two workers monkeyed up the parallel beams high in the air. The crane lifted a fifteen-foot section toward them. The men worked in tandem to slide the ends into place between the two goalpost-like supports. Once positioned, they hammered in high-strength bolts to secure it. One man slid out to uncouple the beam, and the crane lowered the rigging to the deck below and then raised the next steel section.

Finishing his sandwich, Hector lay back like he was sunning in a lounge chair and sipped his soup from a large thermos cup. "It gives me the willies to watch them, man. Seeing Julio dangling over the side of the platform damn near made me blow chunks."

"Me too. The only reason I didn't was I thought he'd be pissed when he had to pick them out of his hair." Cal was growing expert at deflecting talk about the accident. It was getting old fast. He wished everyone would just forget about it.

Hector threw back his head and guffawed. "That would have been a sight. So who you bringing to dinner tonight at Julio's?"

He'd vacillated back and forth between the urge to call Kathleen and dread of calling. Telling her Jessica and Julio wanted her there gave him leverage. But he hadn't wanted to ride that horse. If she went, he wanted her to arrive as his date. He tugged at the neckline of his T-shirt.

He hadn't had this issue before getting his leg blown off. In the past, he'd reach for the phone and call, and if he got turned down, he dusted himself off and called someone else. But right now there was no one else. Since the last girlfriend's defection over his intimacy issues...her words, not his...it had been months since he'd even been interested in going out. He realized he put up boundaries, but a guy couldn't leave himself so open to a woman that she could rip his heart out. Stacy had come close enough to doing that.

Cal finished chewing a bite of ham and cheese, stuffed his sandwich back in the plastic bag, and jerked his cell phone from his pocket. He hopped down off the side of the truck, caught his balance, and stood with the phone in his hand. Shit, she'd probably turn him down because he'd waited to the last fucking minute. But he'd been rejected before. And survived. And he had a reason for asking her to go with him.

"If you haven't called already it's too late to do it now, man. Women don't like getting invitations at the last minute. They like to have their wardrobe planned out and know everything you're doing."

Hector knew what he was talking about. He had a wife and four daughters.

Cal found the number for the main office. He'd looked it up the night before. He pushed the button and listened while it connected and began to ring. Hector had a few other things to say about what women didn't like and Cal threw up a finger to shut the man up. "You're going to jinx me."

Hector chuckled.

An operator or receptionist answered the call, and he asked to speak to Kathleen O'Connor.

The phone rang again twice, three times. "Kathleen O'Connor."

She sounded a little preoccupied.

"This is Cal Crowes."

A beat of silence followed by a shy, "Hello. How are you?" had his anxiety level dropping a little.

"I'm good." Shit. What was he doing trying to ask her out when they'd had a five-minute conversation and nothing else? Hell it wasn't even five minutes, it was more like two. But she was already on the other end of the phone, and he had to man up and ask.

"I saw the video on the news last night," she said, before he could ask.

He bit back a groan. "I don't know who sent it to the news stations. I've been dodging reporters this morning here at work. They were parked outside the site when I got here."

"It was pretty dramatic stuff. You didn't say anything about grabbing Julio by his safety vest until you could get hold of his hand."

"Well, at the time it was the only thing I could get a grip on." He really didn't want to relive the whole thing over again. "You didn't look too bad in action either."

"Thank God no one knew who I was. Mr. Wiley's already been in to check on me and make sure I'm not going to do any interviews."

That didn't sound good. "I hope he wasn't giving you a hard time."

"No, he just thanked me for responding so quickly, then told me next time to let the men handle things."

He could practically hear the seething anger in her tone. "You're not pissed off at all men about that, are you?"

"No. I'm very selective at the ones I'm aiming that at right now."

"I'm glad to hear that. Julio and his wife are having a big get-together tonight. His wife Jessica called me," Two days ago. Why the hell hadn't he called then? "She said she'd really like to meet you in person so she could thank you for what you did. I was hoping you'd come, too, as my date." He paused and when she remained silent, went on. "I know I'm a stranger, but I thought you'd feel safe having dinner with them and about a hundred other people, so we can get to know each other."

"A hundred other people?" Amusement came across in her tone.

"Julio has about twenty cousins who live here with their families, and half the crew will be there, too, with theirs. Since you're new here, it will give you a chance to get to know some of the people who'll probably be building the structures you design."

She remained silent for a moment.

"It'll be good food and good people. No pressure."

"That sounds like something I'd like. What time?"

His shoulders fell. He hadn't realized how tense he'd become, waiting for her answer. "Seven."

"I have an early meeting in the morning. I'll only be able to stay a couple of hours. If I meet you there, you can stay as long as you like. What's the address?"

Was she giving herself a back door in case things went south? The thought threw him, and his mind blanked. He asked Hector what the address was before giving it to her.

"What's the celebration about?"

"They're having a baby, their second, and after the scare Monday, they wanted to celebrate life."

"That sounds like a good idea. Throw out the bad and embrace the good."

"Exactly."

"I'll try to make it on time. I'm not familiar with the area, but I have a GPS."

"If you like, we can meet after work and get coffee while we wait to go to Julio's. Then you can follow me there." Why hadn't he thought about that before? It wasn't a good idea for her to drive unfamiliar streets in that area.

"Thank you, Cal. I'd like that."

He mentioned a coffee shop close to her office. They made arrangements to meet there at six-thirty. He'd be able to fit in a shower and a change of clothes before they met.

Relieved, he closed his phone and put it in his back pocket.

Hector needled him, "You were sweatin' bullets getting that date. I hope she's worth it."

"She is. She's beautiful, and brave, and she tried to run interference for me with asshole Warren the other day."

"To bad she wasn't here today." Hector's expression went from sour to a smile. "Ah—the hot mama with the curves and the hair. If her skin wasn't so fair I'd think she was Chicana."

Cal grinned. "She's Irish. Her last name is O'Connor."

"I like my women with meat on their bones, too." Hector

waggled his eyebrows. "Gives you something to hold on to at night. My Carmela is soft and warm in all the right places."

"Whoa, Hector, way too much info." Cal threw up a hand as though warding him off, but he grinned.

Hector smirked. "You sure you can handle someone like her? I mean, she had bigger *cojones* than Warren. She was the one who went over the side to help save Julio while Warren was standing there with his thumb up his butt." He frowned, suddenly serious. "Why is Warren on your ass?"

Cal picked up the sandwich he'd stuffed back in its bag. "He thinks my leg makes me more of a risk on-site than other workers. He's trying to goad me into a fight or figure out a reason to fire me."

"*Mierda.* If I didn't already know about your leg, I'd never guess there was anything wrong."

Cal had worked hard to be as versatile as possible on the prosthetic for just that reason. And he'd had a wonderful physical therapist who helped him with it. Cal leaned against the front quarter panel of the truck and finished his sandwich.

"Do you think this chiquita can help you with that?"

Cal shook his head. "She's new to the company. She was just hired a couple of days ago."

"It's good you asked her out because she's beautiful, and not for what she can do for you. That way she won't have to rip your balls off later. You need to get out more, my friend."

If she liked him, that was the plan. If she could hang over the side of a platform to help save a guy, dating a guy with part of a leg missing shouldn't bother her at all.

KATHLEEN HUNG UP the phone and returned her attention to the sheet of paper taped to her drafting table. That moment on the site on Monday had wound its way through her mind like a song, over and over. The wind had kicked up, and Cal stepped close to block the dust billowing up and tucked her hair behind her ear.

Every motion seemed protective and—

She'd responded to him instantly. That had never happened to her before.

It took more than polite behavior to impress her. Having eight brothers, she was used to their rude, crude, and obnoxious jokes and behavior. But they could be tender, caring, and strong, too. Like Zach had been that morning. She was spoiled by their protection and love, since she was the baby in the family. Too bad they still insisted on treating her as if she was two instead of twenty-five.

Her thoughts shifted back to Cal. His quiet strength had stood out from the moment they dragged him up on the platform still gripping Julio. He'd kept his cool then, and maintained his composure when Paul Warren suggested he secure the safety netting. Combine that with his modest avoidance of the limelight and she was...very interested.

Zach would be shocked she was going out. He'd think she'd accepted just to prove she was ready to move on.

Too late now. She had a date. Even though it was just for her to meet Julio's wife. Her heartbeat picked up and nerves played castanets in her stomach. She couldn't allow herself to respond too eagerly. She had to maintain her distance.

Men weren't monogamous by nature. The clues to understanding that had been in her brothers' numerous conquests and in Lee's infidelity. Even two out of her four married brothers had strayed from their spouses, one ending in divorce and the other was still in marriage counseling.

So did that mean she would one day have to accept that her husband would stray, no matter how much she loved him? Would she have to worry constantly about if or when it would happen?

All of this inner agony over the first date she'd accepted in six months since her breakup. Maybe she wasn't ready to date. But it was just a get-together with friends to share a meal. She and Cal wouldn't be spending all that much time together in private.

Needing the distraction, she shifted her attention back to the project. She'd been thrown into the deep end of the pool the morning after the accident, and had been in meetings for two days about the commercial structure she and the others in her pod would be working on.

She felt in her element with a Rapidograph pen and straight-edge ruler in her hands. Every architect had his or her own way of working. Some worked out their design directly on the computer. Others drew them old school onto large sheets of drafting paper by hand. For now, the computer could wait until she had the perspective drawings done.

She'd do the plans on the computer in AutoCAD and turn them into three-dimensional renderings using the software. But on paper she plotted how the structures would look when being approached from different directions. She'd wandered the site with the others, taken photographs, studied the survey diagrams and prospectus, and talked for hours with the client about what kind of structure they wanted.

She finished her drawings, then moved on to setting up the parameters of her AutoCAD program. She was so intent on her work she didn't hear anyone approach until he cleared his throat.

Thinking it was Edward or Dave, she didn't turn. "Need something?"

"I've come to apologize for Monday."

She straightened from her hunched position over the computer and swiveled her desk chair to look at Paul Warren. "Oh, hello, Mr. Warren. No reason to apologize. We had a difference of opinion. It happens."

Paul pulled the spare chair out from beneath the counter and sat down.

Kathleen bit back a sigh. She carefully saved her work before swiveling around to face him.

His smile was sheepish. "We didn't get off to a very good start. I'd like to take you out for a drink to make up for my bad behavior."

Feeling more wary than reassured by the offer, Kathleen said, "That isn't necessary." It wasn't she who deserved an apology, but Cal Crowes. "We're coworkers, and we'll probably have other times when we don't see eye to eye." She shrugged and searched for something to talk about that would head off another attempt to ask her out. "How's the breezeway coming along?"

"The crew will be putting the roof on tomorrow."

"It's a beautiful design. I loved the optical illusion created by the side supports when standing at either end. Whose design was it?"

"It's Hillary's."

"I'll have to tell her how impressed I am. I looked at some of her framed designs and the pictures of them yesterday. She's very talented."

"Yeah, she is." His phone rang and he looked at the screen. "I have to go." He rose from the chair. "I'm sure we'll cross swords—uh—paths again soon." He grinned.

She smiled, relieved he'd been called away. "Thanks for stopping by."

"Later." He threw up a hand and was already hitting redial before he turned away. He strode out the door, the phone pressed to his ear.

Kathleen returned to her computer.

"Was Paul making a second pass?" Hillary asked from behind her.

She was starting to like the open concept of the room less and less. It lent itself too easily to interruptions. "Only a half-hearted one." She swiveled her chair. "He's not really interested in me any more than I am him. I think it might be he's trying to live up to the reputation he built for himself."

Hillary's brow wrinkled, a thoughtful look crossing her face.

Considering the woman's interest in Warren, Kathleen wondered if possibly she had a thing for him. How hard would it be to love someone and watch them date so many other women? She knew exactly how she felt, but at least Kathleen hadn't known until after she broke it off. Hoping to lighten the other woman's load, she said, "Don't worry, you won't have to return the bet money."

"Good thing, since I already spent it on beer and hot wings."

"And I enjoyed every one of them. Thank you. Oh, and I love the design you did for the breezeway. It's truly beautiful."

Hillary smiled. "Thanks. I was really lucky the company who commissioned it was open to paying a little more for what they wanted. It has more steel in the construction than their budget called for. Sometimes you can get away with adding a few elements to a design, but not often."

"I'll keep that in mind."

Hillary wandered in closer, and when she reached for Kathleen's drawing, Kathleen laid a hand on it, holding it beneath the sheets she was using to do computations. "I'm not finished with the design yet. I want it to be a surprise."

Hillary frowned, then smiled, though it appeared a bit stiff. "Okay. Now I'll be curious as hell until I get to see it." She wandered back to her own cubicle.

Kathleen worked for a few minutes longer. Then an idea occurred to her. If the party was going to be a sort of new life celebration, she'd give Julio and his wife a little something for the baby. She went online to look up a number. She'd been able to get most of the wedding preparation money back, but the deposit for the wedding photos was non-refundable. She might be able to get the services transferred to someone else if they had a branch here. It wasn't as though she was going to have her own portrait taken. She found the number and spoke with the representative. She was put on hold for a while, then the man came back on and said it was possible. She asked for a gift certificate to be emailed to her for half the amount, with a list of what it would cover.

She hung up and immediately realized she was dismantling yet another wedding arrangement. A twinge of pain clouded her eyes with tears. Why couldn't she get past this? She quickly brushed them away. She was tempted to call Cal and back out of the date. She could mail the gift certificate later.

But it would be the coward's way out.

Her brothers wouldn't give up when they met with heartache. Zach's girl had dropped him while he was deployed, and he'd moved on.

She could do it, too.

Kathleen threw herself back into work to get the whole issue of men and dating and broken hearts off her mind.

She set up her AutoCAD program parameters and began the work on the lower levels of the structure. She didn't realize it was time to quit until Edward got up and dragged his jacket off the back of his chair to leave.

Her date with Cal loomed, and her nerves jingled. She had a fresh blouse in the car to go along with her skirt, proof against the hazards of drawing with ink and the habits drummed into her during her college courses. She'd go get the blouse and change. Freshen up a bit. She carefully saved the project and closed out her program.

Paul Warren sauntered in and started toward her. A feeling of dread settled in the pit of her stomach. If he was trying to change her impression of him, it wasn't working.

She casually wandered over to Hillary's cubicle.

"Hello, ladies. I was wondering if you'd like to go out for a drink."

Hillary looked up and Kathleen caught the cautious hope in her expression. Kathleen rushed to say, "Thank you for the invitation, Paul, but I have a baby celebration I'm going to with a friend. But I'm sure Hillary would like to go for a drink to unwind."

To his credit, Paul never missed a beat. "Hillary? It will give us some time to celebrate the success of the breezeway. The clients are raving about it."

"Good, I'm glad." She settled back in her chair. "I could use a glass of wine."

"Another time, Kathleen?" he asked.

"Sure." She kept it casual but uneasiness settled in the pit of her stomach. "You two have a good evening." She stepped over to her printer to get the two sheets of paper she'd printed from her email and put them an envelope.

"I didn't think there were that many people you knew here in San Diego. You said you'd just moved here two weeks ago. Do you really have a date, or are you avoiding me?" Paul asked.

What the hell? It was none of his damn business.

Kathleen drew a breath to try and ease the anxious beat of her heart. "Yes, I really have a date. This is a gift certificate I purchased on line for the happy parents, if you'd like proof." She held out the paper.

He eyed the paper and stuffed his hands into his pants pockets. "No, I believe you. I just don't want first impressions to cause an issue between us, Kathleen."

The passive-aggressive bullshit in his demeanor set off nervous alarms. "I don't have an issue." She added a mental *yet.* "Having a comfortable relationship with my coworkers is important to me. But I'm not really comfortable with anything else."

"With me, you mean?"

"Yes. Since you're technically a boss here."

"I see." His expression shifted to a more neutral one. "I understand. But when you've done well on a project, I'll feel slighted if you don't allow me to buy you a drink to celebrate."

Hillary came around the dividing wall to join them.

Kathleen nodded. "That will be fine. You two have a good night." She retrieved her purse from her desk and the lightweight jacket she'd worn to work. She couldn't wait to escape to her car.

It was while she sat in her vehicle and tried to quit shaking that the anger surged. Had she misread Warren? Had he really tried to intimidate her? The passive-aggressive thing threw her, and she waffled back and forth, which further amped up her anger.

She'd have to give it some time and see if he came back for another pass. And if he did, she wasn't going to put up with his shit, whether or not it cost her this job.

CHAPTER 4

CAL SAT AT the coffee shop window closest to the parking lot. He should have asked her what kind of car she drove. He'd been so worked up just talking to her on the phone, his mind had been a sieve. Hell, he hadn't been able to even remember Julio's address, and he'd been there at least twenty times.

He ran a palm over his jaw. He could work two hundred feet in the air, but he couldn't call a woman and ask her out without turning into an idiot. What the fuck was wrong with him?

A dark blue Honda pulled up and parked.

Kathleen got out of the vehicle and looped her purse over her shoulder. Her cherry red blouse enhanced her pale skin and dark hair. Her black skirt hit modestly just above her knee, but hugged her hips and made her waist look tiny by comparison. Hector had called her a hot mama. Oh yeah, she was hot.

Cal rose and ambled to the front door before she made it across the parking lot. When she saw him holding the door open, her expression, a little anxious, changed to relief. When she smiled, he noticed her red lipstick matched her top perfectly. Her mouth looked ripe for kissing and more.

In an instant his body responded, and he smiled. "Glad you made it," he said.

"I had a delay at work and was worried I'd be late."

"No worries. Even if you were, this will be a casual get-together. People will be coming and going for most of the evening." He rested a hand against the small of her back as he guided her to the table he'd claimed. His heart rate spiked just touching her. She smelled like summer, coconut or vanilla. Good enough to eat. His throat thickened and he swallowed. After getting her settled in one of the plastic seats, he asked what she'd like to drink.

"I'd love a hot chai tea."

He went to the counter and placed their orders. He set the sealed cup and a small plastic container with a lemon wedge in front of her.

He didn't want coffee or tea, so got a cup of hot chocolate instead. She eyed the whipped cream poking out of the top of his cup and smiled when he tugged a spoon out of his shirt pocket and offered it to her. "I'll share."

"It looks tempting, but no."

Not as tempting as she was. "When did you move to San Diego?" He had to get his mind on something else.

"Two weeks ago. I drove out for a job interview and got it. I'm staying with my brother, Zach, until I find a place to live."

"And what does he do?"

"He's in the Navy. A medic, among other things." She popped the lid off her steaming tea and put in some lemon and a packet of sweetener.

Noticing her hands were shaking, he laid a hand over hers. "Let me put the lid back on for you," he offered. Was she nervous about the date or something else? "Is something wrong?"

"Just an upset at work earlier. I'll relax in a minute."

"You had nerves of steel Monday. Want to share what it is that's upset you?"

"Just a personality clash at work." She changed the subject abruptly. "What branch of the service were you in?" she asked as he popped the plastic cover on and set it in front of her again.

He let it go, since she seemed to want to avoid talking about it. "I was a corporal in the Marines." He skimmed the whip cream off the top of his cup and put a spoonful in his mouth. The creamy sweetness of it dissolved on his tongue. She'd taste just as sweet.

She was silent a moment. "I'm sorry you had to give it up." He read regret in her expression.

Had she found out about his leg? Had Warren told her? "I had an option to stay in. I could have even been deployed back into combat in a support position, but I chose not to. I was concerned I might not be as good as I needed to be. I couldn't put any of my guys at risk. But you don't ever stop being a Marine."

"Zach has that same mindset. In fact, most of the men in my family do. Mark's a first sergeant in the Marines, Jason's a sergeant major in the Army, and my father and oldest brother Michael are cops back home.

"How many brothers and sisters in all?"

"Eight brothers, no sisters."

"Eight?" It took him a moment to wrap his head around that. "I bet every one of them is protective as hell of you."

She nodded. "Yes, pretty much."

"Where's home?" he asked.

"Boston."

"I thought I heard a hint of Massachusetts in your accent."

"And I thought I heard the south in yours."

"The great state of Texas."

"Oh, the hat tip with the hard hat. I knew it reminded me of something. You know, in westerns, when a man tips his hat to the ladies."

"Yeah, some of us still do that."

"That's nice." Her smile softened, and he groaned inwardly.

"I've never been to Texas. I've only been here to San Diego once before. I've been so busy with school, I haven't had time to do much of anything but study and work. And…" she trailed off.

He took a sip of the hot chocolate. "And," he urged.

"Look for a job." She looked away, her green eyes shadowed.

She'd been going to say something else. What had it been? She seemed an open book, but everyone had secrets. With such strong ties to home and family, why would she relocate so far away from them? Was she running from something, or someone?

"What about your family?" she asked.

"One younger brother, Douglas. My dad's a contractor and runs his own company. My mother does the bookkeeping. They build residential projects and flip houses."

"So you learned the ropes from your dad."

"Yeah, partly. I worked commercial sites right out of high school. It seemed natural to go back to it after I got out of the service. Are you through with that?" he pointed to the tea.

She nodded and pushed the cup toward him. The black bruises on her wrist caught his attention. He drew away the cup and cupped her hand in his. "Julio did that when he latched onto you, didn't he?"

"It's nothing. It's barely sore anymore."

The small talk they'd exchanged, though it helped him to get to know her, didn't come close to cutting to the heart of what kind of person she was the way these bruises did. "Thank you for helping me save him. I didn't know how long I'd be able to hold on with just one hand."

Her throat worked as she swallowed, and her voice was husky as she said, "You're welcome."

He rose to toss the empty containers into the trash. "We should probably go. I'd like to introduce you to Jessica and Julio before the mob arrives." It was natural to offer her his hand. When she took it, he noticed her fingers were stained black with ink.

She started to jerk her hand back, her cheeks red. "It's the hazards of being an architect. My Rapidograph leaked, and I couldn't get it off."

Cal smiled and bent his head to kiss her fingertips. "Just a sign of good, hard work, nothing to be embarrassed about. On the other hand, be grateful I rushed home and took a shower."

Her laughter broke the serious mood they'd fallen into.

CAL WAS A charmer. When he kissed her fingertips, she'd felt that small caress all the way to her…. She wasn't going to think about that. He'd gone out of his way to make her feel relaxed and safe. So safe, she'd agreed for him to drive her to the party and moved her car back into employee parking at the office. As they passed the third street corner with a group of teenagers standing around smoking and eyeing every car that passed, she acknowledged she'd made the right decision.

Distracted by the drive, she'd almost put aside Paul Warren's attempts to intimidate behind her. Something in one of the teenagers' sullen expressions brought it all back.

Why was Warren asking her out for drinks anyway? She'd already made it plain she wasn't interested. Or was he persisting to try and reverse the impression he'd given her that first day? His pushiness increased her anxiety about their working relationship and Cal's situation. She couldn't deny that the project manager was manipulative and determined.

But how was she supposed to warn Cal about the guy without compromising her own situation? She couldn't afford to lose the job. She'd put in hours every summer, and an entire semester to complete her internship, all working toward her licensing test. She could be finished with the requirements in eighteen months if she worked hard. But in order to take the test, she had to be employed in her field.

"When Jessica and Julio decide to celebrate, they do it in a big way," Cal said as they pulled up behind a long line of vehicles parked on the street.

She'd made the right decision in coming with him. She didn't know the area, and with all the twists and turns they'd taken, she'd have had difficulty finding her way back to the main road. And had she gotten lost—she shivered. "Their neighbors won't mind you parking here?"

He shook his head. "They'll all be at the party." He got out and came around to open her door.

She enjoyed his old school manners. It was a long way from the casual treatment she'd accepted from Lee. She'd had some time to think about a lot of things since the breakup, and Lee's infidelity wasn't the only thing she could live without. He'd taken advantage of and diminished her self-worth in more ways than she could count.

When Cal helped her out of the car, she looped her hand through his arm and earned a smile. "These friends of yours seem very popular."

"This neighborhood is very close. They all seem to pitch in when there's an illness in the family, a new baby, that kind of thing."

"And when there's a party?"

"Then, too."

They loped up the sidewalk, Cal's long legs eating up the distance much more easily than hers. What did it say about her when she couldn't keep up with a man with only one normal leg? She was relieved when he slowed his pace to a stroll. The sound of mariachi music rocked straight ahead.

Cal guided her around the side of the house to a gate. The backyard was strung high with plastic lanterns already lit. Tables of every size were positioned around the perimeter of the yard and covered with brightly colored plastic tablecloths. Three large tables filled with food stretched along the side of the concrete patio, and people were already mingling.

Julio rushed to meet them as soon as they entered the yard. His round face was a far healthier color than the last time she'd seen him. Julio gripped Cal's hand and bumped shoulders with him. "*Bienvenida, mi amigo.*"

"*Gracias, Julio. Estamos contentos de estar aquí,*" Cal replied. "You remember Kathleen O'Connor."

Julio tilted his head. "I will never forget her. Gracias, señorita."

"You're welcome."

"What is it you do for Wiley?" he asked.

"I'm an architect. Monday was my first day on the job in Wiley's drafting department. I was just checking out some of the sites with Mr. Warren to get a scope of what they do."

"It was a lucky day for me."

"Congratulations on the baby. I brought something for you and your wife." She withdrew the envelope from her bag and handed it to him. "It's a gift certificate for your first round of baby pictures, or your wife when she starts to show. You can call the number on there and arrange the time."

Surprise blanked Julio's features. "This is very generous of you."

"You'll want pictures of everything."

"Gracias."

"You're welcome."

A petite woman about her own height joined them. Her pale skin and blonde hair were in direct contrast to Julio's dark good looks. Julio was quick to introduce Kathleen to his wife Jessica.

"I'm so glad you could join us," Jessica said, she bypassed the handshake and hugged Kathleen. "Thank you for helping Julio on Monday." Her eyes looked suspiciously shiny as she drew back.

"It was mostly Cal, I just acted as added ballast."

"She brought us a gift certificate for the baby," Julio said, handing Jessica the envelope.

"How sweet of you. Thank you." She clutched the envelope against her chest. "Cal, you know everyone. Be sure to introduce her." She winked at Kathleen. "And don't let him be shy about getting up and dancing. I'm going to make sure to find a song you can do a Texas two-step to."

"I'd like more than one date, Jess. If I step on Kathleen's toes all night, that might be a deal breaker," Cal said.

Jessica shot him a wry look. "If you can walk iron twenty stories off the ground, you can dance with a girl without stepping on her toes."

Cal gave her an aw-shucks smile. "I can give it a shot."

"Good. There's enough food for an army over there. Everyone in the neighborhood brought a dish. I'm going to go put this somewhere safe right now." She waved the envelope.

Cal guided Kathleen around the yard and introduced her to some of the crew and their wives. They were friendly enough, but the moment they learned she was an architect for the company, their attitudes shifted, which was a shame, since she could have used a few friends. She'd left them all behind in Boston.

It really was a family party. Some of the kids were running through the crowd and others playing in a large tree house balanced in the one big tree in the yard.

She and Cal filled paper plates with food and he guided her to an empty table. "That was real nice of you to get Julio and Jessica something."

"It was just a spur-of-the-moment thing," Kathleen shrugged.

"Photographs aren't cheap." His blue-green eyes probed her, making her feel on edge for the first time.

"I had a prepaid thing I wasn't going to use. I couldn't get my money back, so I transferred half of it to them. I'll give the other half to someone else. You know how frugal we Irish are." Kathleen bit into a taco and groaned. These were homemade, even the tortillas, and they were delicious.

Cal finished chewing and swallowed. "Why do I get the feeling there's more to it than you're saying?"

She wiped her mouth and hands on a napkin. Why was she so reticent about it? Lee and Tamara were the ones who'd been in the wrong. But deep down she believed if she'd been paying closer attention, he wouldn't have made such a fool of her. "It was a deposit for wedding photos."

He remained silent for a moment. "I'm sorry, Kathleen."

"I'm not. Studio pictures should be of something happy and precious. They'll be put to good use by Julio and Jessica."

"I wasn't talking about the photos."

"I know. I don't want to talk about it. I left all that behind six months ago."

"It's Callahan and his hot señorita," a voice said from behind them.

Kathleen shifted around to see Hector, the man who'd gone down the elevator with Julio the day of the rescue. Had he just called her hot? And had he and Cal been talking about her?

Hector was short and stocky, with a wide chest. Not exactly

handsome, but something about his overtly masculine features was very attractive. The woman with him was short and round and had a sweet smile.

"Hector." Cal's voice held a warning.

The man's cheeky grin inspired one from Kathleen.

Cal rested his arm along the back of her chair, and she had to quell the urge to lean into him. The heat of his body reached out to her. He smelled of soap and some kind of masculine cologne with a clean citrus note. She was shocked at how strong the urge was to bury her nose in the bend of his neck and just breathe him in.

"Kathleen, allow me to introduce Hector and Carmella Martinez," he said, breaking her momentary lapse of control.

"Nice to meet you. Why don't you join us?"

Hector inclined his head. "Gracias, Ms. O'Connor."

"Call me Kathleen, please. Carmella, that's a lovely name."

"It means garden. My mother named all my sisters after flowers, and I was the first one born, so I ended up being the whole plot."

"You're not going to believe this," Kathleen exclaimed. "My middle name is Rose."

They all laughed.

Carmella sat in the chair to Kathleen's right. Hector left to troll the tables for their dinner. The two didn't seem at all intimidated by her job in the head office, and Kathleen began to relax.

They ate, and the conversation flowed. Occasionally women wandered by, every one of them offering Cal a kiss on the cheek and a thank-you for saving their cousin or brother. Cal seemed embarrassed by the whole thing instead of flattered. After his second apology, Kathleen laid a hand on his arm. "You saved a member of their family, of course they're grateful."

"I'm not used to being kissed by one woman while I'm out with another. I'm sort of a one-lady-at-a-time guy."

He didn't know anything about her situation, but the comment gave her a punch to the gut. Were there really men who felt this way?

Julio and Jessica wandered over to visit. A couple of men followed.

"Is there going to be any change in scheduling for those of us working residential construction?" one of the men asked.

For a moment Kathleen didn't realize he was addressing her. "I don't know, Mr.—"

He glanced around, as if he was uncomfortable giving her his name. "Terrance Monroe."

Cal leaned in closer to her, his body tense. "Terrance, she doesn't have anything to do with the running of Wiley. Claiborne from the head office, Warren, and Tom are in charge of all work scheduling."

Kathleen rested a hand on Cal's knee and felt the edge of his prosthesis. The physical knowledge that his leg was truly gone hit her like a punch, and she swallowed against the sudden sense of loss. He was still a stranger to her, but the empathy she felt at that moment nearly overwhelmed her.

She forced her attention back to Monroe. "I'm in the design section, Mr. Monroe. I'm an architect. They hired me to draw plans for some of the commercial projects they've been hired to build. I went out earlier this week to look at a site and was given the project prospectus. I've already started the design process. So to sort of answer your question, the more commercial projects Wiley brings in, the more workers they'll need to build them."

The man smiled. "Draw good and fast, Miss. We get paid more when we work commercial."

Kathleen nodded. "I'll do my best."

Monroe wandered off with his friend.

"I'm sorry, Kathleen," Cal murmured close to her ear.

His warm breath caressed her neck, triggering a delicious shiver. "It's all right."

Jessica left to mingle with some of the other guests while Julio carried their small daughter into the house to put her to bed. It seemed natural to lean back along Cal's side while they watched Hector and Carmella sway to the music together on the concrete patio.

"I never realized how hard it must be to be stuck in the middle," he said.

Kathleen caught what he meant quickly. "I'm not a boss, so I'm not in charge, and I'm not part of the construction crew. So, yes, I'm stuck in between." Later she'd be working with the crew and the project manager directing her designs, but right now she was just a worker.

"You don't feel uncomfortable with me because I'm on the crew?"

"No." She'd feel more uncomfortable working with Paul Warren when the time came. "I come up with the ideas, and you make them happen. It's a symbiotic relationship. Take one part away, and the whole thing crumbles. It's a shame there's any kind of divide."

Cal studied her for a moment. "Why did you try to run interference for me with Warren?"

She needed to warn him. Right now would be the perfect time. She remained silent for a moment, debating what to say, and decided to be straight with him. "Because he was being an asshole."

Cal laughed, and she felt the effects all the way to her toes.

"Do you want to try that dance?" Cal offered her his hand.

Darn. He'd switched the subject too quickly. "Sure." Kathleen placed her hand in his.

"I'll apologize now in case I step on your toes."

"I've been dancing with my brothers for years; trust me, I won't even notice."

Cal smiled and shook his head. He was so masculine and handsome, yet there was vulnerability in him she couldn't help but respond to.

They wove their way to the patio, and he slipped an arm around her and clasped her hand in his, but hesitated.

"Don't worry. I'll follow you." If he did step on her toes, she'd bite her tongue off before telling him.

But he didn't. As they swayed and shuffled their way around the dance floor, Kathleen relaxed against him and enjoyed being held close. It had been six long months since she'd felt a man's arms around her. He even rested his chin against her temple and clasped her hand against his chest.

She'd seen him with his friends, seen his caring and humor directed at them and at her. How had anyone survived war and ended up so…balanced? Or was that all a façade? Was he really as trustworthy and straightforward as he seemed? Or was she experiencing the same blindness she'd had with Lee?

Was she really going to allow herself to doubt both her instincts and the men she dated from now on?

She wouldn't allow herself to measure every man using the imprint left by an unfaithful asshole.

Cal deserved better than that. She hoped.

But she couldn't get involved. He seemed a nice guy, but she was still grieving the loss of a relationship she'd counted on lasting a lifetime. No, two relationships counting her best friend, ones she'd believed would endure anything.

"You're thinking really loudly," Cal said close to her ear.

"Just enjoying the music and the company."

"Then why have you tensed up?"

Kathleen forced herself to relax. He increased the pressure against her spine, urging her closer.

The physical attraction she'd been trying to ignore all night roared along her nerve endings like static, creating a hypersensitivity to his touch and the brush of his chin against her hair.

But she fought the urge to rest her cheek against his shoulder and lean into him. Her head was saying one thing, her body another.

Before the evening was over, she had to make a decision about whether or not she could trust Cal Crowes. His livelihood might depend on it.

CHAPTER 5

T HE PRESSURE BUILT around the moment he would say good night to Kathleen. Since when did he become so worked up about a good night kiss? It was his leg that had issues. There wasn't a damn thing wrong with his lips. But his mouth seemed to have frozen shut since they left the party.

This lack of confidence with women, and his inability to be open, had cost him dates and destroyed his last relationship. He needed to get over these issues.

Kathleen saved him from himself when she said, "You do realize Callahan is an Irish name."

"Yes. So is Jameson, my middle name."

"But Crowes is Native American."

"Yes. My father's family was originally from Colorado. His great-great grandfather was a Crow warrior."

"That's really interesting. You have the high cheekbones of your Native American ancestors."

He hadn't really thought about it before. "I guess so. Is your middle name really Rose?"

"Yes, after my father's mother. My brothers used to call me Thorn. They said I was a thorn in their side when mom asked them to babysit me."

Cal chuckled. "I only have one brother, and he's a pain in the ass. I can only imagine with eight—"

This woman was so witty and easy to be with. What the hell had happened between her and her fiancé that they'd called the wedding off?

But if he asked, it would kill the moment, and he'd cheat himself of a good night kiss. And he really wanted one. Ah hell, he really wanted more, but he'd have to build up his nerve and then ease her into the idea. But Jesus, he'd have dreams about her mouth. She had the most kissable mouth he'd ever seen. Even now with her lipstick gone it looked sexy.

He hoped she wanted to see him again.

They pulled up in front of Kathleen's car, and he pushed the gearshift into park and turned off the motor. The clicking of the engine as it cooled sounded loud.

"I had a good time. Thanks for asking me, Cal."

The knot of tension released inside him. "Good enough that you'd like to do something else this weekend?"

She remained silent a moment. "I'm not sure I'm ready for any kind of romance. I dated the same man for three years and was engaged to be married a year. I ended the relationship six months ago."

"I'm sorry, Kathleen." His heart had been stomped on by three-inch spiked heels. He could empathize.

The parking lot lights slashed across her face. Her throat worked as she swallowed. "I caught him in bed with my best friend."

"Jesus!" That ranked right up there with being Dear John'ed during deployment.

"Go out with me and shoot them a selfie. Let them know you've moved on with your life."

She smiled. "Use you for revenge, huh?"

"We could get dressed up and go to a Ferrari dealership and take pictures in the car like we're out on the town."

Kathleen giggled. "What did you really have in mind?"

"Since you're new to San Diego, you have a lot of choices."

"Are you okay to walk all day?" she asked.

So she knew about his leg. And didn't seem bothered by it.

But the reality of seeing it was another thing. "Yeah, I'm good. I don't swim anymore, so that knocks surfing out, and I can't roller-skate, but other than those two things, I'm good to go. Who told you about my leg?"

"Someone mentioned it in passing." She tugged at the hem of her skirt, though there was no need. She remained silent for a moment or two.

He released his seat belt and shoved open his door. When he came around Kathleen had already exited the vehicle.

"I'll call you Friday with a plan for Saturday."

She tilted her head. "A plan?"

"Yeah. Hector says women like to know ahead of time every-thing that's going on so they can prepare."

"He does?" She looked thoughtful.

They ambled the few feet to her car, and Cal took her keys to unlock the door. The dim lights in the parking lot reflected off her skin. Her eyes glittered.

"Since Hector has a wife and three daughters, I thought he might be right."

Kathleen grinned. "Someone once told me too much planning took the spontaneity out of things. Just a general idea of where we'll be going will be fine. As long as I have my purse, I'm pretty much prepared for anything."

Yes! He'd worn her down. He hadn't entirely lost his touch. "I've always wondered what you ladies have in there."

"It's kind of like your Marine tactical vests. Every pocket is filled with whatever you might need for any emergency."

Cal chuckled. He'd laughed more being with her than he had in a long time. And despite the worry about his job, she made him feel…lighter. He really didn't want to mess up with her by pushing.

"I've had a good time too, Kathleen." He leaned forward and kissed her cheek. He wanted to linger, but forced himself to step back. "Let's go to the zoo on Saturday. There's a good restaurant called the Tree House where we can eat dinner after we've seen the sights. Does that sound okay?"

"Yes. It sounds great. I'll wear walking shoes and sun screen."

"Sounds like a plan. I'll wait until I know your car will start before I leave."

"Thanks, Cal."

He watched until she drove away. She was something special. But hurt, really hurt. He understood all too well how that felt. He'd—*they'd* take things slow.

A tap on his driver side window startled him and he jerked his head in that direction. Paul Warren stared in at him. Cal took his time turning over the key and rolling down the window.

"What are you doing here, Crowes?"

His aggressive tone gave Cal's self-control a slap, and he gripped the steering wheel hard to curb the desire to reach through the window and punch the guy.

"I gave someone a ride back to their car, which was parked here."

Warren looked around the parking lot. "They're gone now."

"Yeah, they just left." Cal reached for the key and started his truck.

Warren opened his mouth to say more, but Cal cut him off. "You have a nice evening, Mr. Warren." He nodded once, rolled up the window, and pulled away.

There was no escaping it. Warren had a hard-on for him, and he was going to have to be as aggressive about keeping his job as Warren was about trying to get rid of him.

SHE SHOULD HAVE told him. Keeping quiet and letting the chips fall seemed like the coward's way out. It was the coward's way out. Guilt filled her stomach with a sourness that had nothing to do with the tacos she'd eaten.

Maybe nothing would happen with Cal's job, and she'd have gotten all worked up, gotten him all worked up, for nothing. She rubbed the dull ache making itself known in her forehead. If she really believed that, she wouldn't feel this way.

The last time she'd felt like this was....the last night she'd been with Lee.

She cut off the thought. She needed to leave all that behind. Starting now.

Kathleen poured a shallow glass of wine and wandered through the kitchen to the living room. Organized gear in duffle bags sat ready to be loaded along the wall next to the front door. Her brother Zach didn't have to tell her he was going on a training tomorrow. The bags said it all. She worried about him, but he was doing what he loved.

The opposite wall worshipped the electronics gods. In the place of honor was one of the largest flat-screen televisions she'd ever seen, along with an Xbox and several other things she hadn't attempted to even turn on. She ignored the tennis match being played on the screen and settled back on the opposite end of the couch from her brother to sip her wine and unwind before she went to bed.

"You're home early. How was the date?" Zach asked, his attention on the female tennis player as she dove for a ball and returned it.

How could he watch a replay of a tennis match? That would be pure torture for her.

"It's a work day tomorrow for us both." She propped her pink fuzzy slipper-covered feet on the coffee table. "He seems like a nice guy."

She knew what was coming before he even opened his mouth. She'd been listening to brotherly words of wisdom about other men and about dating since she went to her junior prom.

"He's working his way into your good graces, hoping for more."

Kathleen hid her smile behind her glass. "And you know this how?"

"I'm a guy, Kathleen. That's what we do."

"Zach, do you really think we women are so stupid we don't know that?"

He tilted his head to study her. "You know I would be remiss in my responsibilities as your big brother if I didn't warn you about guys."

She cocked an eyebrow at him. "I've been living away from home since I was seventeen. Believe me, I know when a guy is on the make. I spent the last three years in college fending them off." The first three they'd been after Tamara, and she'd been the best friend... Then later, after she worked so hard to lose weight, she'd begun to be noticed in her own right... "I'm a twenty-five-year-old woman with my own life. I don't tell you who to sleep with, and you don't get to tell me who I can't."

"Sleep with!" His voice rose. "You've only been out with this guy once and you're planning to sleep with him?"

"Says the man who had a different SEAL bunny in his bed every week as soon as he graduated BUD/S."

"Who told you that?" His outrage was a mixture of expressions. Possibly a blend of guilty conscience plus wondering who the hell had spilled the beans.

"You just told me. It was a shot in the dark."

He raked his fingers through his thick auburn hair, or was he tearing at it? He turned his narrowed green eyes on her. In that moment she recognized their shared heritage. Anyone could see it in the color of their eyes and the shape of their faces. Thank God he'd gotten the red hair and freckles.

On his masculine features, with the scruff of copper-colored beard darkening his jaw, his freckles just looked like he had a tan rather than the rash it would have looked like on her. She had enough on her plate with the body shape she'd inherited from her mother.

"Relax, Zach. I'm not in a rush to sleep with anyone. Trust me on that. After what Lee did... You've fulfilled your brotherly responsibilities. You've warned me off of all men. Now will you please stop acting like a cliché and let me run something serious by you?"

He leaned forward to plant his elbows on his knees. Because of his training, he'd bulked up since leaving home, and his broad shoulders and muscular arms looked strong enough to carry whatever load she needed help with. "Shoot."

His directness triggered a smile. She told him everything about her first day on the job, Warren's sexist attitude toward newly-hired women, and his aggressive dislike of Cal.

"Document this prick's behavior and take it to your boss. He's a lawsuit for the corporation waiting to happen. They'll make short work of him."

"That's one of the problems, Zach. I can't afford to be known as a whistle-blower this early in my career. That's probably how he gets away with his behavior, in fact. If I go into my boss's office three days in and tell him his project manager is a sexist pig, it won't be Paul Warren who'll be out on his ear, it will be me. I have to wait and give him the opportunity to put his hands on me or do something overt. Then I can knee him in the balls and go to the boss."

Zach flinched.

"There's another consideration, too. I think the woman I work with has real feelings for the jerk. They may have had a relationship. If he continues to ask me out, it's going to put a strain on our working relationship. If I get him fired, the working relationship will be nonexistent. So it benefits me to have a boyfriend. And if I go out with Cal, I can say in good conscience I'm seeing someone and keep Warren at a distance."

"It sounds like you have all this thought out."

"I did until tonight."

His brows went up and he leaned in closer. "What about to-night?"

"If I was a team player, I'd continue to keep my mouth shut, but I feel guilty as hell that I didn't say something to Cal about Warren. I should have warned him the man has it in for him. I don't know what Warren's reasons are, but it's obvious he does."

Zach threaded fingers through his hair to push it out of his eyes. It looked like he'd taken a hatchet to it and cut it himself. "You're holding back telling the head office about this sexist pig you're working with. And you feel guilty because you're straddling the line with this guy, too. Does that pretty much sum it up?"

"Well you didn't have to make me sound so spineless," Kathleen complained.

Zach grinned. "I'm just jerking your chain." He turned serious. "You've been out on one date with this guy. Are you going to see him again?"

"On Saturday. And there's one thing I didn't tell you about Cal, Zach."

"What is it?"

"He's an ex-Marine and an amputee. His right leg below the knee."

"And he's working construction." It was a statement not a question.

"Yeah. And he's as good as the others at it. I didn't know there was anything at all wrong with his leg until he ran on it. He said they offered to allow him to go back into combat, but he turned them down. He didn't want to go back if he wasn't certain he could do the job without putting his guys at risk."

"So you went out with him because you have this connection with guys like Jason, Mark, and me."

"No I didn't. I went out with him because he's the complete opposite of Lee and he's a good guy, like I told you." And he was sexy as hell. And he was the first guy she'd been attracted to since the breakup.

"You're giving this guy Warren ammunition to use against Cal by dating him, Kathleen. Warren is just looking for a way to get to him. He'll say something nasty about you, and if Cal cares at all, he'll feel duty bound to kick the guy's ass, and he'll lose his job."

"I don't intend for Warren to know we're seeing each other."

"And Cal's okay with that?"

"Well, I haven't said anything to him about it. But it will make both our lives easier if Warren stays in the dark about it."

Zach's features grew serious. "Kathleen, the fact that you've decided to avoid letting anyone know you're dating Cal just to avoid conflict with this Warren guy isn't good. You're allowing him to manipulate you."

"I'll handle Warren from my end." She hoped things would

level out once she let him know she was seeing someone. "What do you think Cal should do about the job situation?"

"Shit. I don't know, Kathleen. Bringing suit against the company seems a chickenshit way to keep the job, but threatening it may be his only resort if this guy keeps putting pressure on whoever hired him."

"He won't do it. He's too much of a straight up guy."

Zach's brows rose. "If you're that impressed, maybe you need to bring him around so I can meet him."

Yeah, that was going to happen when snow fell in San Diego. She shook her head. "Nice try. Not happening."

Zach frowned. "Afraid he won't stand up to scrutiny?"

"No. I'm not afraid of that at all. But I know your interview and intimidation tactics. We've only been out once, and I don't want him to think I'm more trouble than he needs."

Zach leaned forward again, his expression earnest. "I'd never do that, Kathleen."

She studied his rugged features. He was a master at lying. Hadn't the Navy trained him to lie under torture? "Yeah, right. If it were up to you and all my other dear brothers, I'd be cloistered in a convent like some seventeenth century heroine in a romance novel."

"If you'd let us vet—" Zach cut himself off, his lips compressed.

If she'd let them vet Lee, he'd never have passed muster. So why the hell had he passed it with her? And what about Tamara, her college roommate, her best friend since sixth grade? "Lee wasn't the only one in that bed when I walked in. And you *all* met Tamara. Would you have thought she'd betray me?"

He studied his laced fingers. "No. I'd never have believed it. She was the sister you never had. I'm sorry I said anything."

At least she hadn't been the only one fooled. Although there was little comfort in knowing that. In some ways Tamara's betrayal and loss hurt more than Lee's. Kathleen stared down into her wine. "I need to know I can judge someone's character without needing backup."

He nodded. "I get it." But he had a morose scowl when he rose to his feet. "But we all need some help now and then."

He'd had his own losses with a girlfriend who dumped him while he was deployed in Iraq or right after. He hadn't let a woman get close emotionally since. Kathleen read that in his avoidance of the subject.

"I have to bug out at zero four thirty. We'll catch breakfast at the base so you don't have to cook for us again. As much as I appreciated it this morning, you're not used to the hours. You look wiped out right now."

"I am a little," she admitted.

"I'll probably be back at nine hundred, but don't worry if you don't see me. I'll have my cell phone with me in case of an emergency."

"Okay. I have a couple of apartments I'm going to check out after work."

He tucked his hands in his back pockets. "I'm not here much anyway. You know you can stay here as long as you want."

"Yes, I do know, and I hope you know just how much I appreciate it. But we need to work out some kind of signal so when we bring dates home there won't be any embarrassing moments. Like I can always leave a bra hanging on the bedroom door, you could hang your underwear out there."

"Kathleen—" He pressed the heels of his hands against his temples as if his head might explode.

Kathleen threw her hand up with a snicker. "Okay. I'll stop." She set aside her wine glass. "You're just so easy to tease." She went over to give him a sisterly hug, then tilted her head back to look up into his eyes. "I'm not anywhere close to the loose woman I've led you to believe. But you need your privacy as much as I need mine, and the plan was that I'd only stay as long as it took me to find my own place."

True, moving out would leave her totally alone in a city she didn't know—yet. But she'd needed some distance from home, room to allow the hurt and humiliation to heal at their own pace. She'd felt just as isolated there as she did here. Somehow Lee's friends had become her friends, and she ended up being the one abandoned after their breakup. Despite his being an unfaithful, lying, conniving asswipe.

Tears threatened, and she closed her eyes against them. "I'll still want to see you as much as possible, Zach." She tightened her arms around him.

"I get it, honey." He gave her a gentle squeeze, and buffed her forehead with a kiss. "But if you need me to have a man-to-man discussion with the asshole, just let me know."

"I will." She stepped away and pretended to retrieve her wine glass to hide her shaky composure. "Be careful tomorrow."

"Always am."

She knew that wasn't necessarily so.

He meandered down the hallway to his bedroom. "And Thorn?"

"Yes."

"Knee that supervisor in the nuts if he fucks with you again. No job is important enough to put up with a bunch of shit."

How much shit would Zach put up with before he walked away from being a SEAL? He put his life on the line every time he was called up. What she was experiencing was nothing by comparison.

She gave him a nod. "I will."

CHAPTER 6

PANIC MADE IT hard for her to breathe. Her heart drummed in her ears so loudly it drowned out everything else.

The AutoCAD program was open on her computer monitor, cursor blinking on a blank page. She'd looked three times, but her project was gone. She saved it when Paul Warren was here. She distinctly remembered doing it. Even if the program hadn't saved the rest of the work she did after he left, what she finished before should all be there.

And that wasn't all that was missing.

She had to calm down. Her drawings and rough designs had to be in this room somewhere. Please let them be here somewhere.

When she left to meet Cal, she'd stacked everything on her drafting table in plain sight. The pristine emptiness of the surface glared at her now.

She swallowed in an attempt to moisten a mouth gone bone dry. Someone had deleted her CAD file and moved the drawings. But why? She backed away from the space to lean against the dividing wall between her cubicle and Edward's.

Hillary sauntered in. She was already shrugging free of her lightweight jacket before she reached her cubicle. "Morning, Kathleen."

"Hey." The word came out breathless and weak.

Hillary paused in midstride, her brows rising. "You're white. What's happened?"

Kathleen struggled to maintain her composure, but tears weren't far off. "All my work from yesterday is gone."

Confusion flitted across Hillary's face. Her jacket still hung from one arm, snagged on the purse dangling from her hand. "Gone? What do you mean *gone*?"

"The project I started in my CAD program is gone, deleted. I left the drawings and my copy of the prospectus stacked on the drafting table. They're not here, either."

Hillary dumped her purse and jacket on the floor. "They can't be gone." She moved to the shallow stack of drafting paper left on the Formica countertop and thumbed through it. When she found nothing there, she bent to look under the counter.

Kathleen hadn't had time to accumulate any clutter. The emptiness of her cubicle stared back at them both. The only thing new was the bulletin board she'd hung beneath a shelf running head-high above the counter with her photos of the project building site.

"You guys aren't playing a practical joke on me, are you?" Kathleen asked.

"No." Hillary's expression was grim. "For one thing, we don't touch each other's work, and for another...this is not one damn bit funny."

Kathleen drew a tiny bit of comfort from Hillary's solid support.

"I'll call down to maintenance and ask them to look through yesterday's trash."

"I didn't throw my work away."

"I know, but if some other idiot did, maybe we can catch the drawings before they've disposed of them." Hillary reached for the phone.

While Hillary was making the call, Ed and Dave came in. Kathleen approached them and explained what had happened. While Dave tried to recover the file on her computer, she, Ed and Hillary—when she wasn't answering the phones—started a systematic search of the room.

At one point Ed went out to ask the secretaries and receptionist to look around the office supply areas.

"I've called down to tech, and they're sending someone right now to see if they can recover your file. Have you looked in the hanging files for your drawings, Kathleen?" Dave asked.

His calm questions were helping her remain hopeful. "No. I don't have a key to the cabinet."

"I'll get mine." He retrieved his key from a desk drawer and opened the cabinet.

Eighteen by twenty-four inch pieces of drafting paper hung in large sections from bars and clamps suspended from a wall unit. Kathleen carefully looked from one side, while Dave started from the other.

"Kathleen," Dave called her attention to a clamped section. Suspended neatly from the file hanger were her drawings of the building façade from different angles, and several other sheets with her calculations.

Relief lifted the weight of anxiety from her, leaving room for tears to rush up, and she bit her lip to still its trembling. Dave laid a hand on her shoulder. "This couldn't have been a mistake. Someone had to put them in there on purpose. I thought you might have deleted your CAD file by mistake, but since the drawings disappeared, too…" He shook his head.

She nodded. What else could she do?

"You need to set up a password on your computer right now to lock out everyone but you. And you might want to transfer all these drawings and calculations to the computer, too, for safekeeping, and then store it on the server so it can't be messed with," he suggested.

"I will."

"How the hell did they get in there?" Ed asked. "Hey, Hillary, Dave's found them."

Hillary hung up the phone, which had rung three times since they arrived. She rushed to join them.

"Kathleen may be the only one besides the receptionist and

the secretaries who doesn't have a key. Whatever practical joke someone was playing, it was damn stupid." He removed the papers from the clamps and handed them to her.

"I'm real sorry this happened, Kathleen. I can't imagine why anyone would touch your work," Ed said.

"Nothing like this has ever happened before," Hillary added.

"I really appreciate you all helping me find them," Kathleen managed around the knot in her throat. "They weren't anything I was going to give the client, but it's just part of my process to work things out on paper before I start the design on the computer."

Dave's features looked set with anger. "Scan them and put them in the computer, just to be safe. Then you can print them out and take the originals home. You should frame that one." He pointed at the montage of the different façades. "The design is beautiful."

She didn't know if he was saying that to make her feel better or if he truly thought it. "I may do that." She forced a smile. "I'd love to take you all out to lunch as a thank-you."

"Not necessary, but…" Ed grinned. "We could all hit Wally's down the street for corn beef sandwiches."

"That sounds good," she agreed.

Hillary gave her shoulder a squeeze. "I'll call maintenance downstairs and tell them to call off the search."

"I'll go out and tell the secretaries," Ed said.

Dave closed the cabinet and locked it. "I'll make sure you get a key to the cabinet. The tech guy should be here in just a few minutes."

As they all dispersed to give her some time to regroup, Kathleen moved back to her cubicle and sat at her desk. She spread the drawings out on the table. For all his oddities and passive-aggressive behavior, she couldn't imagine why Paul Warren would do something like this, or anyone else. She barely knew these people. But this couldn't have been a mistake.

She wouldn't be played for a fool again. She'd watch her back from now on.

CAL ATTEMPTED TO ignore the cell phone raised in his direction as he heaved the last heavy plastic drainage tube onto the truck. Hector and Julio had made a competition out of filming him at work. Every time he started to do anything, they both whipped out their phones.

They'd taken it one step further, too. They wanted to catch him doing something embarrassing. He finally put himself on notice to watch his language—which he had to admit had gotten saltier the longer he was on the crew, as salty as it had been while he was in the Marines. He had to avoid all the things a man did while with his buds that he wouldn't do in mixed company, like adjusting himself when his underwear got him in a bind or everything was sticky with sweat. So far he'd avoided those pitfalls.

They hadn't filmed the titanium pylon with its shock absorber on his prosthetic because he wore work boots to cover the carbon fiber foot. There might come a time when he'd have to bare all in order to protect himself, but he wasn't quite ready for that. Once people saw the prosthetic, their whole perception of him changed. He'd left home because his own father doubted his abilities and treated him like a cripple.

If he'd thought of all this stuff sooner, he might have called the whole thing off. But he was preparing for a siege, just as he had when he was in the military. He might never have to defend his right to do the work he enjoyed, but if it came down to it, he could prove he was just as able-bodied as the next man. Most of the time.

There would come a time when he wouldn't be able to do the work. The skin and tissue on his stump might break down from the stress. He knew it. There were weekends he did without his prosthesis entirely to give himself a break from it.

But not this weekend.

"Guys, we have to take these things over to the other side of the project. They'll be moved next week to another site. Get a move on," he urged. The two men closed their phones and put them away. Julio helped him tie down the plastic tubes while Hector jumped into the truck and started it up.

"How 'bout I record you guys while you unload?" Cal asked while they drove around the perimeter of the building inside the fence.

Julio scowled. "You said you needed us to video you working."

"Not constantly."

Julio and Hector looked at each other and grinned. "We haven't been," Hector admitted.

Cal jerked his head around to stare at them both. Outrage punched him. "You assholes. I've been working my ass off all day."

The two roared with laughter.

Anger heated his face. "I'm sitting in the truck while you two unload all this shit."

"All right, Cal." Hector's shoulders continued to shake with mirth, although he stifled the sounds.

"You can rest tomorrow," Julio said, his tone conciliatory.

Shit. They were forever playing jokes on each other. And they'd thought him friend enough to do the same to him... His anger dissipated. "I have a date tomorrow."

"With the hot señorita Kathleen?"

"Don't call her that, Hector."

Hector's brows rose.

He didn't really know Kathleen, but she was more than a lush body and a beautiful mouth.

"I meant it in a very nice and totally respectful way, Callahan," Hector said.

"I know. I'm just edgy." And tired. All night the repercussions of losing his job had played through his mind, each scenarios worse than the last. The worst being having to return to Texas with his tail between his legs.

His brother had been supportive, but his father and mother had serious reservations about him working on the building sites. His parents' constant worry and coddling had driven him crazy.

Their lack of faith in him would have surely been crippling if he'd stayed around.

He wasn't a cripple. Sure, he had some issues stemming from having lost a leg in combat, but he'd worked through the worst of them. He just had a little further to go.

He took off his hard hat and scrubbed his knuckles over his cropped hair. Hector pulled to a stop.

"You know how you guys feel when some of the guys make those fucked-up remarks about your green cards even though they know you're American citizens?" He turned to Julio. "Or every time the cops roust you, thinking you're a gang member when you're just driving home after work?" These were things he knew happened on a regular basis in their neighborhood.

"Yeah," Julio said. Hector nodded.

"In both cases, people are judging you because of your heritage. Their perception of you is skewed because of their prejudice. If I wore shorts to work and flashed my scars and my prosthetic, every man on this site would see me in a different way. Some of them would refuse to work with me because of it."

He stopped to look at each man. "I haven't said anything to any of the other guys because of that. If it becomes known among the crew, and it causes an issue, it will only support Warren's case to get rid of me."

"We have proof now that you are capable of doing the job," Julio said.

"And they see you do the work, Callahan," Hector added.

"It doesn't matter. Perception is truth."

Julio frowned. "When the other guys find out, what will you do? They're bound to if asshole Warren keeps harping about it."

"I'll deal with it when it happens." He rubbed his hands over his head once more, then put his hard hat back on and climbed out of the truck.

"I thought you said we were unloading," Julio said.

"Three of us working will get it done faster than two, and I'm ready to go home, aren't you?"

"Yeah, I am," Julio was quick to answer.

Hector adjusted his hard hat and pulled on his gloves. "While we are working, Julio and I will tell you the secret of winning a woman's heart and keeping her happy."

Cal raised a brow. "And you two think you have something figured out the rest of us guys don't know already?"

Julio shot him a look. "You know what they say about Latin lovers, Callahan. We have a reputation for a reason."

Cal fought hard not to grin.

Julio grunted as he lifted one of the tubes. "The first thing to remember is to always tell the truth. Women will forgive you for many things, but lying to them isn't one of them. They'll say they forgive you, but they will remember *forever*, and whatever lie you tell them will come back to bite you on the ass."

Hector nodded. "The next thing is to really mean what you say to them. If you tell her she has beautiful *pechos*," Hector held his cupped hands in front of his chest, "believe it. Because if you don't, it is the same as a lie."

Julio added, "And don't just tell her they're beautiful, tell her in a way that will convince her."

Cal slid a tube out of the bed of the truck into Hector's hands. Kathleen did have generous breasts. That small hint of cleavage that had peeked out at him all night had whetted his appetite for more. "How the hell am I supposed to do that?"

"By telling her how it makes you feel when you see them." Hector pointed a glove-covered finger at him. "But you must not say 'seeing your breasts *hace que mi polla dura.*' You must say it in a way that is romantic."

Cal ran a hand over his jaw. He wasn't good about sharing his feelings. Any of his feelings. How was he supposed to say something romantic when what he'd really be feeling is embarrassed and clumsy? And a hard dick was a hard dick. Where was the romance in that? Though as memory served, his ex had at times been very pleased with his.

"Women want to be romanced, Callahan. To know they are desired. My Carmela has grown round since giving me my children. But I still tell her how soft her skin is, how much I desire her. And she still blushes for me. And her smile." Hector blushed himself.

Julio returned from stacking the pipe next to the rest. "Women try to hide those things they don't like about their body. But in order to get naked with one, you must let them know you desire the whole package." He grinned. "And you will be rewarded."

By the time they'd finished unloading the truck, Cal's ass was dragging, but as he drove home he continued to mull over all of Hector and Julio's advice.

He'd flirted with girls in college and never had a problem. But college girls' expectations were much lower than a grown, independent woman's. He'd have to up his game if he intended to impress Kathleen. He kept coming back to that moment when he kissed her fingertips to ease her embarrassment over the ink stains. She'd been worked up about something at work and had remained tense, but after that one small gesture she'd relaxed with him. And her smile—those lips…

As soon as he was home he shed his clothes and prosthetic and climbed into a hot tub of water to soak his tired muscles. He bathed his stump in antibacterial soap and massaged it, making certain he had no red spots or soreness. He'd pushed himself too hard today. Which meant he didn't really need to be on his leg all day tomorrow.

Out of all the difficult things he'd learned over the last three years, accepting the signals his body sent when he'd overdone was one of them. He wasn't even thirty yet, and yet he had to curtail his activities on occasion. Not often, but enough to make him resent it.

But he was still better off than others. Better off than his men who'd died in the Humvee. He pressed the heels of his hands into his eyes until the sting subsided.

He'd have to call Kathleen and change their plans. Maybe see if she'd be open to a drive, a movie, and dinner instead. They could do the zoo another time. If she didn't change her mind about going out with him altogether.

He could understand her reluctance. To trust another man

after the betrayals she'd experienced would be difficult. Although he'd be a pretty safe bet. It was hard enough for him to take on one woman, let alone several.

The water was cold by the time he climbed out of the tub and dried off. He sat on a towel on the toilet lid and put on underwear, sweat pants and a T-shirt. He balanced against the sink on one leg and washed his liner and hung it on the plastic form it was shipped on to dry, then grabbed the crutches he'd propped against the wall.

Once in the living room, he reached for his cell on the coffee table and texted Hector and Julio to send him their videos from today on the job site. He'd piece the clips together into some kind of sequence, like a day on the job type of thing. He settled on the couch with his laptop in his lap, and pulled up the website for a local cinema to see what was playing.

The awkward feeling that dogged him every time he thought about asking a woman out was already building to undermine his confidence.

Why was he still letting Stacy's attitude mess with his mind? It had been damn near three fucking years since she rushed out of his hospital room and out of his life. Kathleen was a totally different woman. Stronger, more independent. He found her number and punched it.

"Hello, Callahan," she greeted him. "How was your day?"

The helpless feeling subsided and he found himself smiling. "More than I bargained for. I was wondering if we could do something a little more laid back tomorrow and save the zoo for another day."

"Sure. What do you have in mind?"

"How does a drive up the coast, dinner, and a movie sound?"

"Perfect."

"Comedy or drama?"

"Definitely comedy. We'll save the drama for another time."

They spent a few minutes talking about the movies and decided on one.

"How was your day?" he asked.

"More than I expected, too."

He heard the stress behind her words and frowned. "Anything you'd like to talk about?"

"Maybe tomorrow after I've had a couple of glasses of wine and a good night's sleep."

"Sounds like your first week on the job hasn't met your expectations."

"No, it hasn't." Once again the distress came through.

"Next week will be better, Kathleen. Just take it a day at a time until you hit your stride."

She remained silent for a moment. "It wasn't the work, Cal."

The invitation came without him even thinking about it. "Would you like to come over and share a pizza? I was going to order one. I have beer, but no wine."

She hesitated only a moment. "Sure. What's the address? I'll bring the wine."

"Where are you coming from?"

They spent some time talking about the easiest way for her to travel from her brother's house to his apartment. "If you get lost, call me and I'll come find you."

"I have Lolita to show me the way. I've named my GPS since I use it so much. If she doesn't get me lost, I'll see you in twenty-five minutes."

"I'll wait and order the pizza once you get here."

Cal glanced around his place. It wasn't spotless, but it would do. He stared at his absent ankle and foot. He could put his prosthetic back on, but the sweatpants wouldn't hide a damn thing. Kathleen knew his lower leg was gone. It was best to get it out in the open and let her come to terms with it.

Maybe that's what he'd done wrong before. Hiding the damn thing didn't seem to make it any easier to accept. And why the hell had he attempted to do that anyway? It was a fact of life for him. Part of who he was. If she couldn't deal with it…they'd only have invested one date and a pizza.

The pep talk wasn't making too much headway against the knot of anxiety taking root in the pit of his stomach. He didn't want Kathleen to be turned off by something he couldn't control. He felt more carefree when he was with her. Her sense of humor kept him smiling.

And he'd dreamed more than once of those lips, painted bright red and leaving a trail of lipstick everywhere they went.

CHAPTER 7

TRY AS SHE might, Kathleen hadn't been able to shake the heartsick, angry feeling that dogged her all day. The promise of a slice of pizza and a glass of white wine didn't ease it one damn bit. She'd never felt less hungry.

The thought of seeing Cal helped a little, though. Her response to him had guided her to say yes to his offer of an escape from her empty house and her thoughts.

She ached to be held for just a few moments. She wondered if it would be too soon for something like that.

Lolita's voice instructed her to turn left, cutting through her emotional distraction. She flipped on her blinker and swung off the busy thoroughfare and onto a fractionally quieter, less frantic street.

She spied the sign for the four-plex at the same time Lolita said, "Destination on left." The feminine voice projected satisfaction, or was that just her imagination? If the old girl had some pride in a job well done, who was she to question it? That was better than she'd felt today.

God, she had to shake this off and quit wallowing.

She fished her cell phone out of her purse, found Cal's number, and punched it. "I'm in the parking lot."

"Just climb the stairs. I'm the second door on the landing.

"Be right there." She gathered her purse and the bottle of

wine and got out. The wind had picked up and whipped her hair across her face, so she tucked the wine under her arm while she held her hair to one side and climbed the stairs.

The two apartments she'd looked at after work were farther away from the office and had been way too expensive. It might be smart to look into a place like this instead.

Cal stood at the door and held it open for her with a carefully placed crutch. Her gaze swept down to the bottom of his right pant leg, which hung empty. Pain punched at her shaky emotions, but she plastered a smile on her face.

"Thanks for asking me over. Zach's doing maneuvers and hasn't called or shown up."

"I wanted to see you, Kathleen."

Those simple words and his direct gaze triggered a smile.

"After we order our pizza, you can tell me what happened today that's got you so worked up." He swung forward on his crutches, releasing the door behind her. He was as skillful and athletic using crutches as on his feet. When he swung close, she caught the clean scent of soap, fabric softener, and him. His T-shirt, faded and worn, hugged his chest and shoulders like an old friend. His sweat pants hung low on his hips.

Even dressed for comfort he looked sexy as hell.

When he turned his intent, searching gaze on her, she experienced a buoyant sensation in the pit of her stomach, and tingling ache of arousal ignited between her legs. Her mouth went dry, and she couldn't think of a thing to say to break the silence.

He grinned. "Did you work late?" he asked, his fingers plucking at the sleeve of her blouse. Every nerve cell in her arm suddenly rose to attention.

"No. I'm apartment hunting, and I went directly to two different units right after work."

"Any luck?"

She shook her head. "Both were too expensive for the space they had to offer, but then they were closer to the beach, too. I'd settle for something closer to work with lower rent."

"Rent's eighteen hundred a month here, but you have about

nine hundred square feet of space."

"That sounds wonderful." As opposed to the twenty-four hundred a month for an area about as big as the interior of her car.

"I'll give you the super's number. He has other units in the neighborhood. There might be a vacancy."

"I'd like that."

"Want me to open that for you?" Cal asked, indicating the wine bottle she was clutching.

"Yes. Please." She wandered around his living room while he opened the bottle. It was a typical bachelor pad, with a large flat-screen television, leather couch and chair, and a matching ottoman big enough to drive to work on. The shelving unit under the television held an eclectic collection of music CDs, DVDs, and books. She tugged free a volume on engineering as technical as some of her college textbooks.

"Why didn't you go to college after you were discharged?"

"I actually enlisted in the Marines hoping to go to the Combat Engineering School. I thought with my experience...but by the time I got through boot camp, I learned I didn't have enough college, and there weren't any slots open, plus, what the Marine Corps needs at the moment is what you get when you enlist."

She heard no bitterness in his voice and wondered at it. But even working in the Engineering Corps, he could have still been killed or injured.

He twisted the corkscrew in and pushed the mechanism handles down to pop the cork. "I'd just gotten out of a regimented field, and my schedule was regimented because of physical therapy and all that. I wasn't ready to sit in a classroom. Then I decided I liked the active side of construction better than the design part of it, for the time being." He opened an overhead cabinet, lifted down one of two wine glasses, and poured her a half a glass of wine.

"The hard work suits you. You're staying in shape and doing something you love." She shoved the book back in place. "I've been sitting behind a drafting table drawing, designing on a computer, or studying in a library for the last six years." She joined him at the island that divided the kitchen from the living room and reached for the glass. "My brother Zach wants me to go running with him on the beach on the weekends to get in shape. He runs five miles a day or more."

Cal's brows quirked in a semi-frown. "I wouldn't suggest you take on five miles to start with."

"I won't. Not without an oxygen tank and an ambulance standing by."

His masculine laughter triggered a smile.

She took a sip of the wine. "I told him I needed to learn to walk before I could run."

His blue-green eyes crinkled at the corners as he smiled. "Sounds like a good idea. You don't plan to end up like a string bean, do you?" He swiveled to the refrigerator and got a beer.

"It couldn't happen if I ate only one bean a week. It isn't in my genetic makeup to be a twig."

He ran his gaze down over her, then back up to her face. "I think you're perfect just the way you are, Kathleen."

Her heart turned over. She took a sip of wine to cover the effect of both his words and the touch of his gaze. Heat stormed her cheeks. "That was nicely done, Callahan. Would you like me to carry your drink so we can sit on the couch?"

He grinned. "Sure." He handed over his beer and swung around the island to go into the living room.

She learned why the ottoman was the size of a car when he tugged it close so they could both use it to prop their legs on.

"What do you like on your pizza?" he asked.

"Anything but anchovies or pineapple."

"Why anyone would ruin a perfectly good pie with either of those beats the hell out of me," he agreed. "How about pepperoni, sausage, mushrooms, sweet peppers, black olives, and extra cheese."

"Sold."

He leaned over to the end table to retrieve his cell phone. The movement stretched the material over the rounded curve of his hip and outlined his tight buns.

Hit by a desire to touch, Kathleen gulped her wine. Maybe she should have brought another bottle. One wasn't going to be enough. On second thought, she needed to keep a clear head. She set the glass on the coffee table.

She leaned back, kicked off her shoes and propped her feet up on the ottoman. She stared at the empty space where Cal's ankle and foot should have been and weren't. The ache over his loss hit her again.

Cal finished the call and tossed the phone onto the couch next to him. "They'll deliver it in about thirty minutes. Now tell me what happened at work today."

The guilt she'd been carrying with her for days rose up full force. "There's something I need to tell you first."

"What is it?"

"I think Paul Warren really has it in for you. You need to watch your back." There, she'd said it.

"I know."

Surprised she jerked her head up.

"He's been riding my ass at work for days. I don't know why he has it in for me. It's probably my leg." He ran a distracted hand over his close-cropped hair.

The tight, worrisome feeling of guilt she'd carried around all week eased. "What do you plan to do about it?"

"I'm building up evidence of my competence on the job. Hector and Julio taped me with their cell phones working all day today. I thought I'd compile the clips into a day-on-the-job thing to show the powers that be if he keeps pushing."

"That's a really good idea. I can help you do that if you'd like. I'm pretty good on the computer."

He smiled. "Thanks. I could use some help. By the time I left the site today, I'd done two men's jobs, and those assholes had used the excuse of taping me to sucker me into doing just that...their two jobs. Plus mine."

Kathleen chuckled.

He rested his fingertips on her forearm and ran them up and

down. "Now tell me what's been going on with you."

She told him everything that had happened that morning. Her anger built again just thinking about it.

"Who do you think did it?" he asked, his expression grim.

She couldn't say anything about Paul Warren. It would only throw fuel on the fire between them. "I work with three other architects. They all seemed upset as I was. I don't believe any of them did it. Or I'm hoping none of them did it." She dropped her legs from the ottoman and reached for her wine. "I've password-protected my computer, and during my lunch break I bought an external hard drive and saved everything to that as well. I'll keep it with me when I'm not in the office."

"And your drawings?"

"I scanned them into the computer and took the hard copy home."

Cal gripped her hand. "Do you think Warren might have anything to do with this?"

"Why do you ask?"

"He was in the parking lot when I dropped you off. He wanted to know what I was doing there. I just told him I'd given someone a ride to their car. I didn't mention it was you."

"But he might have seen me."

"Yes."

Kathleen swallowed. Well one problem was either solved or would complicate things for her. "It's none of his business who I see."

"But he might start projecting his anger at me onto you."

She remained silent a moment. She couldn't allow him to take responsibility. "Things got off to a rocky start between us from the first day, Cal. It may not have anything at all to do with you. The tech guy said my file was deleted around seven. We were in the parking lot around nine-thirty. He and Hillary, one of my coworkers, went out for drinks right after work. He'd have had to delete the file after that. So you weren't what inspired it, if it was him." She sipped her wine. "There's no way to know for certain who might have done it."

"Are you sure you can get past this?"

She set aside her empty wine glass and relaxed back against the couch again. "I don't have a choice. I've already scheduled my licensing exam. I have to be currently employed in my field to take it." Her attention snagged on a small scar running along the underside of his jaw. The beard dusting his firm jawline made his features appear all the more masculine.

His unusual teal eyes traced over her features. "Do you think you can put it behind you?"

"I'll be on guard from now on, but I'll get through it. I'll take it a day at a time, like you suggested. If things don't level out, I'll look for another job."

When he put his arm around her, it seemed natural to lean into him. The sturdy, muscular width of his chest lay beneath her hand. The comfort he offered drained away the rest of her tension. The weight of worry resting squarely on her shoulders seemed to shift.

After a few moments, every thought of what had happened at work flew from her mind to be replaced by awareness of him. A sensual lassitude invaded her muscles, draining the last of her tension. How could being in his arms create such a firestorm of need?

CAL'S HAND RESTED against her waist. His blood raced. She smelled sweet, and the generous swell of her breast pressing against his side was the most tempting weight he'd ever felt. Adrenaline stormed his system, and he swallowed against the accompanying breathlessness. He wanted to tilt her face up and kiss her. He wanted to drink her in. He traced the curve of her cheek with his fingertips.

The phone rang. "That's probably the pizza guy." His voice sounded husky. He reached for his cell.

"Mr. Crowes this is Nora Harper. I'm a reporter for Channel 8 news."

Cal bit back a curse.

"I'd really like to interview you. We've been looking into your background and learned you're a veteran and an amputee. You must realize how rare it is for someone with your issue to work in the field of commercial construction. We think you could be a real inspiration to other people with disabilities."

Cal reluctantly drew away from Kathleen. "Look, Ms. Harper. I'm not interested in being on television. Like I told all the other news people who showed up at the site, I just want to be able to work and live my life. There are other guys out there who have given more than I have who deserve your attention. Get out there and find them."

"We're already doing that, but we want to include you in our broadcast. Since we released the video on Tuesday morning and mentioned that you were a retired vet and an amputee, a great many viewers have commented on the story. There's been some back and forth about whether, as an amputee, you'd be competent doing the same job as the other workers. That you might be a token disabled employee for Wiley to show their diversity."

Cal remained silent as the pain resonated through him. "What people believe doesn't matter to me, Ms. Harper. I'm working at something I'm good at. If I lose that job, it will be because you stirred the pot."

"What do you mean by that—"

He cut off the conversation. When her number flashed again he blocked it.

Kathleen grasped his hand, concern in her expression. "Maybe we should spend some time tomorrow working on that video, Callahan."

He swallowed. "Maybe so."

"There are people in this world who are so miserable it makes them feel better to tear other people down. Don't buy into anything they say."

It sounded like she was speaking from experience. "I won't." He gave her hand a squeeze. "But if you really want me to feel better, you could give me the kiss I was hoping to ease into before the phone rang."

Kathleen studied his face, her expression serious despite his attempt at levity. She leaned forward and pressed her lips to his. Her mouth, soft and warm, parted to caress his. Heat rocketed through him, and he reached for her, but she pulled back and his hands slid down her arms and away.

Her eyes betrayed uncertainty. "I'm not ready for anything serious yet, Callahan."

Anger at the faceless fiancé stormed through him. She was so open and straightforward about everything else. To see her hesitant about anything was painful. The asshole had really hurt her.

But he had his own reasons for being cautious, too. "I'm good with taking it slow, Kathleen."

The uncertainty in her expression eased.

"My girlfriend broke things off because she couldn't stand the sight of my leg or my scars."

Kathleen flinched.

"I was still in the hospital with my foot gone, my jaw wired shut, and the rest of me cut up by shrapnel when she walked—no, ran away. So I do understand how you feel."

"I'm sorry, Cal." He read real pain in her face, pain he didn't want her experiencing on his behalf, because it could too easily trip over into pity.

"She did me a favor. I didn't need her to pretend to have my back when she didn't. Nobody wants lip service where there should be love. Nobody deserves that."

"No they don't. And I understand about that, too."

He suppressed a sigh. "Yeah, I guess you do. So out of all the things we have in common, it seems we've discovered the worst."

"We'll just have to poke around and see if we can find something more positive."

He nodded. That kiss they'd just shared seemed like the place to start.

CHAPTER 8

KATHLEEN RAN A quick brush through her hair, and, using a scrunchie, tried to tame her thick, dark hair into a ponytail at the base of her neck.

She checked her light makeup, and after spreading on pale pink lip gloss with a fingertip, washed her hands and dried them. Earlier she'd cleaned the house in preparation for Cal's visit, not that men seemed to notice much about things like that. Zach rarely did. But she still scanned the living room for her brother's random clutter. Why on earth would he leave a cleaning kit for his Sig balanced on the edge of the flat-screen television?

For a guy who didn't want anyone to know what he did for a living, he didn't make much effort to organize his living space so visitors wouldn't guess. But then since she'd lived here, the only people who visited his house were his teammates when they dropped by to pick him up.

She shook her head. Her brother's social life sucked worse than hers. Or had he cut back on his normal routines because she was rooming with him? She didn't think so. If she had to guess, she'd say he had no social life, only his job. That was sad.

And his continued absence without word was worrying.

A decisive knock on the door broke into her worry-fest and sent her heartbeat soaring. Even though she was expecting Cal, she still looked through the peephole. She was already smiling when she opened it. "Hey."

Instead of an answering smile, Cal frowned. "I hate to tell you this, Kathleen, but you have two flat tires."

"What?"

He pointed at her vehicle.

She stepped out on the stoop and automatically shut the door behind her. On the right side both tires were completely flat. Shock froze her vocal chords, otherwise she'd have been making free use of some of Zach's favorite swear words. She strode across the drive to look at the damage and squatted down to look over the face of the tire. There was no damage on the sides, but the tread was too heavy to see any punctures in that area.

"Could you have run over something last night on your way home?" Cal asked, offering her a hand up.

"I don't know. If I did, I didn't notice it. Everything was fine when I got home."

"If it's a slow leak, it can take a little while for them to go completely flat."

She brushed a hand across her forehead. Her face felt stiff. "They're brand new tires. My parents didn't want me driving across country without having the old ones replaced. I'll have to call for a tow."

"They'll charge you an arm and a leg. I can take the wheels off and run them to a garage. If you ran over something, they can be plugged."

"It's too much, Cal."

"Naw. It will only take me a few minutes."

"You mean hours. Nothing takes a few minutes here."

He grinned. "Well—The tow will probably cost you about a hundred bucks. If you have to replace the tires it will be between a hundred and hundred fifty apiece, depending on the type of tire you want, plus the service fee to put them on. If I take them in and all they need is to be plugged, you'll just be out the cost of the repair."

At a time when she was saving every dime for the deposit, hookup fees, and first month's rent for an apartment, the projected cost was mind-boggling. And she had to have her car to get to work.

"All right, you've convinced me." She brushed a hand over her forehead and smoothed away a few stray tendrils that from sides of her face. "This is unbelievable."

"Relax. We'll deal with this then go out for something to eat and hit the movies later."

"I wanted time to work on your video clips. You may need them on Monday."

"We can work on them tomorrow. Unless you have something else planned."

She shook her head. "No, I don't have anything planned. I haven't heard from Zach, and I was just going to hang here."

"If he's out in the desert doing maneuvers, they may have decided to extend their stay."

"I didn't say he was out in the desert." How had he guessed?

"You said he runs five miles or more a day, he's in the Navy, and he's been gone for two days without word. It doesn't take a mental giant to figure out he's a SEAL, Kathleen. My Marine division worked with some of them in Afghanistan. In fact, it was a SEAL Team who saved my life after the IED exploded under our Humvee. I'm not going to say anything to anyone about him.

"Oh, and I'll need your keys to get the jack out of the trunk."

Her throat burned and tightened at his reference to the IED which had taken his lower leg. She turned away before he could read her expression. "I'll get them."

"I've never changed a tire in my life that I didn't get dirty doing it." Cal removed his button up cotton shirt and his T-shirt, exposing a well-toned chest with a light coating of brown hair and muscular shoulders. A small tattoo consisting of three names crossed his pectoral muscle on the left side.

He held out the shirts. "If you'll put those somewhere, I'd appreciate it."

Kathleen draped his shirt over the back of one of the kitchen chairs and tried not to stare. There was one deep scar on the back of his right arm and another at the waistband of his jeans above his hip. They did nothing to detract from the masculine beauty of his body.

What was she doing getting mixed up with someone as attractive as he was? He could be beating women off with a stick. He probably did. Although he didn't act like it. But how was she to know? Lee hadn't acted like it either.

Using her jack and his, Cal positioned them where they'd create the best stability. "You can crank one while I do the other. Then I'll take the lug nuts off and we'll be good to go."

They worked together to keep the car level as it rose high enough for him to remove the flats.

He had to work hard at some of the lug nuts, most likely put on by machine. On a whim, Kathleen filmed him with her cell phone while he worked. His muscular biceps bunched every time he put pressure on the lug wrench, and her video of it proved he was capable of doing things physical even off-site.

It also gave her an opportunity to admire him from behind a camera, so he couldn't tell how affected she was by all that bare, manly skin. The early morning sun glinted off the blondish highlights in his hair. If he let it grow out, would it be wavy or straight?

Once he got both wheels off, he was sweating. Kathleen went inside and came back with a hand towel and offered it to him.

"I'm sorry, Callahan."

"What for?" He wiped his face and the back of his neck with the towel.

"This isn't the way I wanted our day together to go."

He winked at her. "This is just a small bump in the road, darlin'. We'll get over it and move on."

The way he said darlin' in his Texas drawl made her smile. They went in so he could clean up.

AT THE GARAGE, Cal returned from washing his hands in the restroom and slouched into one of the uncomfortable plastic seats in the waiting area of True Tire Company.

Kathleen fidgeted in her seat, then stood up, placing the heels of her hands against her lower back and stretching. The bowlike curve of her spine thrust her generous breasts out. The three employees at the counter snapped to attention, their eyes following her every move while she was totally oblivious. With her hourglass figure, lush mouth, and green eyes surrounded by thick dark lashes, she was gorgeous…and didn't even realize it.

She'd only eaten one slice of pizza the night before and drunk two shallow glasses of wine. Who had convinced her she needed to work on her figure or anything else?

A sudden fierce possessiveness rushed through him. Who the hell were these guys to ogle his woman? Getting to his feet, Cal suggested, "Let's walk across the street and get an ice cream."

"No ice cream for me. But I'd like something to drink."

Once outside the garage, he caught her hand and gave it a squeeze. "What has you so worked up?"

"Will they be able to tell what punctured my tires?"

"Probably not. Why?"

"I'm just being paranoid after all the stuff that happened at work yesterday."

Cal remained silent, thinking it through. "Why would they puncture two tires and not all four?"

She shook her head. "This coming on top of what happened yesterday just has me jumpy and restless. And Zach not calling to let me know he's okay…"

"I'm sure he's fine, Kathleen. Someone would call you if he weren't."

The sound of the vehicles rushing by made it too noisy to talk. Walking across four lanes of traffic took some maneuvering, but they made it. Cal held open the door to the Baskin Robbins for her to precede him.

The scent of freshly baked brownies filled the air. A man ambled by with a sundae topped with them and covered with whipped cream. "What would you like?"

She looked at the brownie concoction with open longing.

"Just some ice water will be fine."

Cal didn't argue. He ordered two ice waters and one of the brownie sundaes with two spoons. He nodded toward a booth and waited for her to slide in before he set the ice water down in front of her and slid the sundae to the middle of the table.

Kathleen's gaze settled on his face.

"A bite or two won't hurt you."

She drew a deep breath. "It seems we have a theme going here. Feed Kathleen."

It did seem they'd spent more time eating together and talking than anything else. He couldn't just ignore the opportunity. "Maybe we need to think of something more interesting and physical we can do together." He spooned up some whipped cream and offered it to her.

Soft color touched her cheeks, and after a moment's pause, she leaned forward, opened her mouth, and eased the whipped cream from the spoon. The response he'd hoped for boomeranged right back to him and he was hard in an instant.

Was he ready to drop his pants and bare all? Was she? He sure wished they both were. But no, neither of them was ready to take the plunge.

When Kathleen reciprocated with a spoonful of brownie and ice cream, he smiled and took the sweet into his mouth.

After her second bite, she rested a hand over his. "If you think the way to my heart is through my stomach, you could be right. And you being handy as pockets on a shirt doesn't hurt any, either." She spooned up another bite of ice cream and brownie.

"I'm handy in other ways, too," he said before leaning forward to take it. This seduction thing was easier than he'd thought it would be, and every time Kathleen's eyes softened or lit with emotion, it encouraged him to be bolder.

She bit her lip. "Are you flirting with me like this because you think I'll put the brakes on before you have to?"

"I'm flirting with you like this because I like the way you blush when I do it." He tucked a strand of dark hair behind her ear. She lowered her face, but not before he caught the parting of her lips.

Maybe if he made her want him, really want him, she wouldn't get all fixated on his leg. "I want you, and I want you to know it. Aren't you used to guys flirting with you?"

She shook her head. "My first few years at college I was a chunk and the guys weren't all that interested. After I lost some weight, my ex and I started dating. He wasn't much of a flirt."

"From what you told me about him, he wasn't much of a boyfriend, either." He offered her another bite of ice cream and she shook her head.

"After some introspection, I have to agree." She leaned her elbows on the table and folded her arms, which pushed her breasts together and gave him a drool-worthy view of her cleavage.

He could no more keep his eyes from feasting on the view than he could stop things south from rising to the occasion. If he got any harder, his zipper was going to leave a permanent imprint on his dick.

"The way you're looking at me right now already makes you a much better boyfriend than he ever was."

"It also guarantees I'm going to have to sit here a few minutes and cool down before I can walk out of here." He reached for his ice water.

Kathleen leaned back in her chair, removing temptation from sight and reach. "Me too, Callahan."

CHAPTER 9

K ATHLEEN STUDIED THE San Diego scenery while Cal drove
them back to Zach's house. Moving to California from Boston
was like blasting off to the moon. The light here seemed more
intense, the styles of the cities were totally different. And she was
still surprised every time she saw palm trees. The more moderate
changes in temperature in California were rather pleasant, too.

She still missed home and family. Missed the few friends she'd
been able to keep after the breakup. And there were still days she
woke and reached for her phone to call Tamara. But not Lee.

Thinking of Lee brought her attention back to Cal. How
could two men be so completely different? Though her sexual
experience was limited to a few heavy petting sessions in high
school and sex with Lee, she at least knew the basics of attraction.
But Cal Crowes was teaching her something altogether different.

With Cal she was primed and ready for sex after just a look.
She'd wanted to climb across the table and straddle his lap right
there in the ice cream shop.

He wanted her. She wanted him. It was a good thing. But too
much of a good thing could be bad for you. This wild sexual
response she had to him could end up hurting her, hurting him.
And having sex without an emotional connection just wasn't
something she could do.

"You're thinking loudly again," Cal said as he laced his fingers with hers on the console between the seats.

"I know." She needed to learn to relax and just let things happen. That had been one of Lee's many criticisms. She could never be spontaneous. She had to analyze and plan everything. But she'd been on a rigorous schedule of classes and work. What had he expected?

He no doubt believed she was supposed to put him first. But when they did have time to spend together... She had to let this go and quit dragging up the hurtful things she'd experienced with Lee.

Cal was different. And she had been spontaneous with him. It was easy to be when you had the time. "Thanks for helping me today."

"Don't thank me yet. I don't have the wheels back on."

Kathleen gave his hand a squeeze. "I'm not worried."

Cal backed the truck into the drive and they got out. For the second time since she'd known him, he had a small difficulty with his prosthetic. The uneven liner inside the truck bed threw his balance off, and he had to grip the edge of the bed while he shoved the wheels down to the tailgate.

Kathleen dropped one of the wheels off the tailgate, then rolled it to her car. The damn thing was heavy, and she had trouble controlling it, which pissed her off. Or was she angry because of Cal's struggle? Every time she thought about a part of him not being there, it hurt her. It didn't make her nauseous or freak her out like his ex. It made her ache for him. He would have to struggle with it the rest of his life. And whoever loved him would be a part of that struggle.

When he removed his shirt for the second time that day, she forgot about everything but enjoying the scenery.

Putting the wheels on was nothing compared to getting them off. Within half an hour, Cal had the wheels back on and the lug nuts tightened.

"Come inside for a cold drink." She offered him the hand towel she'd retrieved from the house to wipe his face.

He followed her into the house, through the bland, personality-starved living room, and into the kitchen. She got him a bottle of cold water from the fridge and waited for him to open his bottle and take a drink before she moved in close.

"I'm sweaty," he warned.

"You're fine." She smiled and ran a hand down over his shoulder to the tattoo. "And I appreciate your helping me get the car roadworthy again." She rose on tiptoe and kissed him.

Cal wasn't slow on the uptake. His hand splayed against her spine urged her to lean into him. His lips parted and his tongue brushed the seam between hers.

Kathleen accepted the slow thrust between her lips, and nearly groaned at the act of penetration. With the promising bulge beneath his jeans pressing into her belly, she wanted to just part her legs and invite him in.

The sound of a masculine throat being cleared broke the spell, and Cal raised his head, but didn't release her.

Kathleen looked over her shoulder at her brother's scowling, disapproving face. This coming from the man who unashamedly admitted to sleeping around, wanting nothing more than a quick roll in the hay.

She fought the urge to roll her eyes and said, "Hey, Zach."

"Hey." His green gaze settled on Cal, intent and searching. She didn't miss the air of bristling big brother that radiated off him like heat off of asphalt. With his scruffy, unshaven face, butchered hair, and unsmiling demeanor, he looked deadly.

"This is Cal Crowes. I mentioned him the other night."

"Yeah, I remember." His deadpan tone sounded less than enthused.

Cal released her in order to step forward and offer his hand. His attention on her brother was just as intent as Zach's was on him. And he didn't seem intimidated, despite Zach's posturing. "We've met before, under pretty intense circumstances."

"We have?" Zach's features relaxed enough to show mild curiosity.

"Yeah. You and your team saved my life."

CAL NEVER DREAMED he'd ever see any of the men who saved his life that day. He'd thought about trying to find them to say thanks, but because of the way they operated, hadn't pursued it. They were like shadows over there, doing the job with complete anonymity. They didn't want or expect to be acknowledged in any way.

He'd known a couple who'd gone on patrol with them. Flash and Greenback. And now, dressed again, he was sitting across the coffee table from the medic who worked on him before they loaded him into the chopper.

"Flash and Greenback, they're okay?"

"Yeah. Both are doing well."

"Good, I'm glad. They used to tag along with my unit sometimes."

"Yeah, I know. Crazy fuckers."

Cal grinned. "Yeah." Kathleen's hand came to rest on his thigh in comfort and support, and he placed a hand over it.

Zach followed the gesture with narrowed eyes. "You're back on your feet, and Kathleen says you're working construction."

"Yeah. Commercial. I'm working with the crew who's building the tower downtown."

Zach raised a brow. "Didn't get enough of danger in the sandbox?"

"We sometimes have to dodge falling supplies or dropped tools, but for the most part it's tame stuff." He shrugged.

"Kathleen told me about what happened her first day on the job. Doesn't sound all that tame to me."

"Nothing like Afghanistan. I'd have bled to death if you and the others hadn't gotten me out of the wreckage when you did." It took all his will to maintain his composure.

"We were just in the right place at the right time, the same as you were that day on the job."

Cal rose. "I want to thank you anyway." He extended his hand.

Zach rose and took it. "You've passed it on, man. It was meant to be."

Cal met Zach's gaze. The shared experience was written there in his face. Dodged bullets, explosions, IEDs, and the deaths they'd seen, like the three men sealed in body bags they'd loaded on the chopper with him.

Zach's mouth quirked up in a smirk. "You wouldn't want to pay me back by keeping your distance from my sister, would you?"

"Zach!"

At Kathleen's protest, Cal turned to study her flushed cheeks and outraged expression. He grinned and shook his head. "Not a chance."

Zach laughed. "It was worth a shot." His expression grew serious. "I'll still rip off your head and stuff it up your ass if you hurt her."

Cal nodded. "Noted."

Zach slapped his shoulder. "Thanks for getting her car squared away."

"No problem." He turned to Kathleen. "How 'bout that drive we talked about? We'll stop for dinner up the coast."

"That sounds nice." She went to Zach and gave him a hug. "Get some rest."

"Will do."

She grabbed a hand of his wildly curly red locks. "I'll cut your hair tomorrow. Stop chopping at it, or I'll have to shave your head."

Cal turned his laugh into a cough. He got the feeling that both he and Zach only thought they were in charge, while it was Kathleen who really was.

Zach shot him a look, then grinned. "No problem. I'm taking a shower and hitting my bunk. I may sleep for a week."

"Good. That way you won't be waiting up for me when I get home."

Zach narrowed his eyes, first at her, then him.

She got her purse, and Cal rested a hand against the small of her back as they left.

"Real modest guy," Cal said.

"Like someone else I know," she said, with a raised brow.

"Aren't SEALs supposed to have better timing than that?" He opened the passenger door of his truck and Kathleen slid in.

"His timing did suck, but he approves of you."

Cal didn't care one way or the other about that. Well, maybe a little. Kathleen's feelings were the only ones he was interested in. He strode around and got behind the wheel. Curiosity had him asking, "How could you tell?"

"He eased back on the 'let's try and intimidate Kathleen's date into making a break for it' routine. And he was smiling before we left. Always a good sign."

Cal chuckled. "I can't wait to meet the rest of your family."

"Be careful what you wish for, Callahan. You might think Zach's a hard nut to crack, but he doesn't hold a candle to my dad."

Cal pulled out onto the street.

After everything he'd been through, facing the men in Kathleen's family didn't worry him. What concerned him was the possibility of getting naked with her and seeing all the passion she'd offered him in her kiss die. For all the confidence he could project in his work, his daily life, meeting people, he had no confidence at all when it came to lowering the boundaries and leaving himself vulnerable in that way.

The last girl he'd dated told him he closed himself off to intimacy. She hadn't realized it was because he'd been scared the one time they made love. It was his first time since leaving the hospital. His body had worked, but his mind and heart had been preparing for that moment of rejection. After a month of dating, and one night of sex, she'd called it quits. Which hadn't been great for his confidence.

Would he feel the same way with Kathleen? She was already winding her way into his feelings with every laugh, every sign of support. She hadn't cautioned him to be careful, or said a word about his stumbling in the truck bed when he was unable to stabilize his prosthetic foot on the liner.

Kathleen had been around enough men to know how saying anything would make him feel.

"Now who's thinking loudly?" Kathleen murmured. "Did the thought of meeting my dad send you into a funk?"

"I'm not worried about your dad, Kathleen. You're the one I'm dating, so your opinion is the only one that matters." He felt the weight of her interest for several moments as he wound his way to Highway 1.

"Thanks, Callahan."

She spoke with such feeling he glanced in her direction.

KATHLEEN'S PHONE RANG and she dug inside her purse to retrieve it. Seeing her mother's number, she hit the receive button. "Hey, Mom.

"Hey, Kathleen. I haven't heard from you this week so I thought I'd call."

Kathleen tried to push back the immediate resentment that tightened her jaw. She shouldn't feel this way about her mother. But her constant sympathy after the breakup had been hard to take. She kept telling herself her mom worried about her, like she herself had been worrying about Zach for the last two days.

But there always seemed to be a hint of criticism in her mother's voice every time they talked. As though the breakup had been her fault instead of Lee's. Again, it wasn't her mom's fault, because Kathleen hadn't been completely honest with her, but it was damn hard to admit to being a fool. "I've been working, Mom." She glanced at Cal. "And I've had a couple of dates this week."

"Already? You've only been out there a couple of weeks."

"And I've been ignoring my social life for the last six months so I could finish school and my internship. It's time I got back out into the world."

"You're not jumping into something too quickly are you?"

"No, it's been six months."

"Good, because there's someone here who wants to speak to

you. Please don't hang up."

"Kathleen."

At the sound of Lee's voice every muscle in her body went taut.

"I made a big mistake, Kathleen."

Rage shot heat into her face, and for a moment she went deaf as her heart beat like a drum in her ears, drowning out everything he was saying. When the hammering in head cleared, he ran on. "Tamara and I both know we made a mistake."

"She's found out about your serial dating, hasn't she? I knew you'd screw her over just like you did me. I even told her, but she wouldn't listen."

"I know what I did was reprehensible."

"You don't understand the half of it, Lee. And you never will, because you're incapable of basic human decency. Put my Mom back on the phone."

"Kathleen… please listen to me. I still love you."

"Put my mom back on the *fucking* phone!"

"Not until you listen to what I have to say."

Kathleen hit the off button. "I need you to pull over, Cal." The movement of his truck was making her more nauseous than the sound of Lee's voice.

Cal whipped the truck into a parking lot in front of an insurance agency.

When the phone rang again she blocked the call. Her hands shook as she dialed her father's number.

"Kathleen, how are you, honey?"

"I'm fine. Are you at the house, Dad?"

"Yeah. I'm in my workshop repairing a lamp. What's up?"

"I need you to go into the house and give Mom your cell phone."

"She has hers. Has she turned it off? Is something wrong?"

His concern had quick tears burning her eyes. "I've blocked her number because Lee is at the house, and he's used her phone to call me. I need to speak to her."

For several seconds total silence filled the distance between them. "All right." She could hear him moving, a door opened and closed, then another. His breathing quickened while he presumably rushed to the house. "She loves you, Kathleen. She just wants you to be happy. Don't say something you'll regret later."

"I don't intend to. I know firsthand what a lying, conniving con man he is, and how he can look you right in the eye without the slightest tell and talk his way around every lie. She wants to believe in the goodness of people, so she's an easy mark. But she needs to hear the truth, and I'm going to give it to her."

"You're going to have to explain all that to me later, Kathleen. Olivia, it's our daughter."

"Kathleen?" The tentative anxiety in her mother's voice angered her all the more. She gripped the oh-shit handle over the door to keep from punching something.

"I want you to listen, Mom. Lee is using you. He used me for three years, he's used Tamara for six months, and now he's using you. Do you think Tamara was the only one he cheated with while we were together, Mom? There were more. Many more. At least eight women came out of the woodwork after we broke up to let me know he'd gone out with them, and he'd slept with at least four of them, maybe more.

"While I was in class, he was getting busy. While I was planning a wedding, he was screwing my best friend in *my bed*. It wasn't just a breakup, it was a divorce, and he took everything. Everything but my self-respect, and I'm not letting him have that."

She drew a deep breath. "I know you think you know what's best for my happiness, but you don't. I'm making my own happiness, and it won't be tied to a lying, cheating, scumbag like him."

"Why didn't you tell me all this before, Kathleen? Not just about Tamara?"

"Because it was my business, not yours. I'm a grown woman, not a two-year-old. And I wasn't going to let him make me feel anymore a fool than I already did. And I didn't want you to be disappointed in me, in my judgment."

For several beats the only thing she heard on the line was

breathing. "I could never be disappointed in you, Kathleen. I love you. I need to go." Her mother's voice shook. "If I had known any of this…Please unblock my number so I can call you in a few days."

"Don't ever let him back in the house, Mom."

"I won't." Her mom sounded entirely too calm. Spooky calm. "I love you."

"Are you okay?"

"Yes, I'm fine. Your father is here, and Lee will be leaving in just a few minutes. We'll speak again later."

Alarm jangled every nerve. That deadpan voice sounded a lot like Zach's when he was at his most intense. "Mom?"

Silence met her inquiry. Kathleen looked at the screen. Her mother had ended the call. She found her mother's number and unblocked it. She felt as if she'd just dumped a ten-ton weight off her shoulders. She tilted her head back and rolled it to loosen her taut neck muscles. She set aside the phone, and for the first time since her mother's call, looked at Cal.

He scanned her face, then raised his brows. "Do you need me to take you home?"

God, he was gorgeous. And what made him even more attractive was his genuine look of concern.

"No. I'm good." She studied him and her heart sank. She groaned and covered her face with her hands for a moment. "Has hearing all that changed your mind about us going out?"

"No. It hasn't changed my mind."

She might as well start everything with a clean slate, since he knew everything else about this particular disgusting and painful situation. "There's one more thing I want to tell you that I didn't mention to her."

"What is it?"

"After I found out about…everything…and we split, I had myself tested for sexually transmitted diseases. They did follow-up tests some months later to make certain, and I'm clear." She couldn't bring herself to look at him. "I think that was the worst humiliation, and the most painful. I'd saved myself for the one man I wanted to spend my life with, and he put me at risk without a second's thought. I dodged more than one bullet by ending things with him."

Cal Leaned across the console, cupped her cheek with his hand, and turned her face to him. He brushed her lips with a soft kiss. "You won't have to dodge any bullets with me, Kathleen. That's a promise."

A gorgeous guy like him? Despite his leg, he probably had women begging to go to bed with him.

What if she just let everything go and believed him? How hard would that be?

Hard. But she really wanted to.

CHAPTER 10

CAL WATCHED THE cursor skip from one thing to another while Kathleen sat at the kitchen table building the clips of taped activity into a consolidated whole. She was a whiz at the program she was using to splice them together. "I'm going to add the part I taped yesterday while you changed my tires," Kathleen said, reaching for her phone. Her fingers flew across the keyboard as she emailed the clip to her computer.

The savory aroma of simmering pot roast filled the room and Cal's stomach growled. "I don't have a shirt on."

"So? You look hot without your shirt."

"Yeah, I was. I was sweating." He glanced at Zach, who was sitting on the couch, and caught the momentary flash of his teeth as he grinned.

"That wasn't the kind of hot I meant."

"Stop trying to rattle your brother's chain," he murmured close to her ear.

Her green eyes held a gleam of mischief. "But it's so much fun."

He was glad she'd bounced back from yesterday's upset. She'd been subdued for most of the day after her ex's phone call and her admission. Coming on top of the quick hit at work, then the two flats, he understood why she needed some time to regroup. But he could tell she enjoyed the drive, dinner, and the late movie. Her good night kiss had left him with a sexual buzz that lasted halfway across town.

They had some powerful chemistry going on. Just being in the room with her was a turn-on.

A cell phone rang behind them. Zach answered it, "Hey, Dad."

Kathleen looked over at Zach.

"She what? Is she okay?"

Kathleen twisted in her seat at those two questions in quick succession, worry tweaking her brows. "Zach?"

"Mom broke her hand, but she's okay," he answered and gave a clenched-fist signal to hold up. "How long will she be in a cast?"

Though Kathleen continued to work on the video, Cal could tell her attention was on the unenlightening conversation going on behind them, which consisted of yeahs and nos.

As soon as Zach hung up, Kathleen swiveled around to face him. "Is she really okay?"

"Yeah. They've put her in some kind of plastic brace thing she'll have to wear for a couple of months, but she's okay."

"Well, how did she break it?"

"She broke your ex-boyfriend's nose with a sucker punch."

Cal's bark of laughter was spontaneous and uncontrolled. He cut it off at Kathleen's quick look of worry.

"Oh my God! Oh my God!" Kathleen covered her mouth with a hand.

Zach grinned like a Cheshire cat. "I can't wait to tell the guys."

"Is she in trouble?"

"Dad doesn't think so, but he had a long talk with their attorney last night. He'll reach out and offer the boyfriend compensation for the hospital bills. But he'll also warn him that if he ever wants to date another woman in the Boston area, he'd best not rock the boat. It seems your best friend Tamara—"

"Ex best friend," Kathleen corrected him.

"When she found out he'd cheated on her, she put an ad in the paper, and all of the women he's slept with in the past three years have banded together to spread the word on social media sites about what a scumbag he is."

"So he calls me. That's just perfect."

"Well, he won't call again," Zach said, a gleam of satisfaction in his eyes. "He was probably hoping you'd call Tamara off."

"Not a chance." Kathleen went back to the program. "I'm publishing the video to the web, Cal."

"Wait a minute. Is that a good thing for it to be out there for anyone to see?" He'd flown under the radar for so long, in so many ways, he wasn't sure how he'd feel if the video went public.

"It's just one of a million unless we draw attention to it. Public opinion might be a good thing to have on your side later."

Zach cut in. "Or it could be a double-edged sword. We avoid it like the plague for a reason. People think they have the right to know everything, even if it puts our lives in jeopardy, or their own."

"We're not talking about state secrets here, Zach. It's Callahan doing his job."

It was him lifting things, tightening bolts with a hydraulic wrench, walking steel, and doing manual labor on the site. Nothing unusual for a construction job. What harm could it do, even if someone else saw it besides him and Kathleen?

Zach quirked a brow at her. "Do you fish, Cal?"

"Yeah. I haven't been in a while." The last time he'd gone with his brother. For a while he and Douglas spent quite a bit of time out on the water every weekend. He'd needed that undemanding time to sort things out mentally, emotionally.

"Bowie and I are going this coming Sunday. Want to come along?"

Surprised by the invitation, he studied Zach. "All my gear is in Texas."

"Most of the guys leave their gear on board my boat. We'll find you a pole and I'll furnish the bait and the beer."

If this was some kind of get to know the boyfriend thing... Was he a boyfriend after four dates? With Kathleen's hand resting on his arm, he felt like one. "Sure. I'd like to come. I'll bring some food."

"Good. Zero six hundred at the Fiddler's Cove Marina. Just come here and we'll drive over together."

"I'll be here."

"If our schedule changes for some reason, Kathleen will let you know."

"Okay. Thanks."

Zach flipped off the television. "I'm going to test drive the haircut," he announced and ran his fingers through the freshly trimmed rust-colored hair that fell over his forehead in waves. Kathleen had done a professional job, leaving it longer on top and shortening the sides and back. "I'll be back at five for dinner."

He kissed Kathleen's cheek, then sauntered out the door.

The silence that followed his departure was steeped in intimacy. There was just something wrong about jumping a guy's sister under his roof. "Want to go for a walk on the beach?" Cal asked.

Kathleen smiled as though she'd read his mind. "Sure."

Cal laced his fingers with hers as they wandered down close to the water. "Did you really want to go fishing with Zach and Bowie?" Kathleen asked.

Would she have rather he didn't? "Sure. I haven't been in a while. Not since I moved here."

"Good. I didn't want you to feel obligated because Zach's my brother."

"And because he probably asked me so he could give me the third degree without you being there to run interference?"

She grinned. "Probably. I hope you'll have a good time despite all the BS."

"My brother and I used to drive across from Houston to the coast and rent a boat. There's something calming about being out on the water. Your brother probably needs it as much as I did." And still do, he realized.

Kathleen remained silent for a beat or two. "How bad were your injuries besides your leg?"

"I had a severe concussion and two cracked vertebra in my neck. My jaw was broken in three places, and I lost some teeth. I had shrapnel from the car embedded in my hip and legs. Cuts, bruises, but I was alive." He swallowed. "The other three men with me were killed almost instantly. The brunt of the explosion went up and over me."

Kathleen looped her arm through his and leaned in close. He chewed back a groan at the way her breast brushed his arm. "You're a walking miracle."

"Yeah, I am." He brushed his fingertips along her arm. Kathleen pulled him to a stop. She slid her arms around his waist and held him tight.

He shouldn't have told her. He wanted, needed something normal in his life. Holding her, feeling her body tight against his, he realized he hadn't had normal since…. since he'd left for Afghanistan.

He needed a woman's touch and everything that went with it. Kathleen was the first woman he'd felt an instant connection to since his breakup with Stacy, and he didn't want it to disintegrate into pity. They fell into a silence while they continued down the beach. In his jeans and T-shirt, he didn't fit into the carefree Sunday afternoon crowd stretched out on towels and soaking in the sun despite the breeze. How long had it been since he'd felt the ocean breeze on his legs?

"The tattoo on your chest?" she asked. "They were with you?"

He nodded. "After they died, I promised myself I was going to live as full a life as I could to honor them. That meant not allowing this thing to hold me back." He raised his leg, kicking up sand. "I've been able to live up to that promise in some ways, not so much others."

"What do you mean?"

"I wear steel toe boots with my prosthetic at work so the crew doesn't see it. In order to be able to do the work, I've been hiding that part of myself from the rest of the world. The physical therapist who got me up on this thing and walking was five foot nothing, and her legs were scarred from an accident. She strutted her stuff anyway, wore shorts all the time." And she'd be the first to kick his ass for being such a coward.

"Is it Zoe Yazzie? She works at the naval hospital as a physical therapist."

"If it's the same woman, I knew her as Zoe Weaver. How do you know her?"

"Her husband, Hawk, is Zach's commanding officer and team leader. Big guy, tall, with dark hair and piercing gray eyes. I went over to their house for a barbecue when I first got here. The calf muscle of one of her legs is damaged."

"That's her. I didn't meet her husband; he was deployed."

"It's a small world."

"Yeah," he agreed.

"Why do you feel like you need to hide anything?" The ocean breeze gusted and blew her hair every which way, so she gripped the heavy fall of hair and secured it with a rubber band.

He breathed in the sea air and studied the curve of her bottom lip until her lips parted and he dragged his mind back to her question. "If I was doing a desk job, I wouldn't have to go through any of this." He ran his hand over his hair, bristling it. "A lot of times, when someone sees you with a prosthetic attached, they automatically view you as…less capable. Even when you prove you can do something, there's still a lingering doubt in the back of their minds that undermines their confidence in you."

If a man's father couldn't believe in him—But Tom Hill had given him a shot, and he'd proven himself. "I can't chance that with the work I do."

"But you don't have to hide anything with me, Cal."

Didn't he?

She'd told him about the most humiliating things she'd been through in the past six months. Just because the scars didn't show on the outside didn't mean they weren't there. Some of them weren't healed yet, and might never completely go away.

But he wasn't ready yet to match her courage and honesty.

They returned to the house to tend to the pot roast. Cal leaned back against the counter while she whipped up some corn muffins. She was so easy to be with.

Too easy. It made him want more too quickly. She wasn't

ready yet. He wasn't ready.

"I have to leave after dinner. There are things I have to do for next week." Fuck! He knew he was running. But he couldn't help himself.

Kathleen glanced up after putting the batter in the muffin tins. "Okay."

Her undemanding acceptance was disappointing.

"Will you be free Tuesday to come over for a meal at my place?"

"I have an appointment to view an apartment at six, so it will probably be seven before I can get there. That isn't too late is it?"

"No. It isn't."

She rinsed the bowl and spoon she'd been using.

Feeling guilty for reasons he didn't even understand, he slid in behind her to press close. He tugged the band holding her hair free and brushed it forward over her shoulder before skimming the nape of her neck with a kiss. She shivered at the caress. Her response triggered a raging hard-on, and he slid an arm around her waist to cup her belly, holding her against him so she could feel how his body responded to her.

When he scraped his teeth along the sensitive area between her neck and shoulder, Kathleen reached back to cup the back of his thigh and pull him in closer. He caressed her breast and felt the nipple harden beneath her T-shirt. God, she had beautiful breasts. Large and soft. She pressed back against him harder.

His heart raced so fast it was hard to catch a full breath. It had been too long. He wanted to lose himself in the moist heat of her body and forget everything.

But the aftermath of doing it too soon might bring reality crashing down on them both. If he wanted whatever this was to survive beyond one encounter, he had to wait.

The sound of a car door slamming saved him from having to make a firm decision. Kathleen spun to face him. "I think you are a tease, Callahan," she accused without heat.

"Your brother's home—early."

Understanding suffused her cheeks with color.

He leaned down and kissed her. "It makes me feel like a teenager again, sneaking around with you," he breathed against her ear.

The apartment door opened. She turned back to the sink, hiding her flushed cheeks. "I'm getting my own place this week," she murmured.

CAL HADN'T BEEN gone even an hour before he regretted his quick retreat. To take his mind off of what was really eating at him, he filled his evening with grocery shopping for the week and doing laundry and household chores.

By bedtime he decided if he didn't get his act together he was going to blow it with Kathleen. He needed to get his head out of his ass and just go for it. If her brother hadn't shown up when he did, they might have gotten farther along, and all this self-recrimination would be hindsight. But how would she have felt if they'd made love before she'd seen exactly what she was getting?

The one had to come before the other.

Settling back on his bed, he reached for his cell phone, and keyed in Kathleen's number.

"Hey, Callahan." Her voice had the softness of approaching slumber.

"Hey, Rose." He could feel her smile across the line and his tension eased. "I should have brought you home with me. Doing shopping, chores, and laundry alone sucks."

"We could have entertained each other between loads," she murmured.

"Maybe we could have finished what we started while we were cooking dinner."

"You are such a tease," she complained.

"Would you have been ready for more, Kathleen?"

She remained silent for a moment. "When I'm with you, I want to say yes. When you're not here, my mind runs in circles with all the reasons we should take it slow."

His tension eased. "In case I miss the message when or if you are ready…be sure to hit me over the head or something," he teased. "Guys usually need a road map to understand what women want."

"I've noticed that with every one of my brothers. I was hoping you were a cut above."

He caught himself grinning like a fool. "Naw. Just a regular guy like all the rest."

"Well there's comfort in that, too. I wouldn't want you to gain too much insight into my feminine mystique."

He chuckled. "Have you spoken to your mom? Is she okay?"

"Yes, I called her earlier. Her hand is going to be fine."

"Good."

"If you ever decide you want to date someone else, Callahan…"

Damn. He hadn't meant to remind her of her ex. All he could do was continue to reassure her. "I won't lie or cheat on you, Kathleen."

"The same goes for me, Callahan."

He started to say he trusted her, but thought of everything it entailed. He had to stick to his plan. "Want to know what I've been dreaming of since we first met, Kathleen?"

"I'm going to be brave and ask what?"

"Your mouth. You have the sexiest damn mouth I've ever seen, and I dream of how many ways we can kiss…among other things."

She caught her breath.

"Does that sound like a man who's interested in anyone but you?"

"No." Her breathing sounded ragged.

His was, too. He was hard as stone again and aching for her. If he so much as touched his cock he'd probably go off. "I'll call you tomorrow."

"Callahan—"

The way she said his name nearly did him in. "Sweet dreams, honey."

THE MOMENT HE hung up, Kathleen clenched her legs together and bit her lip. He wasn't even in the room and he'd seduced her. The way he looked at her at the ice cream shop came to mind, and she stifled a groan, because the memory made the sensitive ache in the most intimate part of her body intensify.

Her desire for Lee had been lukewarm compared to this. Thank God she hadn't married him. She never would have known this kind of passion with him.

If making love with Cal even came close to the excitement of the buildup, she wasn't sure she'd be able to stand it.

She'd just met him, and she was already in trouble. He called to her emotions in ways Lee never had.

Had she instinctively held back from Lee, somehow recognizing his feelings only skimmed the surface? She sensed Cal's emotions ran deeper because of everything he'd experienced.

She had to be careful. She had to keep things light, at least until they were both ready for more. Otherwise she wouldn't be the only one who ended up hurt.

CHAPTER 11

KATHLEEN STUDIED THE plan she was building in AutoCAD. The bare bones were taking shape. The four-story structure wasn't the tallest building she'd worked on, but it was the most complex. It was going to take time and many more meetings with the client.

She rubbed her eyes and tilted her head back to relieve the tight muscles in her neck and shoulders. She needed a break. She saved her work, then saved it again to the external hard drive and the cloud, plus she sent a link to the latter to J.D. Allison, her immediate supervisor, with a note about her progress, before shutting down her computer.

She rose and stretched, then rubbed her hands together to create friction and placed her warmed palms over her eyes. The shadowed blackness of her eyelids soothed her eyestrain, but it also provided an opportunity for Cal to pop into her mind. He had a way of doing that if she wasn't busy.

Instead of waiting for Tuesday, he'd called her and invited her over for dinner on Monday. They'd been together nearly every night since then for a meal, a movie, looking at apartments for her, and, of all things, miniature golf.

Every time she was with him she wanted to throw caution to the wind and jump his bones. When they were apart she was grateful he was taking it slow.

He seemed to want more, but something kept him from easing things to the next step. It didn't take a mental giant to guess what held him back.

She'd yet to figure out a way to approach the subject without making him feel exposed. Men didn't react well when you uncovered their vulnerabilities. And Cal had a doozy.

She could push things along physically and just sweep right past it. But... She'd have to deal with her own vulnerabilities first, however. Despite her reservations, her body warmed to the idea, and heat rushed into her face.

She was at work, for heaven's sakes. She couldn't think about this right now. She dropped her hands.

"Need a break?" Hillary asked from where she leaned against the edge of the dividing wall between their cubicles.

Kathleen shifted to face her. She definitely needed a distraction. "Yes. I think I do."

"Let's go fix a cup of tea or something," Hillary suggested.

"Okay." She reached for the ceramic mug she'd brought from home and her baggie of green tea bags and artificial sweetener.

"You've come prepared today," Hillary said.

"Yeah. If I'm going to make the deposit and first month's rent for my own apartment, I'll have to economize until I get my first paycheck."

They wandered down the brightly lit corridor to the staff break room, which was actually a full kitchen with white Shaker-style cabinets set off by a gray countertop. Three round tables painted white with their padded gray upholstered seats sat empty. The room was always in use during lunch, but right now they were the only ones. Kathleen filled her coffee cup with water and put it in the microwave to heat while Hillary found a cup in one of the cabinets to use.

"So, any plans this weekend?" Hillary asked when they settled at one of the tables with their drinks.

After what happened the week before, Kathleen felt reluctant to share things about her personal life with this woman. "I woke up this past Saturday to two flat tires, and ended up spending all morning getting them fixed. Luckily I had a friend who volunteered to help me."

"It sounds like you're having a round of bad luck."

"Yes, I am. They were new tires, too. We're going to some of the museums in Balboa Park this Saturday. I forgot to ask how your evening went with Mr. Warren."

Hillary shrugged one shoulder. "We had drinks and came back here. I picked up my belongings, and he went one way while I went the other."

So they'd both been in the office when her files were deleted and her drawings locked in the plan hangers. Cal was right. She wasn't going to be able to get beyond it until she knew what had happened.

Kathleen leaned forward and lowered her voice. "Hillary, if you're interested in him, why don't you tell him?"

She remained silent for a moment. "He knows. He's still too busy chasing after the new kids to see what's right in front of him."

Kathleen turned her cup in her hands. "Well, I can promise you I'm not one of them."

Hillary eyed her. "I'm surprised."

Kathleen raised her brows. "Why?"

"He's an attractive man."

For once in his life Lee was handy. "My fiancé and I broke up and called off our wedding before I moved out here. We were together for three years, so I'm still a little raw."

"I'm sorry."

"I just want to concentrate on my career right now." And office romances seldom worked out well.

"I felt the same way after my marriage ended."

Kathleen nodded, encouragement. "How long were you married?"

"Five long, lonely years. Steve was a Marine, and deployed for most of our marriage. While he was gone I finished my degree and found this job. When he came home, he received transfer orders. We'd become strangers by then, and neither of us had the energy to try and fight our way back from it. He left and I stayed."

"I'm sorry, Hillary." She felt real sympathy for her. "Any children?"

"No. He wasn't really home enough for us to discuss having any. Now my biological clock is ticking and I'd like to have one, but I don't have a volunteer." She smiled, but there was an emptiness to it.

"I can't even picture my ex with a child." Lee had been all about Lee. With all his serial screwing, he'd run the risk of fathering a child. Hadn't it even worried him? "I'm glad I escaped before it was too late. I come from a big family, and I want children. Not as many as my parents have, but two would be nice." She took a sip of her tea. "Maybe it's time to get back out there and search for what you need, Hillary. Life's too short to settle for anything less."

Hillary's eyes narrowed and her cheeks flushed. Her mouth thinned with anger. "Paul isn't less. You don't know him like I do."

Shocked at the woman's sudden anger, Kathleen eased back in her seat and stirred her tea. "You're right. I don't. But if he homes in on the less experienced employees, maybe he's looking for someone who needs him. You and I both want to do everything ourselves. Ask for his help with something. If he feels you really need him, he might come around."

Hillary's expression cleared, and Kathleen could see her working to regain her composure. "You could be right. Thanks for the suggestion." She rubbed a hand over her face. "I'm sorry I snapped your head off."

"Love is an emotional minefield sometimes. I understand."

"That's a good way of putting it." She stared at a point just over Kathleen's shoulder. "I've held on for so long, I just can't give up yet."

There had never been any question of holding onto Lee. The betrayal had been too much. But then Hillary and Paul Warren weren't in a committed relationship.

Kathleen gladly returned to work. The whole conversation

had been very uncomfortable. Hillary's lightning quick flash of rage had been frightening. Though Hillary had been friendly from the first, Kathleen didn't really know her. But she knew enough that she didn't want to take their relationship past a working one. The only podmate she felt comfortable with was Dave. He had a fatherly air about him, encouraging trust.

She missed the team of graduate students she'd worked with on projects. They had built a comradeship among them almost immediately because they had a common goal. That was still the case here. She just had to find the key to making it work. But sharing anything personal with her team was off limits.

THE HEAVY APRON filled with metal dragged at Cal's waist. He reached in and grabbed one of the high strength tension control bolts and worked it into place. After he fitted several more, he reached down to lift the hydraulic shear wrench. He plugged the hub over the bolt and flipped the switch. Once the correct tension was reached, the end of the bolt twisted off, and he dropped the small stub into a container to be thrown away later. He wondered idly how many bolts and nuts would eventually be used in the structure. It seemed he had placed at least a quarter of them since he'd been working this job. At a tap on his shoulder, he turned to find Ron Rains standing behind him.

"Tom needs to see you in the office. He sent me up to take your place."

Cal nodded. Ron backed off the beam, giving Cal room. Even though he wore a safety harness and was tied off to a security line, Cal took care as he walked along the metal beam until he reached the stability of the concrete floor poured days ago. Because he couldn't feel his foot and was placing it through motor memory rather than feel, he always got a small buzz of adrenaline after getting off the beams. He presented the wrench to Ron like he was passing a torch and the guy grinned. He removed his apron and passed it on as well.

Ron had hooked onto the security line and was tightening the bolts he'd just placed by the time Cal reached the elevator. The pounding, revving sound of the work going on changed in tempo and pitch as he rode down to the bottom floor.

He crossed the fifty feet or so to foreman's trailer, and barely made it inside when Tom looked up and said, "The head office wants to see you, Cal."

Though he'd been waiting for it to happen, the punch of it still left him with a sour burn in the pit of his stomach. The hope that it might be over something other than his job was slim. "Did they say why?"

"No." Tom's expression remained deadpan.

The temptation to ask if Tom was going to stand behind him was strong, but pride held his tongue. "Who am I supposed to ask for once I get there?"

"Mr. Wiley."

So the owner wanted to see him. This couldn't be good. "I'll be back to finish my shift."

"Take the rest of the day with pay. If you're dealing with company business, you get paid for it. Tomorrow will be soon enough for you to fill me in on what he says."

Yeah, kick in a few extra bucks to make losing his job go down easier. As if it would. He left the trailer, crossed the yard to the turnstile box, and shoved through onto the street before removing his hard hat. With every mile his anger swung from full out boil to a simmer and back again. Driving some of the less busy roads, he made it to the office in half an hour.

He spotted Kathleen's vehicle in the parking lot and wondered if he could swing by and see her after the meeting. If he was upset by the outcome, he might not want her to see him.

Despite the emotion tightening his chest and stomach, he felt in control. If he was getting fired, he didn't have anything left to lose by speaking his mind. He pulled off his safety vest and left it in the front seat with his hard hat.

The reception area of the building opened up to a wide staircase leading up to the second floor. Wrought iron spindles twisted in a decorative pattern supported the highly glossed bentwood handrails on either side. His eyes lingered on the fine craftsmanship as he wandered to the reception desk.

A young woman sat at the desk behind a computer. As he approached, she ran her eyes over him and smiled. "May I help you?"

"I have an appointment with Mr. Wiley."

She flipped her long blond hair to her back. "And your name, please?"

"Cal Crowes."

"Mr. Crowes, you can have a seat right over there while I call upstairs." She pointed to one of the brown and cream upholstered chairs placed around a squat, heavy coffee table in front of her desk.

"I just came off the job and I'd like to wash up." And get his temper under control.

"The restrooms are just on the other side of the staircase to your right."

"Thanks." He strode around the staircase, and, finding the men's room, quickly washed his hands and face. Finding only an electric hand dryer, he used the sleeve of his shirt to dry his face and folded back the cuffs to his elbows.

When he returned, the receptionist smiled again. "Mr. Wiley will see you now, Mr. Crowes. You can take the elevator over there or climb the stairs to the second floor. His secretary will be sitting at the desk outside his office to show you in." She handed him a business card. Absently he tucked it in his shirt pocket.

She smiled again. "Hope to see you again, Mr. Crowes."

"Thanks."

He took the stairs and spotted a woman sitting at a desk, so he headed in that direction. She rose before he reached her.

"Mr. Wiley will see you now, Mr. Crowes." She opened the door for him.

Cal drew a deep breath to try and steady the heavy kick of his heart. He rubbed his palms against his jeans and stepped through the door.

The head of Wiley construction was facing him, pouring a glass of diet soda over ice. A man closing on sixty-five, Wiley looked like he'd spent his entire life out in the sun on construction sites. He strode toward Cal, his hand extended. His palm as it met Cal's wasn't the soft, callus-free grip of a businessman, but the hard, worn hand of a worker. "It's nice to meet you face-to-face, Cal. May I call you Cal?"

"Sure."

Wiley motioned toward a small grouping of upholstered chairs. "Have a seat. Can I get you something to drink?"

Cal swallowed, though his mouth was dry. "A bottle of water?"

"Sure." He moved to a large cabinet and opened one of the doors to reveal a small refrigerator. He removed a bottle of water. "Want a glass?"

"No, sir. The bottle will be fine."

Wiley carried his own drink to the coffee table and handed the bottle over. He waited for Cal to take a drink and settled back into his seat. "You've worked for Wiley Construction for how long, Cal?"

So it began. Cal screwed the lid back on the half empty bottle and set it on a coaster on the coffee table. "Just over a year."

"Are you satisfied with your job here, Cal?"

"Sure, Mr. Wiley."

"Have you seen Nora Harper's reports on her show?" Deep grooves carved the man's forehead as he raised his brows.

"Not recently, sir." In fact he avoided watching the news or interview shows most of the time.

"She does a four-minute human interest piece every night on the news, and a longer one on her show. She's been doing one on injured vets and how they've put their lives back together after coming home. The struggles they've faced finding a job, that kind of thing. She mentioned Wiley Construction and some of the responses she had after broadcasting the footage taped the other day of the near miss on-site."

"She called me for an interview and I turned her down, sir."

Wiley scooted forward in his chair, rested his elbows on his knees, and laced his fingers. "I'd like for you to reconsider your position on that, Cal."

Shock jolted Cal's system. "I don't understand."

"We're getting some negative publicity, not because we don't hire according to the disability laws, but because you seem to be the only commercial construction worker in the area with a disability."

Angry heat hit Cal's face. "I'm not disabled, sir. If I were, I wouldn't be on the job."

"You do have a prosthetic limb, don't you?"

"Yeah, I do. But it doesn't keep me from doing the work."

"Tom Hill has told me that repeatedly. He's one of my best foremen, and I believe him. And watching you walk in here, I'd never guess you had any kind of challenge. It has to be a challenge at times."

Cal remained silent.

"I'm not firing you or trying to talk you into taking a less active job, Cal. I'm asking for your help in heading off a small publicity issue. So far all I'm hearing are negative responses, not just for the company, but because we're allowing you to do the work. So it would be a win for you too if we could turn things around. Some of the comments I've read so far state that we're unnecessarily putting you and others at risk allowing you to walk steel. Tom said you enjoyed the work and wouldn't stick around if we put you on deliveries."

Cal shook his head. "That's not what I signed on for sir. If I was just starting out and my skill level was less advanced, I'd understand being demoted, but I'm a trained welder among other things. I'm an asset on-site, not the opposite."

"Tom said you are damn good at what you do. So I'd like to balance things out with some positive public responses."

"They're pushing the negative because it triggers more reaction from their viewers?" Cal commented.

"Probably. And it's certainly generated some pointed phone calls here from several agencies."

Cal leaned back in the chair, rested an elbow on the arm, and cupped his forehead in his hand. Jesus! He didn't want to go on television. He didn't want to be looked at with sympathy or pity. He cleared his throat and dropped his hand. "Sir, the reason I've been able to do the job is because I don't draw attention to my leg. It isn't something I talk about. The men I work with, there's only a couple who know about it."

"There's bound to be more now, Cal. Ms. Harper has been belaboring the issue since Wednesday of last week."

Fuck! It took all his self-control to keep from saying the word out loud. "No one's said anything."

"Well, they see you every day doing the job, why would they?"

Had he really been worried for nothing? Why the hell hadn't Julio or Hector said something? Both of them watched the news.

"If I go on television, sir, I'm not just protecting Wiley Construction from negative publicity, I'm laying my private life wide open to—everyone." He swept one hand toward the surrounding buildings visible from the windows.

"And what do you have to hide? We do a background check on all our employees, Cal. There's nothing in yours to worry about. You're a decorated war veteran who sacrificed a limb for his country. Go on and make these people eat their words. And I'll look at it as a personal favor."

Shit! What did you say when the owner of the company said he owed you one? He didn't really have a choice. But he didn't want any of this. "All right. But there's only so far I'm willing to go with her interview, Mr. Wiley. She asks me to show off my prosthetic, then I'm out of there. And I'd like to see a copy of the questions before the interview."

"I'll make that clear to her when I call. You're not the only one who'll be on the hot seat. She's asked to interview me, too."

Somehow Cal didn't get any comfort from that.

Wiley stood, and Cal followed suit, recognizing his dismissal.

"I'll have my secretary call you with the particulars as soon as we know them. Please give her your number," Wiley offered his hand.

"Yes, sir." Cal shook his hand and headed for the door.

While he stood outside of Wiley's office door, his first thought was he wanted to talk to Kathleen about the interview.

She'd been in his thoughts every morning when he got up. Lying alone in bed, he went to sleep thinking of her. They'd done little more than kiss and grope like teenagers, but he'd dreamed of more with her. His heart kicked into high gear. He was falling for her.

Ah, hell, he wasn't just falling, he was already there.

CHAPTER 12

KATHLEEN DETACHED THE external hard drive from her computer and tucked it into her purse. Her cell phone rang and she reached for it. "Hello, Callahan."

"I'm in the building downstairs and it's just shy of quitting time. I'd like to see where you work if the coast is clear," Cal said.

"I think Mr. Warren left earlier. I'm on the fourth floor. If you take the elevator, I'll meet you in reception."

"I'm on my way."

Kathleen rushed down the hall to the large square reception area where the secretarial staff was already shutting down their computers. The elevator opened and Cal stepped out.

"Hey, Rose." He surprised her by leaning down and brushing a kiss against her cheek.

"What brings you here?"

"Mr. Wiley wanted to see me. I'll tell you about it later."

She eyed his expression, searching for some key to how he felt about the meeting. He didn't seem angry, but he wasn't totally at ease either. "Come this way and I'll show you my work space." She guided him down the wide hall past three other offices, the restrooms, and the break room. "This is my pod."

"Pod?"

"Well, that's what we call it. I haven't had much time to personalize my space yet."

He paused before the photograph-covered bulletin board, then studied the drawing she'd done the week before and framed just that morning.

Nerves fluttered beneath her ribs at his silence. Would he like it?

"This design is going to be something special, Kathleen."

She breathed a sigh of relief. "Thanks. It's just my vision of what the façade will look like once it's built—if the client is pleased with the design."

Hillary wandered in with a bottle of water. Reluctantly Kathleen introduced her to Cal.

"Are you the friend who helped her get her tires fixed this weekend?" she asked.

"Yeah."

"You're a good man." She patted Cal on the shoulder. She was just behind the partition when she paused and shook her hand and blew on it as if touching Cal had burned it. Kathleen bit her lip to keep from laughing.

"Are you ready to leave for the day?" Cal asked.

"Oh, yeah." Chiding herself for her paranoia, Kathleen opened her purse to make sure the hard drive was inside and checked to be sure she'd closed out her computer.

Cal motioned her out the door ahead of him. She was aware of his hand against her hip, and the way his body heat seemed to envelop her as they proceeded down the hall to the elevator. The two receptionist/secretaries who worked on the floor paused to eye him as they strolled by.

"You're being checked out, Callahan."

His brows hiked up. They stepped on the elevator and he glanced up at the two women with his aw-shucks grin. They both smiled. He made a motion as though tipping his hat. The two giggled like schoolgirls.

The elevator door closed and Kathleen looked up at him. "You really didn't notice until I pointed it out to you?"

"I'm interested in you, Kathleen. Not other random women."

Her breasts tightened as her nipples budded and an instant

heat trailed down her body to nestle deep. She ran her fingertips over the buttons on his shirt. "I am interested in you too, Callahan."

His arm tightened around her, his blue-green gaze narrowed as he focused so intently on her, her legs went rubbery and she wondered if it was possible to have an orgasm from just a look.

"Will you come back to my apartment with me?"

His voice held a masculine rasp that played along her supercharged nerve endings and gave her goose bumps. He was what she wanted. She didn't hesitate. "Yes."

The elevator door opened and they stepped out together.

The two of them entered the reception area and were almost to the door when Paul Warren strode through the front entrance. The moment he spotted Cal he stiffened and his eyes narrowed. When his attention shifted to Kathleen, color suffused his features.

"What's your business here, Crowes?" he demanded.

Cal ran a soothing hand down Kathleen's back and settled into a relaxed but alert stance. "I was invited, Mr. Warren."

Warren's gaze raked Kathleen. "This is a place of business, not a bar to pick up women."

The receptionist behind them caught her breath.

Color stormed Cal's cheeks and his eyes narrowed. "I've had enough of this shit." He started forward.

With Zach's warning blaring in her mind, Kathleen threw up an arm to block Cal's forward momentum. It was like trying to stop a boulder from rolling downhill. Every muscle in his body was charged with aggression, and she had to step in front of him and brace her hands against his wide chest to stop him. "He's goading you, Cal. Don't allow him to use me to provoke you."

She turned to face Warren at the same moment the security guard sauntered up. "Is there a problem, Mr. Warren?"

"Yes, there is," Kathleen answered for him and focused on Warren. "What is wrong with you, Mr. Warren? Your behavior towards me is inappropriate and offensive, as it is toward Mr. Crowes. Cal is here at Mr. Wiley's request and by my invitation. If you don't back off, I will file a harassment complaint against you."

Warren's cheeks grew flushed and he clenched his fists at his sides. "That isn't what's going on here."

"Then why don't you explain what is so we will all know?"

Warren ground his teeth as though he were searching for words. "He's not who you think he is. You're making a bad decision going out with him."

She shook her head. There was something seriously wrong with the man. "I've only been working here nine days. I don't know you, and you don't know me. Certainly not well enough to tell me who I should and shouldn't date. That's harassment. When you demand to know whether I really have a date with someone else when you invite me out for drinks, that's harassment. When you refer to me as a bar pickup, that's harassment. Please—stay away from me, Mr. Warren."

The security guard placed a hand on Warren's shoulder. He twisted away from him. "Keep your hands off me."

Kathleen gripped Cal's hand and tugged him away while Warren was occupied. Once outside, Kathleen took a deep breath and tried to control her trembling.

When they reached her car, Cal leaned back against it and pulled her against him. "Are you okay?"

She pressed in tight and rested her forehead against his shoulder. "It's adrenaline. It'll ease off."

"What the hell is going on here, Kathleen? Has he really been harassing you?"

"It's hard to explain." A rush of embarrassment made it difficult to meet his eyes. "As satisfying as it would have been, I couldn't let you punch him. You'd have been fired, or arrested for assault." She leaned back to look up at him. "I know I turned it so it sounded like it was aimed at me, but he only did it to get a rise out of you. He's fixated on you, Cal. We have to figure out why."

"I don't know. I never met the guy until he took over the tower project from one of the other project supervisors, Shelton Cobb. From the moment he met me he's been riding my ass. I thought he was just prejudiced against me because of my leg." Cal raised her chin to look down into her face and asked again. "Has he really been harassing you?"

She didn't want to go into this with him. It only fueled whatever was going on between him and Warren. "The night you took me to Julio and Jessica's he asked Hillary and me out for a drink. When I said I already had a date, he questioned whether I really did have one. He said it was because he didn't want the argument we'd had that first day to make it difficult for us to work together, but he has a kind of passive-aggressive way of saying things—" She shook her head. "It shook me up."

"And then the next morning your files were deleted and your drawings gone."

"Yes."

Cal's eyes took on a flat cold rage. "You should have let me punch him."

"I didn't tell you about it to begin with because I thought it would only feed the situation between you and him. Zach warned me what he might do if he found out we were dating."

"So you've talked it over with your brother but not me?" Cal stepped back and gripped her arms. "I'm a grown man, Kathleen. You don't have to protect me."

"I know that. I thought we were protecting each other."

"It doesn't feel that way to me." Cal shifted back, leaving her feeling bereft. "Just what kind of argument was it you had that first day. Was it about me?"

Kathleen bit her bottom lip. She didn't want to tell him. He'd misunderstand. "He'd made some derogatory comments about your ability to do the job and that you were reminding the rest of the men what a hero you were by wearing the cracked hard hat. So I reminded him you'd just saved the company from a lawsuit and of the laws governing hiring and firing."

Cal's cheekbones reddened, and for the second time she saw anger directed at her. It tightened his mouth and made him look as intimidating as her brothers. "You've been running interference for me since day one."

God save her from a bruised male ego. "It wasn't because of

your leg. And it wasn't because I felt you couldn't handle things on your own. I didn't even know you then. It was because right is right and wrong is wrong, Callahan."

"I left home because I couldn't take my parents treating me like a cripple. My dad wouldn't even let me work with him. This is the same thing, Kathleen."

She could deal with the anger, but the pain in his expression sliced at her. "No it's not, Callahan. I've never looked at you and seen anything but a strong, virile, sexy man. You're rock steady. I trusted you to protect me when we went to Julio's neighborhood. I trusted you to hold me and comfort me after the worst workday I've ever had. And if you're looking for a way to welch on what you've been promising me since the first time you touched me, then get in your truck and make tracks. But you'll regret it as much as I will."

Cal stormed away from her two strides, then two more. Her heart sank and quick tears blurred her eyes. The pain, sharper and deeper than she expected, took root and left her breathless.

"Damn it." He pivoted on his good leg to face her. "Jesus!" He threw up his hands in frustration. "You should have been a lawyer instead of an architect."

Kathleen blinked to clear her vision.

"I don't need your pity, Kathleen." With his hands clenched at his sides and his jaw taut, he looked formidable.

"I've never felt pity for you, Callahan." She'd felt grief, admiration, lust, and maybe even—She couldn't go there. Not yet. She wiped at the tears dampening her cheeks. Pride led her to turn aside when a male employee walked between the cars to get into his vehicle. She refused to be one of those weeping females who played the tears card to win a fight.

"Can you drive?" Cal asked.

"Of course I can drive." She wasn't hysterical or weeping and wailing like some fool.

"Are you coming to my place?"

"I didn't realize I was still invited."

"I haven't made good on my promise yet."

Kathleen's face burned with a sudden rush of embarrassment, her head jerked up and she twisted around to face him. "Callahan—" she warned.

When he turned his aw-shucks grin on her, she didn't know whether to throw something at his head or breathe a sigh of relief.

"I'm not making tracks without you, Kathleen. I'm a Marine, I don't run from a fight, either. You can ride with me in my truck and I'll bring you back to pick up your car, or you can follow me home."

"I prefer you follow me." She raised her chin. "I'm not a pickup."

His lips twitched. He gave a deep bow and gestured grandly to her car. "Lead on, Rose."

CHAPTER 13

CAL WAS SWEATING with anger by the time he got into the truck. Eating his feelings cost him more in the long run than finding some release for it. His counselor had encouraged him not to hold so much back, but he be damned if he'd blow up in front of Kathleen and destroy the tentative relationship they were stumbling toward.

That moment in the elevator had been perfect. Until that fucker Warren bulldozed up and ruined it.

The idea of Kathleen putting him in the position of hiding behind a woman's skirts still stung. He didn't need to be protected from shit. He'd by God faced down Taliban fuckers. He'd faced death and survived.

She'd kept him from punching that asshole, which was probably a good thing. He'd have wiped the floor with his pansy ass.

And if he'd gone to jail for it, it would have been worth it.

And what the fuck was Warren doing harassing Kathleen? That was some creepy shit. She needed to file a complaint with the company and nip that shit in the bud.

Jesus, he needed to calm down and throw off this anger. He didn't need to be in a room with Kathleen when he was worked up like this. He'd end up saying something that would ruin everything between them.

While he drove, he practiced some of his breathing techniques to get his heart rate down and leach away his anger.

By the time they turned onto his street, he was calmed down and his thoughts had turned to Kathleen. He'd called her on the promise remark. He'd follow through if she wanted him. He certainly wanted her. Jesus, not just wanted.

He was feeling more in control when he pulled into the parking lot next to his apartment. He slid out of his truck and sauntered up to meet Kathleen as she got out of her car. He smiled when he saw soft color tinting her cheeks.

He watched the rounded curve of her ass as she climbed the stairs, and whipped out his door key before he reached the landing.

"Would you like something to drink?" he asked as he closed the door behind them.

"A bottle of water if you have it."

"Cold?" he asked as she followed him into the kitchen. When she nodded, he pulled a bottle from the refrigerator. He leaned back against the counter and offered it to her. "Why didn't you tell me Warren was harassing you?"

"Because it's easy to misinterpret a word or a gesture, and I want to be sure I've got him pegged right before I do that. He made himself scarce this week until this blowup today, so I was hoping I'd misread him."

He rubbed a hand over his face. The fact she had to deal with Warren at all made his anger simmer again.

"You don't need to *deal* with him. You need to file a grievance against him tomorrow."

She propped her hand on her hip, the gesture full of attitude. "He's been riding you longer than he has me. Are you going to file your grievance?"

Her choice of words brought a flush to his cheeks. The whole point was to make certain Warren didn't try to carry things any further with her.

"I'm going to ask for a private meeting and find out what the fuck's been eating at him for the last two months."

She twisted the lid off the water bottle but didn't drink any.

"And who's going to be there to act as referee?"

"I thought I'd ask Tom Hill, our foreman."

She drank some water and set the bottle on the counter.

He searched her face. "I couldn't tell if he was pissed off at my being there, or if he was angry because you were with me. Could you?"

"I don't care what he was angry about. I just need him to stay away from us both."

She looked so down, Cal eased in close and drew her to him. Her arms went around his waist and she rested her head against his shoulder. He smoothed her hair and tucked it behind her ear. "When he and I meet, we'll come to an understanding about you."

"That's just a grand idea, Cal. You need to deal with your issues and let me deal with my own."

"What does it matter how it's resolved, as long as it works?"

"I won't have settled it on my own. You'll have settled it for me. You'll be doing exactly what you accused me of doing."

"Wasn't it you who said you were protecting us both? Let me do this for you, Kathleen, if I can. He may refuse to meet with me."

She leaned back to look up at him. "No, he won't. He's angry about something. Every time he sees you he looks like he's ready to pounce."

Cal shook his head. "I don't have a clue."

"There has to be a connection between you. Otherwise there's no reason for him to react the way he does."

She was right. But he couldn't figure out what it could be. "I guess we'll have to wait until I'm face-to-face with him to figure it out." He slid his hand down her arm. "Let's have a seat and unwind. I think I've had enough of work and work-related bullshit for the day."

He handed her the water bottle and towed her into the living room with a smile. "Have a seat. I'll be right back."

He went into his bedroom and stripped off his work shirt and his steel toe work boots, then tugged off the heavy socks. He studied his bare foot and the prosthetic foot.

Maybe after they'd calmed down and had something to eat later… Who was he kidding? Just the idea of Kathleen seeing him without his leg was enough to send his anxiety level spiraling into the stratosphere.

The only way to get past it was to let her see…

Kathleen came to the bedroom door and paused to lean against the frame. Her attention rested for a long moment on his rucked-up pant leg and the metal pylon and shock absorber above the foot.

He swallowed. "Come on in if you want to."

She wandered closer and sat down on the bed next to him. "I know this probably isn't the time, Callahan, but I just have to say something—something I've wanted to say for the last three days.

"What is it?"

"If your leg is what's holding you back, I don't give a damn about it. I mean I do, but it doesn't bother me in any way that would keep me from wanting to make love with you."

"How can you know for sure?" His throat felt tight, and he swallowed again.

She surprised him when she slipped off her shoes and climbed up on the bed to straddle his lap. Her arms went around his neck and she cupped the back of his head to hold him close.

"What is it, Kathleen?"

"It isn't pity I feel when I see that empty spot where your foot should be, it's grief. For what you've lost, for everything you had to go through to get here." She leaned back to look at him, and her dark lashes were spiked with tears. "No matter what anyone else says, you're not less because of it, Cal. You're more."

The wary tension coiled inside him released. He'd spent all week hoping. Cal brushed at her wet cheeks with his fingertips. "Don't cry, Kathleen. I've made my peace with it." As much as he could.

For several moments he continued to hold her. "Are you by any chance hitting me over the head?" he asked.

Her laugh was a little soggy, but it was filled with relief. "Yeah, I am. We just had our first fight, and you know what they say about make-up sex…"

He was so grateful he hadn't been fool enough to walk away from her in that parking lot.

He kissed her, offering her comfort, and tasted the salt of her tears. Kathleen raised the hem of his T-shirt and he allowed her to drag it up and off. She dried her face with the garment and dropped it on the bed. When she nestled her breasts in against his chest and pressed her lips to his, his sigh was smothered beneath the tangle of their tongues.

He tugged her blouse free of her skirt and ran his hands up over the smooth skin of her back to unhook her bra. She pulled back, offering him access to the buttons. He made short work of them, and slid the shirt down her arms and off. She did a little shimmy he found sexy as hell, allowing her bra to drop forward so she slipped free of it.

Her breasts were perfect, heavy and round, the dusky rose nipples peaked. He cupped one in his hand, bent his head and took the nipple in mouth and sucked, then feathered the underside with his tongue.

Kathleen rose up on her knees to give him better access and caressed the back of his neck. He trailed kisses upward to her shoulder, and when she bent to meet him halfway, caught her lips again.

It had been a long, lonely, dry spell, and he couldn't get enough of her…her smell, her soft skin and lush curves, her sexy little noises. He couldn't stop touching her, kissing her. Couldn't get enough of her touching him.

He worked his hands up under her skirt to find her bare except for a thong and groaned. He eased her off his lap, down on the bed, and turned to run a hand up the inside of her leg. When he slid his fingers beneath the lacy triangle covering her, he found her wet and ready. He slid a finger inside her, then another, and her body gripped them as he caught the rhythm of her moments.

"Cal?"

"I want to watch you come for me this first time."

Her breathing grew ragged as he stroked her deep inside,

found that one spot that had her catching her breath time and again. He flicked his fingers and she arched beneath the added stimulation. When he applied pressure to her clit with his palm, she gripped his arm and cried out, her orgasm taking her. He had never seen anything as beautiful as Kathleen O'Connor, cheeks flushed rosy, her lips parted, as she gasped her release.

When she reached for his belt he caught her hand. "If you touch me right now, things are going to be over before they ever start." He was so aroused he had trouble pushing to his feet to reach the bedside table and the box of condoms he'd purchased on Sunday night. "I have to take my prosthetic off to get my jeans off, Kathleen," he warned.

"It's okay."

He couldn't watch her reaction, instead focusing on jerking the pants down, pushing the valve to release the vacuum holding his socket in place, and removing the prosthesis. It wasn't until he kicked free of his pants that he looked up. From neck to waist Kathleen was naked, the beautiful slope of shoulder to breast snagged his attention. He wanted to bury his face against that slope and taste her skin, breathe in her scent.

Kathleen broke the seal on the box of condoms he'd tossed on the bed, plucked one out and opened it. Since they were hiding nothing, he slipped off his boxer briefs and lay back on the bed.

Her attention slid down his body to settle on his erection. Having her gaze focused on him was almost enough to set him off. He started working numbers in his head to ease back his need.

Kathleen unzipped her skirt and allowed it to fall. She was all woman, soft, curvaceous, feminine. Her dark hair cascaded forward, hiding her face and breasts as, with a small wiggle, she peeled her thong down and stepped out of it.

He'd have her practice that little move over and over for him later, when it didn't threaten to destroy his self-control.

She climbed back on the bed and crawled up to perch on her knees next to him. "Have I told you what a good boyfriend you're turning out to be, Callahan?" It was sensual torture when she slowly rolled the condom down over his erection and lingered to wrap her fingers around him.

"No," he managed between gritted teeth.

"You're not only a much better man than the only other one I've ever made love with," she straddled his hips and leaned down to kiss him, "you're a bigger one, too."

"It's all from wanting you, darlin'," he managed as she sank down over him, taking him in. She was so warm and tight, for a moment the pleasure was so intense he thought he might disappoint them both.

Kathleen gripped her hair in one hand, leaned down and kissed him again. "Relax, Cal. You've already taken care of me. I want to do the same for you." The rhythm she set suited him just fine, though with every downward thrust he had to recite building specs to keep from flying over the edge. He cupped her breasts again and toyed with her beautiful, taut nipples. When that rosy hue started building in her cheeks again, he knew she was close. He cupped her hips, guiding her into a slower pace as he pistoned up beneath her, deepening the penetration.

"Cal?" The breathless sound of her voice was too much for him, and he couldn't hold back any longer. The rush of his release went on for several seconds, static filled his ears, and he groaned aloud. Finally he opened his eyes to Kathleen's smile.

"I think I may have gone blind for a minute," he complained.

Kathleen chuckled. "How long has it been, Callahan?"

He raised a hand to shield his embarrassment. "Ten months."

Her lips parted in surprise. "But why?"

That was the question.

CHAPTER 14

WHILE CAL DEALT with the condom in the bathroom, Kathleen reached for his discarded work shirt and slipped it on. It smelled of fabric softener and hard work with just a hint of his cologne. She hugged it around her, settling against the pillows on his bed. He knew so much about her personal history, but she knew very little about his. He'd told her about his ex-girlfriend, and mentioned his brother, but he hadn't opened up about his parents and why he'd left Texas until he was angry with Wallace.

And now he'd avoided this. What was he hiding?

The toilet flushed and was followed by the sound of running water. The door swung open. Cal wasn't hiding anything physically as he balanced in the doorway on his crutches. His lean, muscular body was roped with muscle. His chest and stomach muscles were defined. Even his scarred left leg and the upper thigh of his right were toned. His sex, flaccid now, was still impressive.

His left leg was peppered with scars, some still pink, like a cut just healed, others looked flat and shiny like healed burns. His right leg, from his stump to just above the knee, was covered by some kind of formfitting liner and a heavy knit sock. What did it look like uncovered?

A phone rang and Cal changed direction on the crutches and swung toward the foot of the bed. His bare behind looked just as good as the rest of him when he sat down on the end of the bed, dropped the crutches next to him, and reached for his discarded pants. He jerked the phone free, and after a moment's pause, ran his thumb over the screen to answer the call.

As he spoke, Kathleen saw the change in his body language. His shoulders and back went rigid with tension.

"Yes, I'll read them so I'll be prepared." He paused listening. "I have to work until five." He braced his elbow on his left knee and cradled his forehead in his hand. "Yeah, I understand." He began to run his palm back and forth over his hair, bristling it up.

Kathleen drew the rumpled bedclothes up and over her bare legs. His tension affected her to the point that her hands balled into fists in her lap. She nearly breathed a sigh when he ended the call and dropped the phone on top of his pants.

He rubbed his hands over his face.

"What is it, Cal?"

"I have to go into the television station for an interview tomorrow. Wiley called me into his office today and asked me to do it." He twisted around to face her and grimaced. "As a personal favor."

He looked up and smiled and Kathleen could practically see the effort he made to shake off what was bothering him. "That shirt looks better on you than it ever has me." He crawled up the bed to join her and tugged the blanket up over his lap.

When he slid an arm around her, Kathleen curled into him and rested her head against his chest.

"You don't want to do the interview?"

"No. But I don't really have a choice."

"Well, if he's asking you to do this, he isn't planning to fire you."

"At least not yet. He said there'd be some questions asked about hiring disabled workers."

"But you're not disabled."

His arm tightened around her. "That's what I told him."

Kathleen turned to slide her arms around him and felt something stiff against her breast. She stuck her fingers inside the shirt pocket to find a business card printed with a Wiley Design and

Construction logo. She flipped it over to find a woman's name written on it and a phone number.

Her breath hitched. It was a new business card only recently placed in his pocket. Possibly only within the last few hours. "The woman who's supposed to interview you, her name wouldn't be Amy, would it?"

"No. It's Nora Harper."

Kathleen held up the card for him to see. "Is there something you're not telling me, Cal?"

He took the card from her and flipped it over to read the front. "Where did you get this?"

"It was in your shirt pocket."

The confusion in his expression seemed real, but she'd been lied to before by a master and never suspected a thing. Could she trust her own judgment to read what was true anymore? Her throat felt dry.

Cal stared off into space a moment and suddenly his expression cleared. "The receptionist at the desk handed me the card as I was getting ready to go upstairs to meet with Wiley. I didn't even look at it. I just stuck it in my pocket.

"Did she say anything to you when she gave it to you?"

He looked down into her eyes. Was that a tiny bit of wariness she read in the frown between his brows? "Yeah. She said she hoped to see me again soon."

Remembering how oblivious he'd been to the secretaries' scrutiny, Kathleen could picture it going down just as he described. "Is she going to see you soon?"

"Not unless it's with you."

She patted his chest. "Good answer, Callahan."

He tossed the card over the side of the bed. "You can burn that later."

Kathleen laughed and snuggled close to him again. "Why are you so—" She started to say anxious and changed it to "—opposed to doing the interview?"

"I'm not good at talking about personal stuff."

She could attest to that. "Like why it's been ten months since you've gotten laid."

"Well, hopefully she won't be asking about my sex life."

Kathleen's arms tightened around him and she let the question lie between them.

"How would you feel if every man you're attracted to wants to see your breasts before you go out on a date, Kathleen?"

She flinched inwardly. "Embarrassed, insulted." And a little less than what she was.

"Every time I've asked a woman out since losing my leg—it's felt like that. They're wondering what's beneath my clothes, and not in a good way. It becomes more about the limitations than the possibilities. Eventually I just quit asking."

"But you asked me."

"I probably sounded like an idiot on the phone."

"If you'd sounded like an idiot, I wouldn't have said yes." She tightened her arms around him this time.

"Then there's the getting up close and personal part of dating. Eventually if you get close enough you're expected to get naked, want to get naked, and that opens up a whole different closet full of junk to sort through."

She ran a caressing hand over his chest. "You're naked with me, Cal."

"Yeah." His smile turned into a very pleased grin. "I noticed." His hand caressed her bare leg from knee to thigh and traced the curve of her hip.

"You didn't seem to have to sort through anything while we made love."

"You weren't focused on my leg, not even when I had to take my prosthetic off."

Watching him do that had given her another jolt of grief and pain, and her desire had taken a stumble, until she'd seen how aroused he was, and her feelings had shifted to what he needed and more.

She wasn't ready to think about it yet, and things had gotten entirely too serious. "I was focused on your magic wand."

Cal threw back his head and laughed. "My magic wand? I've

heard it called a number of things, Kathleen, but never that."

"What about Mr. Feel Good?"

"That's better."

"Love muscle?"

"Have you been watching porn?"

"No. I've never watched porn. Why watch when you can do?"

"Aww, honey," he sighed. "With that kind of attitude, and the rest of the package, you're every man's dream woman."

"Excellent thing to say, Callahan, but I think one man is enough. I do draw the line there."

He slid down beneath the covers, taking her with him. "I'm glad to hear it." The way he looked at her as he ran a thumb along her cheekbone was enough to jumpstart her heart into a sprint and cause other parts of her body to tingle with anticipation. She propped her knee on his hip and pressed as close to him as possible. His bare skin brushing hers quickened the feelings. The promise of more rested against her thigh, so close to where she wanted it, she had to bite back a groan.

He kissed her, slowly, thoroughly, and with such tenderness and passion she felt it from the top of her head to the bottoms of her feet. She ran her hand up his back, then back down to the base of his spine urging him closer.

He raised his head. "What did you do with that box of condoms, Kathleen?"

Her mind completely blank, she glanced around the room before she spotted them on the chest of drawers across the room. "I'll get them."

She wiggled out from beneath him, tugging the tail of the shirt down over her butt.

"I'm looking forward to seeing you walk away from me in your thong, then coming right back to take it off again."

She grabbed the box of condoms, then paused to study him. All those women who'd made him feel uncomfortable were fools. She'd never had a man tell her his fantasies. When he did, he made her feel sexy and beautiful.

"I can do that now." She knew men liked her breasts. She was more uncertain about other parts of her body. "Or…" She shrugged the shirt off first one shoulder, then the other, but caught it before it fell. Clutching the fabric so it rested just over her nipples, she turned to face him. She folded her arms and pushed her breasts together, giving him a show of cleavage. The shirt camouflaged all the areas she was less confident about, and showcased the rest. With an exaggerated sway of her hips, she sauntered back to the bed.

From five feet away, she easily read the hawk-like intensity of Cal's reaction. Her legs grew weak and she shivered with anticipation. Reaching him, she dropped the box of condoms on the bed.

He ran his fingers up the back of her leg, and the small caress ignited nerves, carrying the sensation on to more intimate places. "From the moment we first met I thought you looked like a movie star from back in the fifties."

"Which one?" she asked, her voice losing its strength so it came out a whisper.

"Ava Gardner."

"She was beautiful, Callahan."

"Yeah. So's the woman standing right here in front of me." His voice was husky as he raised the sheet and said, "Come back to bed, Kathleen."

She dropped the shirt on her way in.

CHAPTER 15

WHILE SHE AND Cal were eating Chinese food in bed, Kathleen left Zach a message around seven-thirty to let him know where she was. She left Cal's at midnight, thinking her brother would be ready to send out a posse. Instead she found a note propped on the kitchen table. Zach had been called out to do some kind of night training, which saved her from having to deal with what would have happened if he'd seen her. One look and he'd be able to tell she and Cal had been together. She had a beard burn on her neck, among other places, and she was sure she had a glow to her that broadcasted "Kathleen had sex last night. *Lots* of sex."

OMG! She'd slept with a man she'd only known for ten days. Ten days if she counted today. Where was her common sense, her caution? Gone with a snap of her fingers the moment she'd seen the need in Callahan's eyes. And now this morning she felt a little sore in spots, but otherwise relaxed as hell.

Her emotional state was a little more chaotic. Everything was happening too fast. What she'd been through in the last six months had been hell. She couldn't go through it again.

But she couldn't turn off her feelings for the man she'd made love with last night. His need had reached out to her. Cal had a way of making her feel special, cared for, safe, and… It was too soon for those words to be spoken by either of them.

The car in front of her flashed its brake lights and she slowed. She couldn't think about emotional issues right now when she had the situation at work to deal with.

Cal had encouraged her more than once last night to file a grievance against Warren. But to do so would put a permanent record in both her file and his. Him for harassment and her as a whistle-blower. It just seemed an irrevocable step to take without first making one more attempt to defuse the situation.

As she wove through the morning traffic, the closer she got to Wiley Design and Construction the more her anxiety level spiraled tighter, wiping out her sex-induced euphoria with a vengeance. She hadn't allowed herself to think last night about what returning to work today would be like. Now it came roaring to life with negative possibilities.

When Warren caused the scene, the only witnesses were him, the security guard, the receptionist, Cal and her. Unless one of them had shot their mouth off, the situation would be contained. She didn't want to blow up anyone's career, including her own. But someone always talked.

Nerves knotted her stomach and made her feel slightly nauseous as she pushed the glass doors open and entered the building. The receptionist who'd been there on Monday wasn't at the desk. Instead, a taller, dark-haired woman had taken her place. Well, unless the receptionist had a network of friends here, she'd only had a limited number of hours to shoot her mouth off.

So that just left the security guard. Who was nowhere in sight.

Her phone was ringing when she entered her office, and she rushed to answer it. "Hello Ms. O'Connor. This is Jodi, Mr. Allison's secretary. He'd like to see you before your eight-thirty meeting with Mr. Edgerton. If you could come straight down now, it would be good."

"Okay, I'll be right there."

Jack Allison, her direct supervisor, had been the one to hire her. If Warren had stuck around to write up his side of the confrontation yesterday, Allison could be calling her in to confront her about it. Warren had already proven his value to the company. It would be easier for them to get rid of her and sweep the issue under the rug.

Or Mr. Allison could be calling her in just to get her side of the story. Cal's idea about talking things out seemed a much more prudent course of action. Allison could act as arbiter while they discussed things and cleared the air.

Kathleen locked her purse inside her desk, then took a detour to the ladies' room to check her appearance before going to Allison's office. She'd put lotion on the beard burn, and by this morning it had eased off enough to cover it with makeup. She appeared normal except for her deer-in-the-headlights look.

Jesus! Working here was so fucking stressful. She was so over this shit. She swept out of the ladies room on a burst of determination. When she knocked on her supervisor's door, he opened it at once. "Come in, Kathleen."

It took her only a few moments to realize the meeting wasn't about Warren at all, but about the client wanting to see the drawing she'd done of the façade.

"You don't mind showing it to him, do you?" Allison asked.

He was a yes man; Kathleen had recognized it the first day they met. Short and rotund, with iron gray hair and gray eyes, he was all about the customer and really good at wooing them and landing contracts.

"No, of course not."

"And if he asks to have it?"

"Well, it's of Mr. Edgerton's project. I can have a copy printed for him. If he wants the original, I'll have a copy made for myself."

"That will be fine. I think he's going to be very pleased with your vision, Kathleen. The work you've done thus far is spot on."

Allison was beaming as he showed her out. With something more positive to concentrate on, Kathleen had a more upbeat outlook as she prepared for her meeting. She looked up the exchange for Paul Warren's office and dialed the number. When she got his voicemail, she left a message for him to call her to schedule an appointment. "I think we need to talk and attempt to resolve this issue, Mr. Warren."

"What issue is that, Kathleen?"

Kathleen turned to look at Hillary. Jesus Christ, the woman was obsessed with the man, and nosey. She wasn't telling her shit. "It's an issue with the Edgerton account."

"Paul will be out for a week. He's taken some vacation time."

How had Hillary found out about that? But then she found the woman's obsessive behavior creepy as hell. She'd have to call Cal and let him know about Warren's sudden disappearance. "Thanks for telling me. I've left him a voicemail if he wants to get back to me."

"The fellow you were with yesterday, he's quite the hunk."

"Yeah, he is."

"You're dating him?"

"Yes."

She frowned. "Isn't he the same man who saved the other one on the platform?"

"Yes, he is."

"Be careful not to confuse hero worship with the other feelings. It's easy to be swept away by a romantic notion." Hillary's expression held a hint of sadness. "I think that's what drew me to my husband."

"I'll be careful." It wasn't hero worship she felt for Cal. She admired him for persevering despite his challenges. Admired his strength.

Her father and brothers had performed acts of heroism. They helped people every day. And they were as unassuming as Callahan. Maybe it did play into why she was so attracted to him. But it wasn't the only reason.

"I need to go. I have a meeting." With a nod, Hillary moved on to her own cubicle. Kathleen gathered her notes from the last meeting and took the picture down off the top of the cubbies.

The meeting went well. The client wanted a copy of her drawing along with copies of the three dimensional renderings she'd do on the computer after the plans were finished.

She was relieved to get back to work, though. Meetings were

always stressful. Sometimes the client knew exactly what they wanted, and sometime they hadn't a clue. Luckily her vision and Mr. Edgerton's seemed to be in sync.

She worked through lunch and nibbled a sandwich at her desk, having asked to leave early for an appointment.

She was alone in her pod when her computer trilled, signaling an internal email. Better check that in case it was Allison telling her about some last-minute thing she needed to do. She opened the email.

"Cal Crowes may be a hero to the military, but he's not here on American soil. He's responsible for one death here at home. Ask him about it. Don't let him fool you. He'll take you down with him."

Every word sent a shock through her. *Responsible for a death at home. He'll take you down with him.* Kathleen looked at the address, but it didn't follow the regular internal format of surname dot last name @WileyDesign.com.

What was this person talking about? It had to be Warren who sent the message, based on what he'd said the day before. Or was it Hillary?

If Cal had been involved in anything like the person emailing was insinuating, there'd be a record of it online.

But looking for it smacked of disloyalty. She'd ask Cal about it after the interview this afternoon.

She needed to know the man she'd fallen for was worthy of the faith she'd placed in him. But she also needed to know who had accused him of something this serious. And why.

When Hillary, Edward, and Dave returned from lunch, she'd calmed down and was eager to ask a question. She realized she didn't trust Hillary, and Edward, though friendly, seemed less in tune with the people he worked with than he was with the work itself. Dave gave off a fatherly vibe she found more open to being questioned. "Dave, do you have a minute?"

"Sure. Got a problem?"

"Just a question. Can anyone add an email address to the system, or does it take a special password?"

"All of that is handled by the techs hired to work on the system and keep it up to date."

"Have you ever seen this email address, or know whose it could be?" She laid a slip of paper with the email address on his desk.

He shook his head. "I don't recognize it. Besides, it isn't formatted right. It should have the person's first name or initial listed before the rest. I don't understand how it even got to you."

"I got an email from this address during lunch."

"Was it something work-related?"

"No. Something personal."

Dave frowned. "Was what they said in any way harassment?"

"In a way, yes."

His expression grew more concerned. He pushed his glasses up in a gesture of impatience. "After what happened your first week here, Kathleen... I'd take it to Allison. He's your direct supervisor, and he has the authority to look into it. If someone is using the system to get to you, it would be a simple thing for the techs to trace how he or she gained access to the system, and where the breach has occurred. If whoever sent this is capable of bypassing this small protocol, they may be capable of a whole lot more."

She nodded. She hadn't thought of that, because it had been a direct affront to her, and only concerned Cal. But did she want to leave Cal's life open to enquiry? And that's exactly what would happen if she took it to Allison. There'd be a rush to judgment before he even had an opportunity to defend himself. And how could you face an accuser who hid behind anonymity?

"Thanks, Dave. I'd appreciate it if you kept this between us."

"Had you ever met any of the people working here prior to being hired?" he asked.

"No. Not a one. I come from Boston, so the chances of me knowing anyone here are astronomically slim."

"If you have any more trouble, you can come to me any time."

Touched, the sting of tears had her blinking. "Thank you,

Dave."

"I have a daughter in high school. One day she may be following in your footsteps. I'd want someone to be there for her if anyone was messing with her like this."

Kathleen smiled her gratitude. "You let me know, and I'll help you kick their ass."

He grinned.

At least something good had come out of it. She knew she had at least one person here at the company in her corner.

CAL TUGGED AT the collar of his light blue dress shirt. His fingers grazed the small microphone the technician had clipped to the fabric, and he checked to make sure he hadn't dislodged it. Two large cameras pointed toward the set. The lights above projected enough heat that sweat ran down along his sides.

He didn't want to be here. And he certainly didn't want to have makeup slathered on his face to do it.

Nora Harper stepped up on stage, her blonde hair shining beneath the lights, her five foot five frame appearing taller because she was so slender. Even without the heavy makeup, she'd be a beautiful woman. She lowered herself into the chair across from him and smiled. "I appreciate you agreeing to the interview, Mr. Crowes." She leaned forward and offered her hand. Cal automatically gripped, then released it. They both knew the only reason he'd agreed was because his boss had pushed him into it.

Nora studied him with pale blue-gray eyes, her smooth brow crinkled by a frown. "We'll be taping more footage than we'll be using, and then edit for content afterwards."

Cal nodded. "Okay."

"Also, there was a video I found online of you at work. I thought it would be good to use the footage and dub your answers to some of the questions behind it. I was wondering if we could get a signed release from the person who shot it."

"Two of my crewmates at work shot the video."

"May I have their contact info so I can ask them to sign the releases?"

A feeling of uneasiness took root in the pit of his stomach. She was too casual about it. "I'd feel better if Mr. Wiley saw it first and gave his okay before it's put on television. It was filmed on the site of one of his projects."

Her features tightened, and she tried to cover her disappointment. "I'll show it to him when he comes in to tape his interview and get him to sign off on it."

"I'll email him when I get home and tell him to expect it."

"You don't trust me do you, Mr. Crowes?"

"I don't know you, Ms. Harper. But when I wouldn't give you an interview, you made comments on the air about my workplace and my competence on the job, which sicced several agencies on my boss and pushed him into encouraging me to do this interview. So, no. I don't trust you."

"You said if I stirred the pot you wouldn't have a job."

"Not because of the company I work for, Ms. Harper. Because of the shitstorm you've already stirred up."

"But you wouldn't answer my question on the phone. You even blocked me from calling back. How was I to know that?"

Cal raised a shoulder in a shrug. "I wanted to be left in peace." He motioned toward the cameras. "But this comes first with you, doesn't it?"

She leaned back in her chair. "Are you going to be hostile while I interview you?"

"I'll do my part because I gave Mr. Wiley my word."

She nodded. But she wasn't happy. She touched her ear bud. "We need to get started."

Cal placed his palms on his thighs to keep from fidgeting while Nora did the introduction to the segment. He had to cool down and remain pleasant whether he wanted to or not. An edgy resentment tightened his shoulder muscles.

"Welcome, Corporal Crowes."

Being called Corporal again gave him a twinge of pain, stronger than he expected. Had he believed he could dive back into his life as a soldier and do the job right… He might have lost out on being part of the Engineering Corps, but he'd loved being a Marine. "It's just Callahan Crowes now."

"Is that a family name, Callahan?"

"Yeah, after my great grandfather."

She eased him into the interview by asking about his background.

He began to relax a little since she was sticking with the questions she'd sent him.

She turned to his service record. "You were highly decorated for your service.

Cal shrugged. "There are a lot of guys out there with more distinguished records. Mine was cut short."

"Cut short when your vehicle hit an IED."

"Yes."

Cal's muscles tensed and his heart rate jumped. She was easing into something she hadn't prepared him for. He could smell it.

"How extensive were your injuries?"

He ran through the list dispassionately.

"You were lucky to have survived."

"Yeah, I was. The three other men with me were killed instantly."

"I know you have a tattoo on your chest honoring them."

Was that why she wanted the video? "Yes." He'd gladly turn this thing to something about them instead of him. "Private 1st Class Jasper Holland. He was from Tennessee. He played the guitar and sang ballads to entertain us when we weren't on patrol. We called him Jazz.

"Private Mitchell Ellison. He was from Sacramento, California. He had a dry wit and a sharp sense of humor. He kept us laughing.

"And Private 1st Class Neil Carter. He was from Oklahoma. He was quiet, but had a quick laugh, and was a master at chess. We covered each other's backs for ten months. I was their commanding officer that day, but I couldn't protect them from a bomb." He swallowed back the emotion.

"I'm sorry for your loss, Cal. For all their families' loss."

He nodded. "Thanks."

"How long did it take you to recover from your injuries?"

"Three months for my bones to knit, a little longer for my body to heal. They fit me for my prosthetic six weeks after I lost my leg, but I had to have several more tune-ups to get it right. As my leg changes with use and age, I'll have to continue doing the tune-ups on my prosthetic, probably for the rest of my life.

"After six more months of physical therapy and exercise, I was back to fighting form, and I had to decide whether to stay in or accept my discharge."

And a six-month overlap of one-on-one counseling had helped him deal with his emotions, but it had taken three more months for the headaches to stop. Severe head trauma was a bitch.

"You decided not to reenlist though you'd been cleared to return to combat." The avid curiosity in her expression made him uncomfortable. It was as though she wanted to get under his skin in some way.

"I could have worked in a support position. But I could never be the kind of Marine I wanted to be again. I decided to accept that and move on."

"I've been told a lot of men experience survivor's guilt. Do you feel guilty having survived when the other men didn't?" She projected sympathy in her expression.

He'd tried to stop, had swung the wheel to avoid something, but he didn't remember what. He'd been eaten up with what-ifs for a while, but had had to leave that thinking behind for his own stability. "The terrorist who built the bomb is responsible for my men's deaths. But I'll always owe Jazz, Mitch, and Neil something. My responsibility to them is to continue to live my life in the best way I can to honor their sacrifice. And to remember them."

She remained silent a moment. "You looked pretty strong on the video I saw of you on the job. It's obvious you found something you can do, despite any limitations you may experience because of your injuries."

"It's something I'm good at. I'm grateful to be able to do it."

"Your father wouldn't hire you to work on his construction sites. Why?"

How had she found out about that? Had she talked to his dad? Betrayal like a brushfire raced through him. Brutal honesty was the only way he could deal with this. "My father couldn't get past what I looked like in the hospital when I was flown home from Germany. He labeled me a cripple before he ever gave me a chance to come back from my injuries. It's his loss that he continues to do so, because he's wrong."

She never missed a beat, though she'd gotten the emotional response she'd been looking for. "So now you walk around on steel beams instead for Wiley Design."

"Yeah. Tom Hill our foreman had faith I could do the job and gave me a shot. I proved I could."

"You do realize how rare it is for an amputee to do the kind of work you do."

"Competence in a field depends on a lot of different factors, Ms. Harper. So far I haven't run up against anything I haven't been able to handle. When I do, I'll be the first to turn it over to someone who can. That's why we call our working unit a crew."

"Has anyone at Wiley Design and Construction ever said anything detrimental to you about your ability to do the job?"

She was fishing for what he'd meant on the phone. "No. I haven't broadcasted that I have a prosthetic lower leg. But it's never been an issue with the work, so why would I?"

"It's still a dangerous job."

"Any job can be without the proper safety measures."

"You recently saved a fellow worker's life. What happened?"

He was really tired of repeating the same thing over and over. Maybe this would be the last time. "We were on our way to the elevators to load safety netting when Julio tripped and fell and went over the side. I snagged his safety vest. The crew helped me pull him back up."

"From the video, he nearly dragged you over the side, didn't he?"

"But he didn't."

"Who was the other person who helped rescue him?"

"I'm not at liberty to say."

Her mouth tightened with impatience.

"I appreciate you agreeing to our interview, Mr. Crowes." She leaned forward to offer her hand.

So now he was Mister. Cal shook it briefly. "You're welcome."

She went into a run down on upcoming shows. Cal remained still until the cameraman signaled clear. A technician appeared to remove the mic and its battery pack.

He rose to leave.

"That wasn't so uncomfortable, was it?" she asked.

"You talked to my parents?"

"To your brother."

The betrayal burrowed even deeper. He studied her face to see if she even understood what she'd done. All he saw was a frown.

He shook his head and stepped down off the stage.

"I don't understand why you're so opposed to talking about your experiences. You're alive, you survived." She threw out a hand in exasperation.

"Because my life, my pain, isn't for your viewers' entertainment. It's as personal as your sex life. Do you want to answer questions on television about that?"

"No, of course not. But sometimes talking about trauma helps, it's cathartic."

"I've talked to other soldiers who've been through similar experiences to mine, and I've talked to doctors who treat men like me. Those moments were cathartic. Going on television to rehash my injuries isn't. It's just an invasion of my privacy."

He moved to walk away but turned back. "Recovering from something like this isn't a six-month or even a year-long process. It takes a lifetime, because we have to live with it for a lifetime. Struggle with it for a lifetime. I don't need my recovery or my life made any more difficult by total strangers taking judgmental pot shots at me from afar."

"That's why I wanted to interview you, Mr. Crowes. To show that you've survived the struggle, you're continuing to live a normal life."

If she only knew. The most normal thing he'd done since coming home from Afghanistan was make love with Kathleen. His emotions were finally starting to thaw, and he was only starting to deal with it.

He was wasting his time trying to point out how wrong this woman's motivations were. She was about the job, not any humanitarian effort.

"Good luck to you, Ms. Harper."

He turned and meandered away through the cable-strewn area behind the cameras. He scanned the room until he found Kathleen waiting at the exit door. When she held out her hand, relief flooded through him and he grabbed it.

CHAPTER 16

KATHLEEN REMAINED SILENT as they worked their way down hallways so shiny and clean the florescent lights reflected off of them like runways leading to the front door. As soon as they made it outside Kathleen turned to face him. "You need to take a deep breath, Callahan."

"I'm okay."

No he wasn't. His cheeks were red and his jaw taut. He rubbed a hand over his hair in a gesture of stress she was becoming familiar with.

"I'm sorry she dragged your father into the broadcast." She had to look away to maintain her composure. When she knew he was hurt, she felt his pain. "I know what a trial parents can sometimes be. How they try to manipulate you through guilt to do what *they* want, instead of what you feel you need to. How their expectations of you can cloud their judgment. And if you're pissed at your brother, call him up and bitch him out. But don't hold it in."

The tension in his body eased and he reached for her. He rested his chin against her temple. "It doesn't matter. I was angry at first, but I'm over it now."

"Corporal Crowes." A shout came from behind them, and they both turned to face a dark-haired young man as he bounded out the front door.

"You never signed the releases for the video footage on line."

"I told Ms. Harper my boss would have to view it first. You can email it to me, and I'll see it's signed and sent back after he's given his okay."

The kid didn't look happy as he turned to walk away.

"Why does she want the video so badly?" Kathleen asked.

"I don't know. Unless she's seen some kind of safety violation in it and wants to drag Wiley through the mud or stir up trouble again. We need to check it over and figure it out."

Cal placed a hand against the small of her back as they ambled across the parking lot to his truck. It was a small show of consideration he always made, but coming on top of his being so worked up, Kathleen felt her eyes sting with tears.

What he'd said about his recovery being an ongoing struggle that would go on for years was true. For all his strengths, she recognized how his anxiety levels triggered his emotions. And how hard he fought to control them.

As they drove back to Cal's apartment, silence stretched between them. Though his color had returned to normal, Kathleen could read the tension in his body.

As soon as he pulled into his parking slot, he said. "I need a cold beer. I bought a bottle of the wine you like."

"I'd appreciate a glass," she agreed. She didn't wait for him to come around and get her door, but met him around the front of the vehicle and slipped an arm around his waist.

"Thanks for giving me some time."

She gave him a hug.

She realized they were falling into a routine with each other when she dropped her purse on the table next to the door just as he did his keys. Both of them headed for the kitchen.

Cal removed the wine bottle from his fridge along with a beer. He tackled the cork with a minimum of bother and poured her a glass.

When they settled on the couch, Kathleen kicked off her shoes and curled her legs up. Cal toed off his tennis shoes.

He laid a hand on her calf and rubbed his thumb back and

forth over her skin, both tickling her and giving her a sudden sensual rush. How was she supposed to control this instant reaction she had to him?

And why did she feel she had to?

Because it left her so completely vulnerable to losing her heart to him. And she was falling in love. She wasn't blind to his issues, but she couldn't help herself. He was trying so hard.

She swallowed a sip of wine to cover how emotionally tender she felt. She wanted to ask him about the message she'd gotten at work today, but now wasn't the time. She couldn't picture Cal hurting anyone outside his duty as a Marine. It just didn't compute with the man who held his temper in and hurt himself rather than let his emotions get away from him.

Cal held his beer in the other hand and balanced it on his thigh, but didn't drink from it. "I have a temper. When I was younger I got into fights—a lot. By high school, I'd learned if I didn't want my Dad to come down on me at home I needed to pour all my aggression into sports." He glanced up at her with a wry smile. "For the most part."

Kathleen remained silent, afraid any comment she might make would dissuade him from continuing.

"The military taught me control and discipline, so I thought I'd left all that rage behind, and that was pretty much true until our Humvee was hit." He took a drink from the beer bottle, then moistened his lips. "I didn't grieve over my leg, I bypassed grief altogether and went straight into a full-fledged meltdown every time something didn't go well. I can tell you part of it was my leg, part of it Stacy's exodus, but most of it was losing my men, my career, everything."

He started rubbing his hand back and forth over his head. "Coming home from a war zone to what everyone else thinks is normal is…surreal. The adjustment to that was—" He swallowed. "Difficult."

"I fought my pain meds. I hated being on the pills and thought I could do without them. Big mistake. I had these headaches that were torture." He traced the ridge just over his brows with his fingertips. "The more pain I was in, the shorter my temper got."

"Then one morning one of the day nurses came in and told me she was tired of my shit and she wasn't taking it anymore. If I didn't take my meds and start cooperating, I was on my own. She gave me a lecture that would have pinned my ears back if I hadn't been concentrating on being such an asshole."

Shocked, Kathleen asked, "She couldn't really do that, could she?"

"Well, she did. She took my vitals and made sure I was fed, but that was pretty much it. I poured all the anger her lecture triggered into learning to do for myself the things they'd been helping me do. If she wouldn't help me, I'd by God do it myself.

"She actually did me a favor. With no one to fight with but me, I figured some things out."

He concentrated on the beer bottle like it was the most important object in the room. His throat worked as he swallowed. "It was a form of survivor's guilt. My thinking was I deserved to be in pain because my guys were dead and I wasn't. They were just nineteen- and twenty-year-old kids. They deserved to have their whole lives ahead of them." He covered his eyes, but the grim set of his mouth said it all.

He hadn't been but a couple of years older than the kids he was talking about.

Kathleen couldn't bear it any longer and scooted closer to lay a hand on his shoulder.

Cal dropped his hand and continued. "By the third day when the nurse came in and offered me my pills, I took them. But anything I could do on my own, I did without help. I'm not saying it was all smooth sailing, emotionally, physically."

He focused on her, his expression earnest. "It was hard at first. I had to fight the feelings that I didn't really deserve to live, to have a life. After I got my prosthetic and got up on my feet, I started to see all the other guys around me struggling to move on and realized I wasn't the only one going through that shit.

"There was this one guy. He'd stepped on an IED and lost

both legs above the knee, his arm had been shredded but they managed to save it, though he was doing physical therapy to recover more range of motion and strength in it. He just wouldn't give up. We talked about everything, nothing held back like you do with the doctor or your family, but the whole, naked truth. He made me see I was alive and going to stay that way, and I needed to get on with it. That I couldn't go back to that moment in the Humvee and change anything, and I had to accept it."

"I still have a temper, Kathleen, but I don't blow up anymore. I still have PTSD, but I'm not depressed, and I still see a counselor twice a month to keep tabs on how I'm doing."

Quick tears pricked her eyes as understanding hit her. Cal wasn't reticent because he wanted to hide anything, but because he felt things so acutely. She had guessed this before, but she was seeing it now.

His blue-green eyes looked almost gray-blue with emotion. "I just wanted you to know the real story instead of the fairy tale Nora Harper settled for."

Seeing he was ready for her to be close, Kathleen wiggled over and pressed against his side. Her heart ached for him, at the same time a deep relief took hold. He'd trusted her enough to share his pain with her. He was finally lowering his emotional boundaries like he had his physical ones.

"Thank you for telling me, Callahan." When she brushed his cheek with her lips, Cal turned and they came together in a kiss, soft, comforting, but Cal lingered over the caress. His tongue slipped forward to reach for hers. He tasted of beer and Cal, sensual and heady. Kathleen's pulse surged, her cheeks heated and she cupped his jaw.

Despite his reticence, Callahan was a better lover and boyfriend than Lee had ever been. She thought less and less about her ex and more and more about the man next to her. The buoyant happiness she experienced when she was with him was almost too much.

She sent out a hopeful prayer: *Please don't let this crash and burn.*

Cal broke the kiss long enough to set the beer on the coffee table and go back for more. "I need to be inside you, Kathleen."

God, that husky voice did it for her. She was already wet and ready for him. She tugged his shirt free of his jeans while he worked her shirt buttons, his fingers trembling. That small outward show of how much he wanted her pushed her desire higher. She hurriedly finished the last few buttons and tugged the blouse off. Cal nipped her shoulder, then smoothed it with his tongue. Her breathing went ragged at the small caress. Kathleen struggled to free herself from her bra while he ditched his shirt.

"I love that you wear skirts," he said as he rucked the skirt up, baring her thighs. With a tug he had her on her back and the fabric bunched up around her waist. The leather felt cool against her bare buttocks, his hands hot as they slid up the outside of her thighs. "Just the thought of you nearly naked under your clothes drives me crazy." Cal braced his left foot on the floor as he slid the lacy thong down her legs and off.

Kathleen sat up and reached for his belt. She unfastened it, unzipped his jeans. His erection bulged beneath his boxer briefs, and she worked them down so it popped free and jutted forward. Cal dug his wallet out of his back pocket and jerked out a condom. He tossed the wallet aside and it went skittering across the coffee table and off the other side. He tore the condom open and rolled it down over his penis.

He bent to kiss her and Kathleen looped her arms up his back to tug him down to her. "Not yet, Rose." He kissed her with long, slow, thoroughness. Then slid down to taste each beaded nipple and roll them with his tongue. Kathleen stroked the back of his neck. When he sucked, tempting sparks burrowed into secret areas of her body, making her ache, and she lifted her hips in response.

Cal braced his arm next to her and lowered his body over her own. "Every time I call you Rose, I think of how you look down here," Cal murmured, against her throat. Finding her with his fingertips, he brushed back and forth across her sensitive clit with a touch so gentle it drove her nearly mad and her stomach muscles contracted.

She fisted her hands against his shoulder blades to keep from scratching him. "Cal, please."

"You're dewy and pink, just waiting to be caressed, kissed. There isn't enough room on the couch for me to do it, but I promise I'll kiss you there next time we make love, Rose."

Her body clenched at the visual he painted of his head between her legs and could almost feel his mouth on her at the mere thought. How was it possible he could arouse her beyond bearing with just words? He eased the head of his penis inside her. She caught her breath at the sensation and ran her hands down his back. She raised her hips, wanting all of him, tempted beyond reason. He thrust in all the way and rocked his hips. Just that first sweep of sensation was enough, and she bucked beneath him as she climaxed.

Kathleen opened her eyes to find him watching her.

"God, you're beautiful when you come for me. Let's try it again." He rocked back, nearly leaving her, then thrust forward again. She captured his rhythm. He seemed to lose himself in the motion, the intensity of his movements rocking her as the leather beneath her held her in place. Her own arousal built again, rising up to meet his while he swelled and hardened inside her. The moment she felt the contraction of his release, her own hit her like a tsunami and she cried out.

Afterwards Kathleen stroked Cal's back as his heart pounded against her and his hot, moist breath fanned her neck. The longer she laid there with his weight poised above her the more time she had to think about all the romantic, seductive things he'd said to her since they'd been dating. He could seduce any woman he wanted. All he had to do was open his mouth, and the most erotic things came out. Why weren't women crawling out of the woodwork to be with him? He was gorgeous, had a silver tongue in more ways than one, and all the right moves.

Was she just one of a long line of women he'd done this with?

She kept her tone conversational, though a deep-seated betrayal began to build in her mind. "How long have you been practicing this technique of seduction through vocal visualization, Callahan?"

Cal raised his head to look down at her, his eyes, heavy-lidded and drowsy, projecting a sexy as hell masculine satisfaction. "What are you talking about, Kathleen?"

"Your erotic talk, during sex. How do you know what to say to get me primed?"

His gaze swept her face. "I just tell you what arouses me when I look at you."

How could she be pissed about that? But she was, and she couldn't quite put her finger on exactly why. No—she knew exactly why she was pissed.

"Have you done this with other women?"

"No."

"No?" she repeated, her tone a blend of challenge and surprise.

"No." His eyes never shifted from her face.

"Why do you do it with me?"

"If you don't want me to do it anymore, I'll stop." He shifted and looked over his shoulder at something.

That idea didn't suit her either. She loved the way he made her feel when he… "Why do you do it with me?"

"Do we have to discuss this now? I'm stuck."

"Stuck for an explanation."

"No. Physically stuck."

She could feel Cal was still inside her, but growing soft so he couldn't be stuck. "Stuck how?"

"I've wedged my prosthetic foot into the couch somehow, and I'm going to have to give it a jerk to get it free, and I can't because I'll hit you with my knee. So you're going to have to slide out from under me."

Kathleen bit her lip to keep from laughing. She couldn't laugh. It might hurt Cal's feelings. She hid her face against his shoulder until the urge went away. She glanced up to find him grinning.

"Hopefully, the first of many adventures of making love with you while keeping my prosthetic on."

He was offering her an olive branch. The urge to laugh died. "Making love with you is always an adventure, Callahan."

"Now who's seducing who?" he shot back. He eased back on his knees and slid free of her body.

Using her arms she pushed up into a sitting position, then slid her leg free from behind his hip. She swiveled her legs over the side of the couch and scooped her blouse up off the floor. With a wiggle she tugged her skirt down and then shrugged into her blouse.

"I'm amazed at how you can go from sexy as hell to businesswoman in a matter of seconds," he commented.

She pointed a finger at him. "You are not going to distract me, Cal. We will continue this conversation." She assessed how he'd wedged his foot between the back of the couch and the cushion. "Lean forward on your hands," she instructed.

He jerked his jeans up over his bare backside and did so. She reached behind him and gripped the metal pylon of his prosthetic. It was the first time she had touch it since feeling the edge of the socket during their first date. The cold metal was so foreign compared to the rest of Cal's body. She set aside the quick jab of grief and gave the limb a tug, freeing his sock-covered foot shell.

"Thanks." Cal adjusted his clothing. When he shifted from the couch to his feet, he favored the knee a few steps before his gait evened out and he disappeared into the bedroom.

Kathleen grabbed her bra off the back of the couch and picked her thong up off the floor. Determination in every step, she followed him into the bedroom just as he disappeared into the bathroom. She hurriedly shimmied back into her thong and removed her blouse to put her bra on.

Once dressed, her armor was back in place. She took a seat on the edge of the bed, facing the bathroom door. They were going to resolve this issue between them or she was going to leave. Because she couldn't live with believing in someone and having them betray her. Not again.

Then another thought came to her. Was this about the email more than his sexy talk? No…Maybe… Or was this more of the pathological distrust Lee had bred with his betrayal? She leaned forward and rested her head in her hands. She didn't know anymore.

CAL DISPOSED OF the condom and cleaned up. He opened the door and paused for a moment to study Kathleen as she sat on the edge of the bed. Shit! He could tell from her expression she had overthought every word he'd said to her. Why had he ever taken Julio's and Hector's advice? Because he hadn't wanted her to walk away without giving him a chance. And at the time he'd thought it might be his only shot.

"To try and explain will spoil the romance for you, Kathleen."

"What will spoil things for me, Callahan, is continuing to feel manipulated."

He drew a deep breath. "That isn't what I intended." He left the bathroom doorway to sit on the bed next to her. "I wanted to make you feel desired."

He leaned forward to rest his elbows on his knees. "I'm not him, Kathleen. I'm not a player, a liar, or a womanizer. I'm not out to manipulate you to get what I want, or disrespect you. I care about you, and I want you to care about me. I want to be with you, not as a notch on my bedpost, but because we fit together in so many ways."

With each word, he could see her anger slip away. She folded her arms around her in a defensive posture. Finally she turned her face aside so he couldn't read her expression.

"The first time we were together, taking my prosthetic off…It's worse than being naked, Kathleen. It's like laying your soul bare. Do you think I could do that with just any woman? That I would want to leave myself open to rejection again?"

"No, I don't believe that." She leaned forward to rest her head in her hands for a moment. "I'm trying to leave it behind, Cal, but sometimes things get inside my head."

"I know how it works Kathleen. I've gone through the same thing myself." He wished to God he hadn't, but he had.

"I'm always on the defensive…looking for things." She finally sat up to face him. "Did you really mean everything you said?"

"Every word." He forced a smile he didn't feel. "Rule number one. Never lie to a woman; she may forgive, but she won't forget, and it will come back to bite you."

"Damn straight. We have memories like elephants. Better than elephants." Her buoyant tone fell flat.

Cal reached for her hand and was relieved when she allowed him to take it. "What makes you believe I didn't mean what I said, Kathleen?"

She remained silent for a long moment. "It had nothing to do with you, Cal, and everything to do with me." She swallowed. "Three months before I ended things, he started making remarks about—my body. Tamara is tall and thin and beautiful. But it turned out she wasn't enough for him, either. I don't think anyone will ever be enough. But…he wanted me to be different in a way I couldn't be. Toward the end I was practically starving myself, trying to please him. When I caught them together, I finally understood."

But the damage had already been done. Cal slipped an arm around her and held her close. Had she cried, he'd have felt better, but she curled into him instead and remained dry-eyed.

"You know how guys always say they're boob men or butt men?" he asked.

"Yeah."

"That isn't my sweet spot, Kathleen."

"What is?"

"Besides your mouth?" He smiled as quick color touched her cheeks. "I found my sweet spot the first time we made love."

She studied his face for a long moment before she asked, "What is it?"

He reached for the buttons on her blouse and was amazed when she didn't pull away. He slid her bra strap out of the way. "It's right here." He trailed the back of his fingers down the slope of her shoulder to the top of her breast. "I could spend days just nestled right in there with my face pressed against your skin, breathing in the way you smell and tasting you."

Kathleen bit her lip, fighting a smile. "You are a strange man, Callahan."

"You're probably right."

"I don't want you to stop telling me what turns you on." Her cheeks got redder.

"Good. I don't think I could resist anyway." He was addicted to it. Addicted to pleasing Kathleen.

Her hand skimmed his while he refastened the buttons her blouse. "Why did you start?"

Hector and Julio had shared the idea, but Kathleen had been the inspiration. "When we met at the coffee shop and you were embarrassed by the ink stains on your fingers." She nodded. "It was the way you responded when I kissed your fingertips. I was turned on the rest of the night."

Kathleen sighed. "So was I."

Relief lightened his mood while he and Kathleen fixed a meal together and ate. She seemed to have sloughed off her earlier upset. "Why don't you go get my laptop out of the bedroom and bring it in here? While I clean up you can go through the video and see if there's anything likely to cause me or the company an issue."

"Okay."

He had just pushed the button to run the dishes when Kathleen came into the kitchen and placed the laptop on the counter. "Cal, you didn't sign the release so someone posted the address to the video on Nora Harper's site and the show's site, *Harping on the Truth*. You've had over three thousand shares and at least two hundred comments since it was done."

"That—" He bit back the word. He ought to have known she'd find a way to get around him. She was probably pissed about the parting shot he'd gotten in. "Take it down, Kathleen."

"I think you need to read some of the comments, before I do. Some of them are pro and con regarding hiring disabled personnel, but most of them are about you."

"What about me?"

Her smile held a hint of amusement. "Read them and find

out."

Wariness took root, and he was slow to approach the computer. He read the first comment, "OMG, that is one hunk of manly male. He can come work on my house any time," then the second "He looks like he can get the job done." The farther down the list he went, the more suggestive the comments became. One commenter even posted her phone number. Didn't she know how dangerous that was?

He glanced up to see Kathleen watching with a smile. "These women are crazy." He shook his head. "I'm a construction worker, not a male stripper.

"I feel so used," he complained in an exaggerated aggrieved tone and flashed her a grin.

Kathleen giggled.

He read a few more and ran across one that disturbed him. "Just because he lost a leg in a war zone doesn't make him a hero. He lived when three other men died. Why was he spared? He promised to watch their back. If that wasn't enough, he caused their families even more grief." He hoped Kathleen hadn't seen that one. And how had the writer known about any of the particulars of what had happened or that he'd visited the families? The television show hadn't aired yet.

Was it someone in one of the men's families? He'd lived through the hell of survivor's guilt, and the grief of losing his men. Some of what the commenter said brought it all back.

He tried to control his tone when he said, "Take it down. If the guys at work see it, I'll never hear the end of it."

"If you're sure."

"Positive."

Kathleen tugged the computer over to her. She typed in some info, a password, and selected the video and deleted it. "All gone. But there's still a copy on my computer at the house if you need it."

"Thanks."

He tried to shake off the emotions the comment had triggered.

"I just wanted you to read some of them so you'd know there are women out there like me who see more than a prosthetic when they look at you, Cal."

He suddenly realized what she was getting at. She had body image issues and so did he. But being with her had gone a long way toward erasing some of the negative he'd experienced. He'd make damn good and sure he did the same for her.

Maybe the next time they went for a walk on the beach he'd wear shorts. He'd have to buy some.

CHAPTER 17

CAL GRIPPED THE ladder mounted alongside the wheelhouse door and braced his feet against the wallowing motion when the cabin cruiser hit the wake of another vessel. Looking east, he followed the flight of a lone gull as it glided on the stiff breeze cutting inland. It had been too long since he'd been on the water. Until they left the dock, he hadn't realized how much he'd missed it.

He breathed in the salt-tinged air and studied the passing scenery as Zach, or Doc, as the other two SEALs on board referred to him, navigated out of the bay and pointed the vessel out to sea.

Flash Carney wandered out of the cabin and gripped the other side of the ladder. Though he had been a member of SEAL Team 5 at the time of Cal's injury, Flash had been transferred to another team. He, Doc, and Bowie still had a bond. It had been apparent as soon as they dropped what they were carrying and moved in to greet each other with handshakes and hugs.

"It's good to see you on your feet, Cal," Flash yelled above the wind.

Cal grinned. These guys wouldn't pussyfoot around his amputation. They'd witnessed it firsthand. They'd all had a hand in saving his life. "It's good to be standing instead of on my back like the last time you saw me."

"You came out of the Humvee with your side arm in your hand ready to fight. I knew you'd make it. So, you're dating Doc's sister?"

He'd wondered how long it would be before one of them would approach him about it. That it was Flash came as a surprise.

"Yeah, I am."

He expected some razzing, but instead all Flash said was, "Funny how things come full circle isn't it?"

Cal studied the man's face. He'd been quiet and introspective most of the time he'd known him back in Iraq and Afghanistan. In fact, Flash had talked more since showing up for the trip than Cal had ever heard him back in the day.

It was like kismet. What were the odds that he would hook up with the sister of the man who'd saved his life? "Yeah, it is. Kathleen kept talking about her brother Zach, but I had no idea he was the guy who dragged me out of the Humvee until we met face-to-face. It was a little surreal."

"I bet."

"He didn't recognize me, but I remembered him."

"Well, your face was pretty messed up, covered in blood and teeth and starting to swell. I wouldn't have recognized you if I hadn't known you before."

"I guess not."

"Looks like the docs put you back together pretty good. You're still as ugly as ever."

Cal laughed. "Yeah. I still have a few pieces of shrapnel here and there and this." He raised his leg. "But I'm good."

"Good."

"And you?" Cal asked.

"Let me show you my girls." Flash whipped out his wallet and pulled a picture free.

Ensign Dan Rivera, aka Bowie, appeared at the top of the ladder leading to the wheelhouse above. "He's doing it again," he said over his shoulder to Doc before mounting the ladder and climbing down.

Flash laughed. "You're just jealous." He extended a picture to

Cal.

It was a candid shot taken out in the desert. The woman had strawberry blond hair and freckles across her nose. Her country girl beauty garnered more than just a passing glance. The little girl she held on her lap resembled her so much there was no mistaking they were mother and daughter.

Flash crowded close. "That's Samantha, my fiancée, and Joy her daughter. Our daughter. As soon as we're married, I'm putting the paperwork through to adopt Joy. She calls me Pop already, but we want it to be official."

Meeting this woman had changed Flash. Cal had been around him for an hour and the difference was obvious. Some of it could be about being home from a war zone, but the way the guy had whipped the picture out... "They're beautiful, man. When's the wedding?"

"Two weeks. My team's going wheels up soon, and we want to do it before that happens. Sam doesn't know why I'm pushing it, but if something were to happen to me in action, I want them to be covered."

Cal nodded. "Understood."

"Besides. Sam and I are talking family. We'd like Joy to have a baby brother or sister soon. I have to make her an honest woman before that happens."

Bowie came to stand on Flash's right and lean against the opposite side of the ladder. "I'm the sixth son in a family of six. I can tell you how to have a boy, Flash."

Flash raised a brow, suspicion in his expression. "All right I'll bite."

"Fill Sam a bubble bath and pour her a glass of wine. While she's in the bath give her a back rub. You want her to be as relaxed as possible. Buy her something really sexy to wear to bed, you know, to get the pump primed. Kiss her and tell her how much you love her. Then..."

"Yeah?"

"Call me and I'll take it from there."

Cal bit his lip to keep from laughing.

"You son of a bitch," Flash growled, eyes narrowed. Then he chuckled. "I've already warned Sam about you."

"Moi?" Bowie pointed at his own chest, dimples flashing in each cheek as he grinned. "Why the hell would you do that? Even I have certain rules."

"Like?"

"Never poach a teammate's woman." He squeezed Flash's shoulder. "Relax, you still qualify. And never date anyone in a teammate's family. I already have too many people shooting at me to chance someone I know doing it."

All three of them laughed.

Bowie's gaze slid to Cal and his lips twitched suspiciously. "You're either a very brave man or you have a death wish."

Cal knew where this was going. He shrugged. "Kathleen's worth the risk."

Bowie studied him for a long moment. "You may be a cooler customer than I am, Crowes."

"Naw. If things went sideways between us…not that it's going to happen…but if it did, it wouldn't be Doc, Kathleen's seven other brothers, or her dad I'd have to look out for."

"Then who is it?"

"Her mom."

Bowie pointed his finger at Cal and grinned. "Flash, you got to hear this story. Come up here and let Doc tell it to you."

The two men climbed the ladder to the wheelhouse so Doc could share the story. Cal followed them and wedged a shoulder against one of the side supports to the awning against the rocking movement of the boat. He smiled while Doc explained how his mother had broken her hand punching Kathleen's ex in the nose. Cal noticed he left out the part about what a cheating bastard the ex was and just called the guy a scumbag who'd tried to use their mom in an end run to get back with Kathleen.

A few minutes later the fish finder started pinging like crazy. Doc pulled back on the boat's throttle and guided the vessel toward a cloud of gulls in the distance. Thirty feet from the disturbance, Doc cut the engine and let the boat glide to a stop.

The large vessel wallowed in its own wake, then settled. "Gulls feeding like this usually means there's a fish frenzy going on. Check that for me, Bowie."

Bowie hunched over the sonar device. "Looks like some action for certain."

"We'll drop anchor here on the outskirts. Yellowfin love to come from the outside and feed off the bigger fish drawn in by the movement."

"Okay, what's the bet this time?" Flash asked.

Doc grinned. "Low man has to buy us each a case of beer and, just to give everyone an incentive, fillet all the fish we catch today."

"Are we going by number or size?" Cal asked.

Doc chuckled. "You are a quick study, Callahan. We'll measure each fish from snout to tail and keep a running tally." He opened one of the seats and removed a marker board with metal hooks attached at the top and a black marker.

This was the first inkling Cal got about how serious these guys were about fishing. He did not want to be the poor sucker who had to clean a cooler full of fish. But he could get off on eating a few.

"Flash, drop anchor," Doc ordered.

"Aye, aye." Flash mounted the ladder and disappeared below.

"Cal, I set out four poles for you to choose from; they're down in the cabin on the bunk. Check them out and take your pick. There's a harness or two down there too."

"Roger that." He descended to the deck and ducked down into the cabin. A saltwater rig could run as much as nine hundred dollars with the reel. The rod alone could be as much as five hundred dollars. In for a penny, in for a pound. Cal chose a shiny new two-piece rod. He checked that the line wasn't tangled and the reel worked properly, then picked up a harness. If he hooked something big he might need it.

He stood back and watched the three other men set up to fish. SEALs were driven and focused by nature, so were Marines. Cal understood the need to be both a teammate and a competitor.

He'd missed being in the mix. Here he could compete. The playing field was even.

Gripping a lawn chair, he flipped it open and set it along the rail and baited his hook with a bait fish from the cooler Doc had furnished. "Casting," he called out as he flipped the reel and whipped the end of his rod forward toward the feeding seagulls.

The line landed just where he wanted it. He braced his knee in the chair and slowly reeled it in to lure whatever was out there into biting.

Five minutes later Flash was the first one to hook something. The sound of his reel spinning was cut short when he set the hook. For several tense minutes he heaved and reeled to bring in his prize. The rest of them cheered him on as they waited to see what he had. "He's surfaced, I need a gaff," Flashed called out. His shoulder and arm muscles bulged beneath his T-shirt as he fought to keep the fish up.

Doc set aside his own rig and grabbed a long gaff secured to the side of the boat. With a practiced move, he leaned over the rail, hooked the large fish and dragged it on board. The yellowfin tuna was still fighting to be free and flopped on the deck. Cal estimated its weight at roughly thirty pounds. A good catch.

Doc measured and recorded Flash's catch on the board while Flash secured it in a large cooler.

"Ladies we're gonna need more than one of those if we're going to feed the hungry hoard at Lang's tonight," Doc said.

Cal cast his line again and felt the immediate tug as the bait was hit. The reel spun as whatever had latched onto the scrod ran with it. He flipped the spindle with his thumb and the reel abruptly stopped, but the force of it nearly jerked the pole out of his hand. Jesus, whatever he'd hooked was *big*. He cranked the handle and felt the pressure of trying to keep the line tight. He pulled back on the rod, the tip bowed as he forced the fish closer and reeled in the line.

"Need any help over there, Cal?" Doc called.

"Not yet. Once I get him close in to the boat, I'll yell."

He took a seat in the lawn chair and braced his feet on the

side of the boat. He took his time, working the fish in toward the vessel by short increments. Six minutes later he dropped his feet and stood, thinking surely he was close.

A gray-blue shadow swam back and forth beneath the water, disappeared beneath the boat, bending the end of the rod down at an angle. Cal pulled up on the pole with steady pressure but didn't try to reel in any more line. He waited for the fish to swim back out. As soon as he saw the shadow again he cranked the reel furiously. When he saw the size of the thing his breath caught. He had no idea how he'd kept it on the hook.

"What is it?" Doc asked.

"I've hooked a yellowfin, and it's big."

Doc and Bowie reeled in their lines and laid aside their poles.

"Jesus!" Doc exclaimed. "That fucker's huge."

"Too big to eat," Bowie said. "That's a mounting weight."

"You want him mounted, Cal?" Doc asked, his green eyes gleaming with excitement.

"No. I'm not a trophy kind of fisherman. I usually eat what I catch." He could just imagine what Kathleen would have to say about a stuffed dead fish on his wall.

"He's too nice to turn loose. Imagine all those tuna steaks on the grill," Doc said, rubbing his hands together. "Keep his head up so he can't go back under the boat. Bowie and I will gaff him and get him on board."

Flash having reeled in his line wandered over to watch. "That might be a record, Cal. That sucker has to be at least five feet long." He whipped out his cell phone and video'd the fish.

Bowie got the longer gaff, while Doc got a shorter one. Doc leaned over the side in order to reach the tuna. Bowie hit the fish in the top of the head with the hook and held on while it thrashed. Blood poured into the water. Doc swung to get a hook on it, too.

A large silver streak advanced on the yellowfin in a rush. Cal had only enough time to yell. "Shark!" A monster heaved up out of the water, jaws open, exposing razor sharp teeth. Its black eyes gleamed flat as it narrowly missed Doc's arm and clamped down on the tuna from the side, shook its head with a frenzied fury and tore half of the yellowtail away.

Doc's hand slipped off the railing and he started to pitch headfirst into the water. Cal dropped the pole and dove for his legs, and managed to grab a calf and part of his shirt. He was hanging by a foot just above the water with the predator likely circling to take another bite. His head was brushing the water.

Bowie jerked what was left of the tuna aboard and threw gaff and fish onto the deck, spreading blood across the polished wooden floor.

"Jesus H. Christ, get me up!" A long string of colorful swear words followed.

Bowie and Flash rushed to help. Bowie grabbed Doc's arm and his belt while Flash fastened onto his other arm and his other leg. The three of them heaved him back onto the deck, and set him on his feet. He still held the gaff he'd been intending to use.

Cal grabbed the rail to regain his feet. "You okay?"

Breathing hard, Doc pushed his dripping hair back from his flushed face, his eyes wide. "Yeah."

As they watched, the sickle-like dorsal and tail of the shark whipped back and forth as it circled past the boat in search of more prey.

"Shit!" Bowie whispered.

Flash bent over what was left of the dead, mangled tuna. "Dude, you were robbed."

An hour later, they'd moved the boat to a different location and paused to eat the sandwiches and potato salad Cal and Kathleen fixed for their trip. They laughed again at Flash's comment as he passed his phone around to view the video of Doc's close call and as Bowie dubbed it "the great tuna tug-o-war."

"It seems saving people is getting to be a habit with you, Cal," Doc commented.

"I've just been at the right place at the right time a time or two. The shark would have been too full of my damn fish to munch on you anyway. But I didn't think you'd want to get your clothes wet."

"That was damn considerate of you." Doc nodded. "The water out here is cold as hell. Makes my balls shrivel up just thinking about it."

Cal grinned, more at ease with the low-key thanks than all the attention he'd gotten recently. He shrugged. "Just passing it on." He realized he felt more relaxed with these guys than he did even with his building crew. They'd let him step back into the military brotherhood and just accepted him.

"Kathleen said you were going to be on television this week."

Cal grimaced. "Yeah. Actually, it's tonight. I got roped into doing an interview with Nora Harper, on *Harping on the Truth*. You were right about the video. We should never have posted it. I had to send her signed releases yesterday so she could use parts of it, but she'd already found it and put a link to it on her website. Women were leaving comments."

"What sort of video and what sort of comments?" Bowie asked.

"It was just me at work doing stuff on the building site. But their comments were—suggestive."

"Man, you should eat that shit up," Bowie said.

Cal shook his head. "Not while I'm dating someone. I had Kathleen delete it and the comments." His glanced at Doc.

Doc nodded his understanding. "Speaking of videos. Flash my man, I'm going to have to ask you to keep the gem you recorded to yourself."

Flash looked up with a frown. "Why?"

"Because I've been halfway around the world and dodged more than bullets at numerous times, in numerous countries and never had a scratch. That damn shark came closer to getting me than any terrorist. I don't want my family to see it. Every time I go out on the boat they'll be thinking Jaws is out to get me."

Cal laughed right along with the others.

Doc pointed his finger at the man. "Do not post it on some kind of social media site."

"I won't." Flash threw up a hand as though swearing in court. "But I will email you and Cal a copy. Cal needs proof of the size of that fish."

CHAPTER 18

KATHLEEN LEANED BACK against the picnic table and shielded her eyes from the setting sun as she scanned the backyard. The hedge of Hibiscus against the deck was in full bloom, and the fuchsia-colored blossoms busy with bees. The deck stretched down one side of the house and across the back. On one side a buffet table was arranged, a white tablecloth stretched over the dishes to protect them from children's marauding fingers and insects.

She'd never been to Langley and Trish Marks's house before, but the couple welcomed her with open arms. And she felt completely at home, even though she wasn't the spouse of a SEAL or even the girlfriend or fiancée of one.

The Langley's three children, Tad, Anna, and Jessica, took turns diving off the board at one end of the pool. They could swim like fish, but Langley kept watch over them out of the corner of his eye while he hung with Jeff Sizemore, another member of the team.

Brett Weaver, Zoe's brother, dangled a beer between two fingers while he hugged his wife Tess to his side. He gestured with the bottle at Hawk, Zoe's husband, while he made a point about something.

Tess, his wife, was everything Kathleen wanted to be. Tall, slender, gorgeous, and successful in her job. Kathleen wanted to hate her, but it was damn hard to hate someone you'd spent the afternoon cooking and talking with, and who was genuine and a straight shooter.

Samantha "call me Sam," Zoe, Trish, Tess, and Selena were all special. Independent, strong, funny, and open. They fit into their husbands' lives in the same way her mom fit into her dad's. They could stand strong alone when they had to, and were fiercely loyal to their husbands, and each other. She had never laughed or cried so much in an afternoon in her life. It had felt wonderful to be part of their group. She missed the female bond she'd had with Tamara and some of her friends.

Selena's husband Oliver, aka Greenback, arrived with their daughter Lucia and his parents. Selena jumped up from the picnic table to greet them. Lucia was already stripping her clothes off in preparation for hitting the pool. Greenback held her back long enough to put floaties on her arms before turning her loose.

Sam sat down next to her. The pretty strawberry blond had a flush to her cheeks. She was so starry-eyed in love she practically glowed with it.

Did Kathleen look like that when Cal was around? She hoped it wasn't that obvious. Not yet. Not until she knew if he felt the same way.

"Think they caught anything?" Sam asked. "They wouldn't be late if they hadn't, right?"

"There's going to be a lot of disappointed people if they didn't."

"I hope they took showers. The last time Flash went fishing with Travis, he had fish guts all the way down his shirt and smelled worse than road kill."

Kathleen giggled. "Well if they haven't, we can always hose them down out here. Is Travis another member of the teams?

"No. He's Flash's foster father. Actually the only father he's ever had. He and Juanita, his foster mother, wanted to take Joy down to Mexico for a few days so we could have some alone time. It's been a little hectic with all the wedding arrangements, even though we're doing a simple ceremony in church and a barbecue similar to this."

"Sometimes the simple things are more memorable, and they don't smart nearly as much as those five thousand dollar price tags." She regretted every last dime she'd spent on the wedding. All the time and effort as well.

Sam nodded. "Since neither of us has any biological family left, Travis and Juanita and their two sons, Josh and Javier, and Flash's teammates have become our family. As long as we're with them, that's all that matters."

A car horn sounded from on the street and they both looked up.

Two minutes later Flash and Bowie came through the side gate, a cooler between them, and wearing clean shorts and T-shirts. Zach and Cal followed behind them. When Kathleen realized the lower half of Cal's leg was visible in a pair of shorts, she half rose from her seat. Cal was strutting his prosthetic as though it was nothing at all. Kathleen's chest filled with pride and her vision blurred.

"Well, they all look like they're in one piece," Samantha observed. "And they must have something in the coolers."

Having to answer helped her gain control of her emotions. "Hopefully it's not just empty beer cans."

"They're all walking upright, so they couldn't have consumed that much beer."

Kathleen flashed her a look. "You haven't seen my family at gatherings and picnics. All the guys have a tolerance. But I think you may be right. They all seem to have that self-satisfied swagger of a job well done."

Sam grinned. "I thought that was just their normal walk."

Kathleen chuckled. "You could be right. None of them lack confidence, do they?" Callahan had that same swagger despite his prosthetic. How much had he had to practice to regain it? She'd never felt such joy for anyone in her life.

"Was Cal a SEAL too?" Sam asked.

"No. He's an ex-Marine."

"How did you two meet?"

"He works on one of the buildings my company is constructing."

"He fits right in with the others."

He did. He and Zach were verbally batting something back and forth. Zach threw his head back and laughed at something Cal said. The two of them seemed to have really bonded over the trip.

Flash and Bowie dropped the cooler next to the grill. Bowie headed for a beer and Flash ambled over to Sam.

"Hey, babe." Flash grabbed her hand, tugged her to her feet and wrapped his arms around her. "How was your day?" He kissed her lightly, but the emotion in his face was so open and intimate, Kathleen had to look away.

Cal was suddenly there to distract her with her own feelings of intimacy as he slid in next to her and slipped his arm around her waist. "Hey, Rose."

Oh, God! Every time he said it now her body went into sexual hyperdrive. Kathleen rested a hand on his knee where the liner and sock covered his thigh. "You had a good time."

"Yeah." His lips twitched. "I'll tell you about it later."

She raised a hand to touch his cheek. "And you're wearing shorts."

"Yeah. And I've already heard several comments about my lily white leg." He was smiling as he stretched it out for her to see and she smiled back in relief even though she felt a little teary.

"How does it feel?" she managed though emotion had her voice bobbling a little.

"It's good. It feels normal."

If nothing else came out of their being together... He'd broken through the boundaries he'd erected, leaving himself open to more possibilities. Had she just come along at a time he needed a nudge to do it? However it had happened, she was happy for him.

When he leaned forward and kissed her, what would have been a soft brush of his mouth, she turned into something warmer by holding his mouth to hers.

Cal searched her face when she drew back.

"I missed you today," she admitted.

The pleasure she read in his face brought heat to her own. "We can make up for it later."

Warmth lit her cheeks. "I'd like that."

Zoe came out of the house and limped toward the picnic table. "Cal?"

Surprise crossed his face, then he smiled and got up to greet her. "Zoe. It's good to see you."

She hugged him, and for a moment Kathleen thought Zoe might cry. "I want you to meet my husband, Hawk. I've told him all about you. Kathleen, would you like to join us?"

She followed them across the yard to where Hawk stood with Langley. He carried a toddler on his hip, his son A.J. The child had his same dark hair and features in miniature. He reached for Zoe as soon as she was close enough. She took him and hiked him on the hip supported by her stable leg.

"Adam, this is Cal Crowes, the man who saved me when the explosion went off at the hospital."

Hawk's brows hiked up and he extended his hand. Cal shook it.

"Thank you for saving my family. Zoe told me what you did that day. I can't tell you how much it meant to us both."

The intensity and emotion in Hawk's face and voice brought tears to Kathleen's eyes.

"I was pregnant with A. J. when you pushed me out of the hall and covered me to keep me safe, Cal. If you hadn't done that, neither of us would be alive."

"I'm glad what I did kept you safe. But I didn't do anything that anyone else faced with that same situation wouldn't have done." He drew Kathleen forward. "Your team protected me and got me to the chopper. Doc and Bowie saved my life. Your wife helped me get back on my feet and back into life. I met Kathleen, and now we've come full circle. It must have been meant to be."

Hawk nodded. "It must have been. How about I buy you a drink?"

Cal looked to Kathleen.

"I'll be around. You two go talk." Kathleen turned to Zoe,

and mindful of her leg and noticeable limp, held her hands out to A.J. "Hey handsome, how about keeping me company?"

The toddler leaned forward and came right to her. She hefted him onto her hip. She and Zoe strolled back to the picnic table together. "If I hadn't already cried and laughed so much today, I think I might be tempted to start all over again."

Zoe slipped an arm around her. "Me too."

THE SMELL OF chlorine from the pool and the smoky scent of mesquite burning in the gas grill sent Cal's mind spinning back to barbecues in his parent's backyard. He wondered what Nora had said to his brother to get him to betray his family's privacy. No doubt she could charm men…all but him, anyway.

When Flash yelled down the table. "Hey, Cal aren't you going to watch *Harping on the Truth*? It comes on in ten minutes."

Cal's stomach knotted. He was well aware of the time, and had hoped no one would notice. "Taping it was enough, thanks. I'm not interested." He kept his tone flat to cover his sudden nerves.

"There's a television in the weight room. You could step in and watch it. It's only a fifteen-minute segment," Kathleen said.

Cal shook his head. "I'm really not interested."

"What if she somehow slanted the footage in some way?" Kathleen asked.

"I want to see it," Zoe said and scooted off the picnic table bench.

Kathleen joined her. "I'll let you know if she tried to pull anything."

The other ladies went inside with her and Zoe, including Greenback's mother.

Well, shit. He continued to chew his food, but it suddenly tasted like sawdust. He had to drink some water to wash it down. His gaze strayed to the door leading into the downstairs weight room.

"You're really not curious how it turned out?" Bowie asked.

"No."

"Well, what was she like, Nora Harper?" Bowie asked.

Cal looked around to make sure no women were still at the table. "You know that shark we ran into today?"

"Yeah."

"The only difference in it and her is it has more teeth."

The man's brows rose. "Whoa. Why did you do the interview, then?"

"My boss at Wiley Design asked me to. They caught some flack about hiring practices because I happen to be their only worker with a prosthetic. He didn't like the negative publicity Nora Harper was stirring up."

"I hate that shit," Brett commented from down the table. "Tess reports, but she digs deep to make sure what she publishes is the full picture. I've seen some of the pieces Harper has done. She's all about the hype, whether it's the full picture or not."

Cal pushed his plate away. "That's the read I got, too. She's using each interview to further her career."

The women were strangely quiet when they came back to the table. Cal searched Kathleen's face. "What's wrong?"

"You'll have to watch it later on You Tube or one of the tele-vision replay services. She used some of the footage of you on the building site, but it was mostly what I filmed the day you changed my tires. She taped what you said at the end of the interview about it taking a lifetime to heal. So it ended well, but there was just something exploitive about the way the footage was done."

Heat climbed in his face, along with a familiar tightening in his chest. "I'm glad I didn't watch it, then." His phone vibrated and he reached for it. An unfamiliar number showed on the screen, so he walked away from the table to answer.

"Hey, Cal. My name is Patrice and I just saw you on Harping on the Truth. I'd love to meet you and have a drink."

Stunned Cal looked at the number again. "How did you get this number?"

"I just went through a cell phone directory service and paid a fee. Don't be mad. I just thought we could hook up."

"Look, I have a steady girlfriend. I don't cheat. I'm flattered, but no thanks."

"They should have mentioned that on the show. You have my number if you change your mind."

He hung up without comment, but the phone vibrated again. Another unknown number came across the screen. Oh shit! He darted a quick look at Kathleen. She was talking to Tess and had her back to him. Maybe this was just a fluke and it would stop. The phone quit vibrating. He breathed a sigh of relief. It started again, a different unknown number. Cal turned the phone off. If this continued, he'd have to change his number.

When he returned to the table, Kathleen asked, "Everything okay?"

"Yeah, just a wrong number." He'd tell her about the phone calls later.

CHAPTER 19

I T WAS NEARLY ten when Kathleen and Cal said their good-byes and left the Marks's house. Cal's hand rested against her hip as they ambled to the car. "Would you like me to drive?"

"No. I think I'm good. I'm trying to learn my way around. If I get off on the wrong street, you can give me directions."

"Okay."

She was grateful he was secure enough to let her drive. She wove past long streams of residences and pulled out onto Palomar Street. She'd purposely made a point of encouraging Cal to catch a ride with her brother so she could drive him home. She'd call Zach if she decided to spend the night.

Cal had saved Zoe's life and Kathleen's curiosity had been piqued about the terrorist attack at the hospital. "Tell me what happened at the hospital. I heard the news reports about the explosion, but reporters usually share only enough to leave you curious as hell."

Cal ran his hands down his thighs to his knees and back up. "Terrorists targeted Zoe's brother, Brett Weaver, and his family. One of them decided to go after Zoe. I had just arrived to do my therapy, and this guy followed me down the hall to the therapy room. He had a prosthetic arm and was holding something in his right hand.

"He called Zoe by name, like he was making sure he had the

right person, so I turned to look behind me and caught a glimpse of the C-4 he'd strapped around his chest. I shoved Zoe through a door into the therapy wing and covered her just as he hit the switch and set the bomb off. The place was pretty beat-up, but the solid cinder block walls limited the damage to part of the ceiling structure, and the only one hurt was the guy who blew himself up. He was pretty much dust.

"It set off a few electrical fires and smoked the place up. I helped Zoe get out of the building and took her to the emergency room to be checked out."

"Amazing."

He wasn't bragging, just telling what happened as though it was an everyday occurrence. He'd just gotten back from a war zone. Just recovered from the IED explosion. How had he dealt with the aftermath?

She quickly found her way onto one of the main roads north.

"It was pretty cool seeing the little guy, A.J. I didn't know Zoe was pregnant, she never said, but then she wouldn't have. I was a patient, not a friend. Well, we were sort of friends after the bombing." He glanced at her. "Completely platonic."

Kathleen nodded. "You seemed to hold your own pretty well with the guys today."

She turned east a few minutes later and merged into the heavier traffic a block from Cal's apartment.

"Doc and the guys kind of took me into the fold."

"Do you still miss it? I know there's a kind of brotherhood among military guys."

"Yeah, I miss it sometimes. Today felt good."

Kathleen studied his face in the dim glow from the streetlights. "I'm glad you had a good day."

"You could make it perfect by coming in with me."

Kathleen turned into the parking lot and her lights flashed over Cal's truck parked in its regular spot. "I thought you'd never ask. ...what's that in your truck, Cal?"

His attention jerked away from her to his pickup. Something large sat in the bed, a heavy gray tarp covering it. "I don't know."

She pulled up and parked next to his truck. Cal was already climbing out before she turned the engine off.

He pulled up a corner of the tarp to look under it. "It's one of the welder/generator units from the construction site." The tension in his stance, in the way he continued to look over the unit triggered her own tension. "I don't know where it could have come from." He circled the truck to see if anything else was disturbed. "I'm calling Tom." He jerked his phone out of his back pocket and dialed the number.

Kathleen leaned against the quarter panel of her car and watched Cal pace back and forth while he waited for the foreman to pick up. "Hey, Tom, it's Cal. Did you send a welding unit over to my place for some reason?"

He listened for a moment. "I've been out on a boat all day fishing and just got home. It's in the bed of my truck, covered with a tarp." They spoke for a moment longer.

Once he hung up, he leaned back against the car beside her. "He doesn't know what the hell's happening, either. He hasn't sent anyone over with any equipment, and he doesn't have any idea why it's here. He's coming over."

There went their plans, but they could make up for it another time. Kathleen looped her arm through Cal's and leaned in against his side. "When he gets here, you could drive it back over to the site and the two of you could unload it."

"We probably will, but first we need to figure out who parked it in my truck and why. Even though it's on wheels, the unit is very, very heavy and hard to maneuver. You'd have to have access to a truck to move it…and why leave it here in my vehicle? That's what I don't get."

Cal remained motionless for several seconds. "If whoever did it sicced the police on me, I could be charged with possessing stolen property. Since one of these units costs a bundle, I'd be in big trouble. If this is a prank, it's not goddamn funny." His body was rigid, his voice rough as sand paper.

"You've called Tom. He knows you didn't take it. Why would you report it being here if you intended to steal it? Besides, it wasn't here this morning when Zach picked you up, and you've been gone all day. And you had witnesses with you all day."

"Yeah. I did. But I'll still be relieved when Tom gets here. I keep expecting to see flashing red and blue lights headed this way."

It was a long, slow ten minutes waiting for Tom to show. As soon as his truck pulled into the parking lot, Kathleen took the first deep breath in what seemed like hours.

Tom swung out of his vehicle, flashlight in hand and hurried to Cal's truck. "Hey, let's check this out." He jerked the tarp back and, using the flashlight, searched for the serial number. "It's one of ours. Who the hell would take it and park it here in your truck?"

Was that a hint of accusation in his tone? Kathleen's stomach cramped with anxiety.

Though calmer, Cal was still grinding his words out. "Possibly the only person I've had any trouble with on any of the sites."

"Warren is on vacation, and I haven't seen him around the site."

"I didn't take this welder, Tom. I'll do whatever you need me to do to prove it. Jump through any hoop."

"He's been out fishing with my brother Zach and two other men all day. And we've just come from a barbecue where we ate their catch. There's like twenty people who will vouch for him."

"It's Ms. O'Connor, isn't it?" He extended his hand.

"Yes." Kathleen shook it briefly.

Tom remained silent for a moment. "I believe you both." His attention shifted to Cal. "I can't imagine you doing anything that would threaten your job, especially since you have so much attention directed at you right now from the top brass. And if someone's setting you up, they did a piss-poor job of planning, since you haven't been home to take the fall. But that doesn't mean it's not going to happen. We need to get this back to the site ASAP."

"I'll get the truck keys," Cal jogged away.

Left alone with Tom, Kathleen reiterated Cal's defense. "My

brother picked him up at six this morning to go fishing. He's been without a vehicle all day. He really didn't do this." She was as close to tears as she'd ever been during the whole mess. "He's worked so hard to get where he is, he wouldn't do anything to jeopardize that."

"Relax. I really do believe you. But we still need to find out who did this. If the police had shown up, even if he was gone, it would have affected his entire future with the company. There's a rush to judgment these days, and once that happens…"

Kathleen's anxiety eased back a notch, but her heartbeat was still a little ragged when Cal appeared on the landing and descended the stairs. He jogged back to them with the strange gait she'd noticed the first day on the site.

"I've left the door unlocked, Kathleen. Will you wait for me?"

"Yes, I'll wait."

When he stepped toward the truck Tom caught his arm. "Hold on, Cal. I think it would be better if I drove it back to the site and got it unloaded. We don't want you anywhere near this thing."

"It weighs upwards of four hundred fifty pounds, Tom. You'll have to have help moving it off the truck."

"Shit!" Tom nodded.

"Maybe we should call the police and report it." Cal sighed. "I know how it looks, but I've called you to let you know it's here and, like Kathleen says, I have witnesses who were with me all day. Maybe one of my neighbors saw something."

"Wiley doesn't want any kind of negative publicity right now. They haven't said anything, but they're working on a huge deal, and if it looks like we aren't staying on top of site security, it might affect negotiations."

Now Kathleen understood this back and forth with the publicity issue.

"Then let's take it back to the site and get it unloaded." Cal's tone had changed to one of careful patience. "I want it off my truck before the police show up and charge me with stealing the damn thing. I keep thinking someone's trying to set me up for a big fall."

"I'd better drive. The security people won't think much if it's me bringing machinery back."

Cal nodded. "Lock yourself in, Kathleen. We'll be right back."

As Kathleen watched the truck disappear her stomach twisted with anxiety. Everything was going to hell at once. When Cal saw the Harper show he was going to be even more upset. Instead of the serious interview the woman led Cal to believe she was doing, she used careful editing to turn it into something very different.

And the nasty email about Cal she'd received at work was still lurking at the back of her mind. She'd been ready to bring it up with Cal several times, but each time something or someone had interrupted her. Or had she let it? She didn't want Cal to be less than what she thought he was, because she loved him. And she needed him to love her.

But she needed to know the truth before the worry ate away at this dream just like Lee's betrayal had gobbled up the other. She had to know the truth.

CHAPTER 20

T HE CLOSER THEY got to the building site, the more Cal calmed
down. They'd get the damn welder off the truck, and he'd no
longer be waiting for the bite of the ax hanging over his head.

"I know you're going out on a limb for me, Tom. I really appreciate it. If any kind of backlash comes of this, it's on me."

"There isn't going to be any. We're going to get this thing
back to the site and be done with it. But I want to talk to the
security people. No one can come on the property, load up a unit,
and drive off with it without authorization. There had to be some
kind of paperwork. Since I didn't put it through, someone else had
to. The only people authorized to shift machinery and tools
around are those directly involved in the project, and they're
supposed to go through me first since I'm foreman."

Cal felt the last bit of anxiety melt away. "If there's a paper
trail, I'll be cleared. I don't have access to any of that."

Tom signaled a turn into the building site, the trucks head-
lights outlining the chain link gate. A security guard came to the
fence, and Tom got out to talk to him, showed him his ID, and
the guy unlocked the gates and opened them. At Tom's gesture,
Cal got out and jogged around to get into the driver's seat and pull
the truck in. Tom hopped in on the passenger side. "After we
unload this thing, I'll go into my office to look through some of
the paperwork that came through yesterday. Pull your truck

around close to the service elevator, and we'll unload it and push it onto the elevator platform. The first load of guys to show up for work can take it back up to the top floor."

"Roger that," Cal said with a nod.

Because it was the weekend, the lights on each floor of the structure were minimal. The security lights in the yard were a little better, but not by much. Cal drove slowly over the rough terrain churned up by the large supply trucks used to deliver materials. He backed the truck in toward the docking area where the freight elevator sat only feet away.

"I'll get the lights," Tom said and opened the door.

"Hey wait." Cal reached into the glove box and pulled out a short metal flashlight and handed it to him.

"Thanks."

Cal got out of the cab and leaned back against the side of the truck to wait. The muggy heat of a long day settled over him, misting his skin with sweat. One minute passed, then two.

"Tom?"

No answer. It shouldn't have taken that long to find the breaker box. It was right behind and to one side of the elevator. By memory rather than the dim glow of a security light, Cal navigated the path from the truck to the steps. "Tom?" He mounted the steps and walked along the side of the freight elevator. "Tom?"

The hairs on the back of his neck stood up and he froze. Adrenaline rushed his system and instinct kicked in.

There was someone else here. He strained to hear any noise over the sound of traffic on the street. Something had happened to Tom. He had to do something.

Cal eased forward and rounded the steel frame of the elevator. Where the emergency lights should have burned, total darkness met him. He sensed rather than saw movement and ducked. Something whizzed by his head and struck the steel support with a dull clang.

Cal dove toward the movement, falling to one knee and catching the next downward swing with his shoulder. The weapon was metal, and he grunted as pain from the blow resonated down his back and arm. He raised the other hand to fend off the next blow and by sheer luck caught the downward swing. He gripped the metal pipe and wrestled it away.

He got a weak grip on the guy's jacket with the hand partially numbed by the blow to his shoulder. The attacker spun away, wrenched the fabric from his grasp, and sprinted down the platform.

Using an awkward backhand, Cal threw the pipe at his attacker and heard a satisfying thud. The guy staggered, but found his feet and kept going.

Cal pushed up from his knee to his feet. Pain ran up his neck and down his arm. He hadn't a hope of catching the guy in the dark on the uneven ground across the site. He'd flounder around on his prosthetic and probably obscure any evidence of the guy's escape. Fuck!

He had to find Tom. Where was the nearest emergency button? He shuffled through the dark to the right and stumbled on something cylindrical and nearly fell. He bent to feel for it and discovered the flashlight he'd given Tom. He flicked the button and its weak light illuminated Tom's prone figure crumpled in front of the breaker box. Cal sidled around him, flipped the switch on the box, and turned on the lights. The dark red emergency alarm button was positioned right beside it. He hit the button, setting off the blaring alarm while he knelt to touch Tom's neck. There was a steady pulse, but a huge bump was forming on the side of his head and his hair was matted with blood. Thank God he was still alive.

The two security guards he'd seen at the gate came running fifteen seconds later, guns drawn. Cal hugged his arm close to his body. Adrenaline had held the pain at bay, but now it ached like a son-of-a-bitch. He hit the switch with his left hand, turning off the alarm. "Did you see anyone in the yard?"

"No." They answered in unison.

"We were both attacked. The guy ran down that way." One of the guards tore off in that direction.

Cal pointed out the obvious when the other guard continued to stand there with the gun in his hand. "We need an ambulance and the police."

HALF AN HOUR passed, and Kathleen went to the door to look out. Her nerves stretched like bungee cords down the back of her neck, and the low hum of the television did nothing to sooth her. The news had long since played, but a fresh wave of anger on Cal's behalf rose. Nora Harper had turned the report from a tribute to survival to injured beefcake, something Cal never would have agreed to. The woman had done everything she could think of to rob the segment of dignity.

Kathleen called Cal, but a message informed her the customer wasn't available. Why did he have his phone turned off?

When someone knocked, she sighed with relief and rushed to the door.

But Cal wouldn't knock, he'd just unlock the door with his key.

She looked through the peephole. Two uniformed police officers stood there, one young and blond, the other dark-haired and muscular.

Oh, God, something had happened to him. Her heart was in her throat as she opened the door.

"Is Mr. Callahan Crowes at home?" the muscular cop asked.

If they were asking for him, he was okay. Her mouth was dry with the residue of fear and she had to swallow before she could answer. "No, he left about an hour ago with his boss."

"Who might that be?"

"Mr. Tom Hill. Has something happened?"

"We need to speak to Mr. Crowes, ma'am. Do you know when he'll be back?"

"No."

"And who might you be ma'am?"

"I'm Kathleen O'Connor, his girlfriend."

"Do you live here, Ms. O'Connor?"

"No, I'm just visiting."

The dark haired cop's deadpan expression set her nerves off. He pulled a business card out of his pocket and handed it to her. "When Mr. Crowes returns, tell him we'd like him to contact us as soon as possible."

"What is this about, officer?"

"I'm not at liberty to say, ma'am, but he needs to contact us right away."

She knew exactly what this might be about. "I'll tell him to call you when he gets back."

They left and she closed the door, but waited for a few minutes before sneaking a peek out of one of the front windows. The police cruiser sat in the parking lot, the two officers inside.

Kathleen settled back on the couch and clenched her folded hands between her knees as worry knotted her stomach. When her cell phone rang she jerked and reached for it in a panic.

"Kathleen." Cal's voice sounded stressed but calm. "There's been an accident. Tom and I were both attacked at the site, and they're taking us to the hospital. I'm okay, but Tom's in pretty bad shape."

Tears flooded her eyes, but she knew Cal needed her to hold it together right now. "What hospital?"

He asked someone in the background. "Sharp Memorial on Frost Street."

"I'll meet you there." She grabbed her bag and her phone. "I've got Lolita to get me there. I'm leaving now."

"Thanks, honey. Be careful and take your time."

Kathleen locked the door and rushed to her car. Once inside, she used her phone to look up the hospital address and plugged it into her GPS. When the police car pulled out behind her, she ignored it and concentrated on just getting there without being stopped.

After parking, she called Zach and explained what had happened.

"Do you need me to come over there?"

"No, but the cops showed up looking for Cal around eleven." She explained about the welder in his truck and the call to his boss. "Was his truck empty when you picked him up this morning?"

"Yes. I'd have noticed if there'd been anything in it. What do you think is going on?"

"Cal was worked up. He kept insisting he didn't know how the unit got in his truck. If it wasn't in there this morning and he was gone all day, someone had to have brought it there and put it in his truck. He called his boss, and they left to take it back to the site. Then they were both attacked."

"It sounds like a deal gone bad, or someone's setting him up for a fall," Zach said.

Just the idea of Zach's instant loss of faith in the man she was dating, the man she was falling in love with, snatched at her heart and made her tear up.

He continued. "I'd bet on the setup. He comes across as too straight an arrow to steal. And besides, I did a thorough background check on him, and he's clean."

"Zach!"

"Did you really think I was going to let my baby sister date some guy without checking him out first? Call me if you need me." He hung up before she could give him the reaming he deserved. Or did he? If he'd done a check on Cal and hadn't found anything...

She was winded by the time she found the emergency room entrance. An ambulance sat in the portico, lights blinking. She moved around the vehicle and saw an EMT grasp Cal's arm to help him climb out of the back. Cal's other arm was wrapped securely against his body, a nurse stood waiting with a wheelchair, and the EMT urged him into it.

Kathleen rushed forward on a wave of relief. Cal glanced up, and at the relief in his expression, she couldn't hold back her tears any longer. He raised his free hand and caught hers. "It looks worse than it is. I got hit across the shoulder by a pipe or something. It hurt like hell, but I think it's just bruised."

The tight band of fear loosened. "How's Tom?"

"He woke up in the ambulance, but drifted back out. I don't know. I called his wife and she's on her way."

Kathleen walked alongside the wheelchair through the waiting room and back into the examination rooms. Since he'd been transported by ambulance, they bypassed the waiting room.

A nurse wheeled Cal into one bay and drew the gold curtains closed around them. Tom was in the bay next to him.

"I think whoever put the welder in my truck was waiting for us."

CHAPTER 21

CAL SMOTHERED A yawn. The pain meds the nurse gave him were making him drowsy. He eyed the two police officers who sat in chairs inside the examination room with a wry wariness.

"We arrived at my apartment about ten-fifteen or ten-twenty. We were with some friends earlier," he answered Officer Walker's.

"We'd like a list of those friends."

"If you'll call Kathleen's brother Ensign Zach O'Connor, he can give you everyone's contact information." Cal opened his cell and ran through the list of contacts and gave them the number.

"You said you'd been gone all day."

He went through every change in location he made all day and who'd he'd been with. Repeating the information was getting tedious. "So you were not here at all today?" Walker asked.

"No."

The younger of the two, Officer Loche, stepped out of the room, presumably to dial Zach's number. Since it was nearly one in the morning, he'd like to be a fly on the wall for that conversation.

"When did Mr. Hill come over?"

"I called him when we arrived at the apartment, and he came right over. I guess it was about ten-thirty, a quarter till eleven. I left Kathleen, my girlfriend, there, because I thought I'd be right back. We drove the welder to the site to unload."

"That's the large machine in the bed of your truck?"

"Yes."

"Did you realize the welder was reported stolen earlier in the day?"

Cal raised his brows in feigned surprise. "No. I was out on the ocean all day. No cell service, and no one called me after I came in from fishing." And why would they call him anyway, since he had nothing to do with it?

"Did you take the welder off site on Friday when you left work?"

"No. I wouldn't have done that unless Tom asked me to drop it at another site on the way. Kathleen and I had an appointment at a broadcasting studio on Friday afternoon at four to tape *Harping on the Truth*, so I picked her up at work an hour early. Then on Saturday I went with her to see an apartment she was interested in, then to Balboa Park to a couple of the museums."

"What was the address of the apartment, and which museums did you go to?"

Walker just wouldn't give up. Fortunately he recalled the street address of the apartment. "Afterwards we went to the photo museum and the Art Institute. She's an architect and draws, so I thought she'd like those."

Officer Walker's cold, hard stare never wavered. "How did the welder get in your truck on Sunday afternoon?"

Cal shook his head. All he had was the truth, and they'd either believe him or they wouldn't. "I really don't have a clue. You could canvas the neighborhood and see if anyone saw another truck dropping it off or something."

The guy gave him the forty-mile stare, like he took exception to being told how to do his job. "When I got home and saw it in my truck, I called Tom to see what was going on. He didn't know how it had gotten there either, so he came over. He decided we should go ahead and take it back to the site and unload it.

"He also said there would be paperwork in the office indicating who took it off site and how it was transported. He was going to check on it while we were there. We were attacked before we even got it unloaded."

Officer Loche returned and murmured something in the other's ear. Walker didn't look happy.

Obviously Zach's backing didn't please him. *Look elsewhere, asshole, this is not my screw-up.*

Cal couldn't allow himself to think about what Kathleen was saying to the other police officers. He'd told her to stick to the truth. If they avoided answering completely, it would make it appear that they had something to hide. Neither of them had any other choice.

"Have you heard anything about Tom's condition?" Cal asked. Head injuries were tricky. The chances of Tom remembering anything about the attack were iffy.

"He's been in and out of consciousness, so we haven't had a chance to talk with him. We will as soon as he's stabilized."

If he was still going in and out…It didn't sound good. The news was disheartening. "He's a good boss, and a stand-up guy." He shook his head. "He's given me a chance to use my skills when other foremen might not have."

The officer eyed his prosthetic. "What kind of work do you do, Mr. Crowes?"

"I do steel work. I'm part of the crew assembling the steel frame for the building, the rebar for the concrete poured to create the floors, that kind of thing."

"Is that how you injured your leg?"

"No. I was injured in an IED explosion in Afghanistan."

"Can you think of anyone who might want to hurt you or Mr. Hill?"

Would Warren go to such lengths to get back at him for whatever wrong he'd imagined?

"No."

"Anyone with a grudge against you who'd try and set you up for something?"

So even the cop was wondering? Well good, he needed someone to. But he couldn't point a finger at Warren. All he'd done was insult him. "No."

The officer stood and the other one got to his feet. Walker, who'd done all the questioning, produced a business card. "If you think of anything else, don't hesitate to call that number."

"I will." Cal cupped the card in his hand for a moment, then laid it on the bedside table.

Kathleen joined him ten minutes later looking very tired. He wanted to ask her how her questioning had gone, but they both needed to distance themselves from it for a while.

"They should be processing the paperwork to send me home. If you want to go on home and try and get some sleep before you go to work in the morning, I can catch a cab."

She shook her head. "No. I'm good. I'm going to call in sick tomorrow."

Cal lay down and scooted over in the narrow bed to make room for her. She slipped in next to him and he folded her in close to spoon. He breathed in the summer sun scent she wore, wanting nothing more than to bury his nose against her neck and go to sleep, but he fought to stay awake.

She half turned to whisper. "How would they have known you were taking the welder back to the site?"

"I don't know. Unless someone was watching."

"It would take someone with a real grudge to plan all this."

"I know Warren has something against me, but would he really take it this far? It's just plain crazy."

She wiggled around to face him. "There's something I need to tell you." She placed a hand against his bare chest, which only partially soothed the instant concern that zinged through him. "I got a strange email on Friday morning. It said you were responsible for someone's death here in the states."

Cal absorbed her words like a punch. He dragged air into his lungs. "And you didn't tell me?"

"After what happened at work, I thought it might be Warren, but it wasn't his normal inter office address. And he wasn't there on Monday, he'd taken some vacation days and wouldn't be back for a week. I had a big meeting that morning, and you had the interview later that day and I just didn't... The opportunity never came up for me to mention it."

"You had all day yesterday, Kathleen."

"I didn't believe what the email said, Cal. I know you had to do things in Iraq and Afghanistan, but I couldn't picture anything you could have done that would make you culpable for someone's death."

"Damn straight, because I'm not." He fought the urge to explode. Warren had to be the person after him. And now he'd tried to drive a wedge between him and Kathleen. Warren was the only one he'd had any kind of confrontation with.

Kathleen broke into his thoughts. "Can you think of anything at all that happened after you got home that this person could be referring to?"

"No. This has gone too far. Did you print out the email?"

"Yes. It's in my purse."

Cal reached for the cell phone in his pocket. "Hand me that card on the table. Maybe I can catch the cops before they get too far away."

KATHLEEN STUDIED THE strong, shadowed jaw of the man she lay next to. Though she'd only slept with one other man, he'd never stolen her breath like Callahan Crowes. There was something about that rugged jaw and beard stubble that just did it for her.

They had shared the same bed all night. Well, from about four-thirty until now. He'd actually shared his space at a time he was at his most vulnerable. Another boundary fallen. But not without some encouragement.

She glanced at the clock on the nightstand. It was seven-thirty and she needed to call in. But instead she wanted to stretch out close against him and enjoy being where she was, where they were. The sling that held his arm stationary crossed over his chest like a warning, and also reminded her of the caution Cal had given her the night before about his dreams and about waking him too suddenly.

He'd admitted it had been another stumbling block to having a steady girlfriend in the past. Was that why he hadn't asked her to stay the night sooner? For every step they took forward as a couple, another issue in his recovery was laid bare. But she wasn't just any woman. She was the sister of several men who had chosen to serve. And she could handle this.

She eased out of bed, tugged the T-shirt down over her behind, and went into the living room to retrieve her purse. She dug her phone out to find it dead. Shit! She couldn't just not show up. She tiptoed into the bedroom and scanned the room for Cal's cell phone. It lay on the dresser. She grabbed it and took it into the living room. If he had a password on it she'd have to wake him to ask what he was.

She pushed the button to turn it on, brushed her finger over the screen to activate the phone icon and keyed in the number. She called Jack Allison, her supervisor, and explained she'd spent the night in the emergency room with a friend. She'd be willing to extend her days the rest of the week to make up the time, but she needed to sleep.

He was understanding and told her not to worry. She had no meetings scheduled. She could make up the work. Company policy was that office staff had three personal days, and this could be one of them.

"Thanks, Mr. Allison. I appreciate it. I'll be back tomorrow."

"Get some rest. I hope your friend is recovering."

"Yes, he is. He has no permanent damage to his arm and will be better soon."

"Good. We'll see you on Tuesday."

She set the phone on the end table and went into the kitchen to make coffee. She hovered around the pot until it was done, then took her first cup into the living room to enjoy. God, she needed this. She'd barely slept. After the grilling the police had given them during the second interview, because they'd both withheld information, she'd been both chastened and relieved to turn everything over to them.

They'd given Cal some serious looks when they left. But if he'd done anything wrong, he wouldn't have called them back, and they knew it.

The screen lit up on the phone next to her. An unfamiliar number flashed, then the light died. Then another call came in. She watched it glow again and again and finally curiosity drew her to it. She pushed the phone button and the number of voice mail messages came up and a warning that the memory was full.

She had no right to listen to any of them, and she backed away. When screen lit up again she tried to ignore it. But her curiosity was piqued. She'd ask him about it later. After finishing her coffee, she lay back on the couch and was sound asleep in minutes. She pushed down the feelings of suspicion and worry. Cal was not Lee. She had to get that through her head.

Cal wandered out of the bedroom around nine-thirty, just as she was getting her second wind. His sprung shoulder made using crutches impossible so he'd put his prosthetic on. His sleep pants hung low on his hips. He looked sexy as hell despite the dark circles under his eyes.

"I just made fresh coffee."

He got a cup of coffee and brought it to the couch with him. The cell phone lit up again as he sat down. "You used my phone?"

"Mine was dead and I had to use yours to call in to the office."

Cal dug at his sleep-deprived eyes and ran a hand over his jaw. "That fucking show started an avalanche of calls and text messages five minutes after it aired."

"You mean the viewers have found your cell phone number and are calling?"

"Yeah. I called my phone service, and there's nothing they can do other than change my number. I'm going to try and ignore them and wait them out. I've already done a blanket purge of all the messages and numbers twice."

"Record a message saying something like please respect my privacy and they'll quit leaving you voice mails."

Cal shook his head. "I worked on that in the hospital, and

they're still calling. It's fucking amazing. People think the rule applies to everyone but them. Do you think Harpy posted my phone number on her website?"

Kathleen struggled not to smile at the name. "I wouldn't think so, but I do believe she went out of her way to give your sequence a different feel than the rest."

He dropped his hand from his face. "How so?"

"She showed you as a sexy, vibrant male instead of the suffering survivor. The public is responding to that."

"If she did, she did it because it benefitted her."

"I'm sure ratings for her show probably had something to do with it."

The phone lit up again and he hit the button to turn it off without looking at the number.

She didn't need an emotional compass to read his mood. "Are you in pain?"

"A little. I'll take some Ibuprofen or something."

"We did get the prescription the doctor gave you filled last night." If she offered to get it for him, he'd think he was being handled. So she got up instead. "I'm going to get dressed." He needed some time alone.

Cal caught her arm and pulled her between his spread legs. He rested his cheek against her belly. "I know I'm being an asshole." He ran his fingertips up and down the back of her leg.

Kathleen tried to ignore the sensual tug of the caress. He needed to rest. She rubbed a spot between his shoulder blades and felt his tension start to dissipate. "You need to go back to sleep. Four hours doesn't constitute a full night's rest."

Cal flashed her an upward glance. "I don't want to wear this sling. It's driving me crazy."

"The doctor said to leave it on for at least a couple of days, not a few hours."

"Fuck the doctor."

"No, thanks. He isn't my type."

Cal drew a deep breath and sighed. "Good thing. If he so much as touched you I'd kick his ass."

Kathleen was woman enough to revel in his possessive proclamation.

He released her. "All right, I'm done bitching. I'll call Beverly, Tom's wife, and check on him while you get dressed."

Kathleen smiled. "I knew you'd come around." She headed for the bedroom. "I'd suggest you eat something and take some pain meds before you make that call."

Cal quirked a brow at her, but he went toward the kitchen.

She leaned against the bedroom doorjamb. "Are you grumpy every morning, or is this a special occasion?"

Cal poured a bowl of cereal and flashed her his aw-shucks grin. "If you'd still been in bed with me when I woke up, I wouldn't have been grumpy at all."

Kathleen laughed. Since dumping the email in the police's lap, her own stress had eased. Had she ever doubted him? No. She'd fought against it because she believed in him. And he was earning her trust despite the phone calls from all the female viewers. She just had to keep boosting her own psyche. He wanted her. And he didn't make it a secret. She'd hold onto that until these feelings of inferiority gave up in disgust. Otherwise those negative feelings might destroy a good thing.

"Why are you up so early?" he asked.

"I have to go and sign the lease agreement for my apartment at one…I was going to go during my lunch break today. I also have a couple of errands I have to run, and it takes my hair like an hour to dry."

"I forgot. I can shower and shave and go with you."

She sauntered back to him. "You need to take things easy." Careful of his arm she went up on tiptoe to kiss him. "Take a pain pill and go back to sleep for a few more hours. I'll come back and we'll go out to lunch to celebrate me signing the lease."

Ten minutes later she came out of the bedroom dressed in the same clothes she'd worn the day before. She'd shower and change at Zach's. Cal ended his call, and she could see some of his tension had eased. "Tom woke up. He's going to be okay."

"That's wonderful." Relief loosened a few more of her knotted muscles. If Tom had died, Cal would have held himself responsible because the attack happened while Tom was helping him.

"The bad thing is, he doesn't remember shit about what happened last night."

CHAPTER 22

AS RELIEF SETTLED in to ease some of his guilt, Cal stirred a bowl of brown flakes without much interest. The pain medication was doing a number on him, and nausea rolled his stomach. Eating anything seemed a bad idea. And his arm hurt every time he moved it, so he'd decided the sling was probably a good thing despite his bitching.

He turned on his phone and once again cleared the unwelcome messages to free up the phone's memory.

What had he ever done to deserve Kathleen? Her reaction to his short bitchfest made him smile. Though they'd only been together a few weeks, she was the real deal for him. He just needed to pick a good time to say the words.

His phone lit up with another call and he picked it up, an idea forming. He'd appeal to the romantic in each caller. He pushed the icon to set up the message for his voicemail and taped a new one.

When a knock came at the door he was grateful for the excuse to set aside the cereal and rose to answer it.

Paul Warren stood on the porch. Cal scanned him from head to toe, looking for a weapon. He'd rather not have to try and kick his ass one-armed. It would hurt like hell.

"The police came to see me today. I didn't email Kathleen a message on Friday. The police are at the office right now going through the computer system, trying to trace it."

With the strong light glancing off his features, Cal saw a man in distress, not the raging man who'd tried to instigate a fight at Wiley Designs the week before.

Warren urged, "I think we need to talk."

Cal stepped back and gave Warren a wide berth as he walked in. Short of asking to frisk him, looking him over was the only way to determine if he was carrying. Warren wore dress slacks and a button up shirt with no jacket, and Cal didn't see any telltale bulges at the small of his back, at his waist, or in his pockets.

"I'm still under investigation, and I probably deserve that," Warren said as he entered. "I don't have an alibi for last night. I was at home alone. But I didn't attack you and Tom Hill at the site, Cal."

Warren had always called him Crowes—making it sound like a swear word—never by his first name. The change made him wary.

Cal scanned the man's appearance once more. He looked thinner, but calmer. Recognition stuck; Warren had the fragile appearance of someone who'd been through an emotional war. He'd seen that fine-lined exhaustion in his own face often enough.

"Have a seat," Cal offered, gesturing toward the couch.

Warren edged toward the matching leather chair, leaving the couch for Cal. He clasped and unclasped his hands as though he didn't know what to do with them. And didn't attempt to hide the tears streaming down his face. "Mitchell Ellison was my nephew."

Cal, staggered by the emotional punch, remained silent. Now he knew who the man was, he could see the family resemblance in the shape of his jaw, hair color, and build. He'd been too busy deflecting Warren's anger to recognize it before.

Cal rose to get several paper towels from the kitchen. "Your nephew was a good man. A good Marine." He handed Warren the towels.

Warren pressed one to his face and struggled for several moments to regain control. "So you told my sister." His face was ravaged by grief.

"It was the truth."

"He was a kid." Some of the anger came through again.

"Yeah, that, too. But he did his duty like a man. Just like we all did."

"But you came back alive."

And Warren hated him for it. And Cal understood. It was all about why. Why had he been spared? Why couldn't it have been Mitchell instead? "If there was some way I could bring him back to you, Mr. Warren. I'd gladly do it. The three men with me were under my command. If I could have protected them, I would have."

Cal swallowed and looked over Warren's shoulder because to look directly in his face would wreck his composure as easily as Warren had wrecked the paper towels Cal gave him earlier.

"We covered each other's backs for ten months, played cards, watched videos on the computer, trash talked about women and shared our news from home. They might have been scared kids when we first got there, but by the tenth month they were men, still covering each other, working together as a team as tight and well-trained as any."

"Is that what you said to my sister when you visited her?"

"No. I took her some pictures of Mitchell. I told her stories about some of the funny things that happened. How he kept us laughing and made the down time bearable." The salt of his own tears burned the back of his throat as he tried to swallow them. His face felt stiff with the effort not to cry. "And I told her how honored I was to have served with him, to have known him."

Warren ground out. "She killed herself two weeks after your visit."

Cal couldn't control the flinch, didn't even try. Dear God. He rose to pace the small space between his couch and kitchen. It couldn't be his fault. She'd been fine when he left. He sat back down, though every inch of skin on his body was jumping with pain and guilt. He forced his hand to remain on his thigh when his need to rub the top of his head rose up like a compulsion. He had to stop it.

"She seemed fine when I left," Cal said. "She wasn't upset or crying. She said she was volunteering at a local AM VET, helping vets get to their therapy sessions and other things."

"He was her only child," Warren spoke softly, watching his hands mangle the paper towels, "and she couldn't cope with the loss. She sent messages to his email as though they might somehow find him. About how much she missed him. How much it hurt to live without him. How proud she was to have been his mother. I found them on her computer, in her sent file."

It took everything Cal had not to lose it. "I'm sorry. Jesus...I'm sorry."

Warren leaned forward and covered his face with his hands. "I am, too." His shoulders shook with sobs.

Cal was moved to offer him comfort, but Warren likely was still too bitter to accept anything from him. His eyes burned with sympathetic tears, though, and he let them fall, finally wiping them away with the back of his hand and drying the hand on his sleep pants while he waited for the other man to regain control. "What do you want from me, Mr. Warren?"

"I've spent the last week with a therapist talking it through and trying to purge this rage I have toward you, toward every service man I see. I've laid the blame for Mitchell's death, for my sister's, at your door. I know neither were your fault. You were just a handy target for my pain." His eyes were red-rimmed when he looked up. "I wish I could say I've conquered my anger, but I haven't. But I'm working on it. I know I've been an asshole, to you, to Kathleen. I wish she were here so I could apologize to her as well."

"You'll see her at work."

Warren shook his head. "I've decided to leave Wiley as soon as this investigation is complete. I need a change."

"It's better to stick with what you know, Mr. Warren, with who you're familiar with...at least for a time. You need a support system of friends and family around you."

Warren turned to study him. "Is that what the counselors say?"

"Yeah. You should talk to the therapist before making any big changes."

"Maybe I will." Warren got to his feet and walked to the door. Cal followed him.

He rested his hand on the doorknob. "Tell Kathleen I'm sorry."

"I will."

The door closed behind Warren, leaving Cal with the salty taste of regret. Was there anything else he could have said or done? He'd never know.

KATHLEEN LET THE hot water flow over her and relieve the tension. She should have slept a little longer, because she was feeling the drag of the long night. But she'd make up for it tonight.

Her errands had taken a little longer than expected, but she still had plenty of time. She used the blow dryer on her hair, but after thirty minutes it was still damp, so she pulled it back into a tail and secured it with a scrunchie. She'd chosen to wear cropped pants and a shirt of brushed cotton, soft and comfortable. They'd go to some place casual for a late lunch. Then, if Callahan felt up to a little celebratory sex… She feathered blush across her cheekbones and glossed her lips with soft pink.

Cal preferred her red lipstick, but the pink looked more casual. She'd wow him with the red once she talked him into going dancing at a club. She wasn't much for clubbing, but he needed the experience. He had great horizontal moves, and there was no reason why he couldn't transition some of those into dancing. He just needed to relax.

She smiled at the thought, took one last look at herself in the bathroom mirror, then went into her room and grabbed her cell phone and purse. The phone showed only a small charge even though she'd plugged it in while she drove home, then again in her room. She could charge it a while longer in the car until she got to the leasing agent's office. It would be enough to call Cal after she signed the paperwork.

Hearing a brief knock, she paused to glance through the peephole and frowned. What was Hillary Bryant doing here? With a baseball cap covering her light brown cap of hair. Kathleen plastered on a smile she didn't feel and opened the door. Her eyes skimmed over the rusty spots on the other woman's shirt that looked like chocolate. "Hillary, it's nice to see you. Is there something wrong?"

"No. I just need to see you for a minute." Hillary lifted her hand at the same time she gripped Kathleen's hair, forcing her back into the house. She pressed something to Kathleen's neck and lightning danced across Kathleen's vision while every muscle in her body locked up tight. She hit the floor, her muscles refusing to follow her instinctive need to catch herself. She crashed into one of the end tables, pain lanced through her head, and blackness took her.

WHEN TWO O'CLOCK came and went, Cal paced the living room and cursed Kathleen's dead cell phone. Surely she'd charged it in the car. He'd called three times, and the phone rang, but she hadn't picked up. Had she left it in the car? What was the name of the leasing agent? Troy something.

He strode into the bedroom and searched for the card the agent had given him when they were introduced. He searched the dresser and nightstand. Nothing. He went to the laundry basket and pulled out the shirt from Saturday, ran his hand over the pocket, and felt something stiff. He pulled the business card free and keyed in the number.

After the initial niceties, Cal asked if she was there. "I'm sorry, Mr. Crowes, she never showed up for our appointment."

Cal's heart stuttered. "She left here to change clothes and said she was going straight there."

"I haven't seen her. And I can't hold the apartment any longer than twenty-four hours."

"She may have had car trouble. And her cell phone wasn't

working when she left. I'll have her call you as soon as I locate her."

"Thanks. I know she was excited about it. I'll give her twenty-four hours more to get back to me, but I can't really hold it any longer than that."

"Thanks. Something's gone wrong; she wouldn't be a no-show unless it had."

"I hope she's okay."

Please let her be okay. He broke contact with the agent and dialed Doc's number. When it went to voice mail, he left a message. "Kathleen didn't show up for her appointment at the leasing agent's, and she hasn't shown up here, either. I'm heading over to your apartment to check on her. After what happened at the site last night, I'm a little concerned. I'll call you from there."

He grabbed his keys from the table next to the door and rushed out to the car.

If he'd asked her to move in with him… But it was too soon. She needed her own space, and because of the symptoms he was still experiencing at times, he did too.

He hadn't slept all night with a woman in three years. Even last night he'd worried about hurting Kathleen if he had to fight his way free of a dream. Why would she want to put up with shit like that when someone else would be so much better for her?

No, now just a damn minute. *He* was so much better with her. She seemed happy with him. And the sex was fantastic, thanks to the off-the-charts chemistry between them.

But was he good for her?

He dwelled on the answer to that one for the rest of the drive, and was still waffling about it when he pulled up to Zach's house. He was relieved to see Kathleen's car in the driveway. All four tires looked normal. He swung out of his truck and went to the vehicle and looked inside. Nothing seemed out of place. He knocked on the door and waited. Each minute stretched to an hour. He rang the bell. Still nothing. Finally he went around the side of the house to the back door and looked into the kitchen. The place was clean, and there was no sign of Kathleen.

His skin felt tight dialed Kathleen's number again. The distant sound of a phone ringing inside the house prompted a fresh wave of concern. He hung up and dialed Doc's number again.

"Hello!"

"Her car is here, her phone's ringing inside the house, but she's not answering the door. Do I have your permission to break into the house? Or do you have a key somewhere out here? Something's wrong."

"Where are you?"

"I'm at the back door."

"Next to the patio you'll see some concrete planters. There's a spare key to the front door under the second one. You'll have to lift up on it to get it."

Cal followed his directions. "Got it. I'll stay on the phone as I go in." He jogged around to the front. His hands were shaking as he shoved the key into the lock and twisted it. His heart beat so hard he could feel it in his throat while he twisted the knob and shoved the door open.

"Kathleen." He stepped into the living room and froze. Her purse lay on the couch, her phone on the floor. One of the end tables was shoved sideways, and the area rug was stained with dark drops of blood on one corner.

Dear God. If she was hurt…"There's blood on the floor. I'm going through the house."

Doc swore, his voice a choked growl.

Cal hit the bathroom next, touched a towel, still damp, folded over the edge of the tub. The house had a silent, waiting feel to it, as suspended as his breathing. He forced air into his lungs as he looked inside both bedrooms. Nothing. "She's not here. I'm calling the police."

"I'm on my way."

Cal bent at the waist and braced a hand against his knee as he attempted to deal with the numbing fear. He had to shake off this shit and dial the damn phone. He had to find Kathleen.

He dialed nine-one-one and tried to hold on to his patience and his sanity until someone answered the call.

CHAPTER 23

KATHLEEN WOKE TO the throb of a headache above one ear which was keeping time with her heartbeat. Nausea surged up her throat, and she gagged, but there was nothing in her stomach to come up.

Afterward she lay in the darkness and waited for her thoughts to catch up with the sensations of stuffy heat and motion. Sweat ran from under her hair down her neck. She raised a hand to wipe it away, then reached upward to explore the surface above her. She was inside the trunk of a car.

She closed her eyes against the darkness and ran her fingertips along the side of her head, the focal point of the pain, and found a large bump on her scalp and a broken place on the skin there. The hair around it was stiff with blood. Touching it triggered the nausea again, and she dropped her hand to her side on the carpet lining.

Her mouth tasted sticky with a need for water. How long it had been since Hillary Tasered her? How long had she been in this miserably hot, stifling box? She had to get out.

She raised both hands and ran them along the top of the trunk. What kind of car did Hillary drive? If she could remember, she might have some idea how it was structured and how to get out. Her hand struck something dangling from a section along the top and she pulled it. The narrow seat in front of her released and she pushed it forward. Air whooshed into the space, and Kathleen drew a deep breath of the cooler air, immediately feeling more alert.

If the car stopped and Hillary got out, she'd try and climb through into the back seat. The single seat was too narrow for her to get through, she realized, so both would have to be down.

She became aware of the steady momentum of the car. There was no stopping and starting, so they might be on an interstate. No sooner had the thought crossed her mind when the vehicle slowed and started down an incline. Hillary must be leaving the state highway, possibly to a more rural road or down onto city streets.

She strained to see a street sign or a familiar building through the narrow slot, but the nausea was swamping her again. She probably had a concussion. She closed her eyes for a moment. The heat had sapped her strength and made her drowsy.

But if she didn't do something right now, she would soon be incapacitated by dehydration. She searched for the other release pull and gave a tug. The seat folded down. She crawled free of the trunk.

As HE QUESTIONED Cal outside in the front seat of his cruiser, Officer King wore the same deadpan expression Walker had the night before.

"What time did you get here?"

"I've already answered that question twice. You're wasting time. Kathleen has been taken. You can look at the scene and tell there was a struggle. She would never leave her cell phone or her purse. She calls her purse her flak jacket. It has everything she needs."

"She could be injured, confused, and wandering the neighborhood on foot, sir. I'm trying to pinpoint how long."

The officer could have a point, but after last night he didn't believe it. "Look. My foreman and I were attacked last night at a construction site. You can contact Officers Walker and Loche and talk to them about it.

"Kathleen and I were in the emergency room last night until zero four thirty. She drove me home and we crashed. She left my house just before ten. She was going to run an errand and then come here to shower and change to go to the realtor's office. There's a damp towel on the tub in the bathroom.

"I think someone caught her at the door ready to leave. In order to get to the office for her appointment she'd have left at noon or a little before. So you have your time, now please, do whatever you need to do to get the word out! I promise you she's not wandering the neighborhood. Someone has her. They've had her for..." he glanced at his watch "...at least three hours now."

"I'll be right back, sir." The officer got out of the vehicle.

Cal hugged his aching arm. The pain medication he'd taken only worked if he didn't move, and right now that wasn't an option.

Cal threw open the door and got out of the car. He was barely holding it together. This was taking too long.

He glanced at Zach and the young police officer sitting in Zach's SUV. It didn't look like Zach was holding it together at all. He was reading the riot act to the officer, questioning him.

Three hours. Someone could be hurting her, and they'd had three hours to do it. Every time he thought about that, he wanted to punch something or someone.

He scanned the quiet street. Empty driveways stared back at him. Everyone was at work. He took out his phone. If they'd tried to call him, his fucking number would be tied up with the viewers from Harpy's show. Fuck!

He turned the phone on anyway. He'd answer every call to get to the right one.

"IF YOU FUCK with me, I'll Taser you again," Hillary warned.

Kathleen jerked at the sound of Hillary's voice. She'd hoped to climb out without being heard.

"Just lie back there and be still and I won't have to hurt you again."

"Why are you doing this, Hillary?"

"I have to do it. That's all you need to know."

Kathleen reached for the doorknob and pulled up on it. Nothing happened. Hillary had turned on the childproof safety locks.

"I need water." How long had she been in the trunk? Long enough to feel groggy from the heat.

"You'll get some as soon as we get to where we're going."

Weak and dizzy, Kathleen lay still on the folded seats' hard surface. The air conditioning against her sweat-slick skin chilled her, and her hair lay wet against her neck, making the chill worse. She shivered. How long had she been out?

The blinker went on and Hillary turned onto a short incline, stopped for a few seconds, then pulled inside a structure. The sound of a garage door closing followed. They were at a private residence if they had a garage door.

"Where are we?" Kathleen asked.

"That's none of your concern either."

Hillary got out of the car, jerked the baseball hat off, tossed it on the front seat, and slammed the door. She pulled the Taser free of a holster on her hip and opened the back door. "Get out."

Kathleen eyed the Taser. It had jolted both her body and mind and made it impossible for her to move. She didn't want any part of it again. How many times could someone be shocked before it affected their heart? Moving slowly, she sat up and pushed the seat back, closing the opening to the trunk. She watched Hillary's actions carefully as she slid out of the car. The moment the woman started toward her, Kathleen backed away.

"Get inside the house."

"No. Not until you tell me what you want and why I'm here."

Hillary rushed toward her with the Taser. Kathleen gripped the woman's wrist and twisted and shoved back against her, forcing Hillary to backpedal until they came up against the car. Hillary cried out in pain.

They struggled. Kathleen head-butted her on the nose. Hillary yelped and swore. The Taser crackled between them when Hillary depressed the trigger. Kathleen shoved down on the barrel of the weapon, trying to break her grip. Hillary inched the weapon closer to Kathleen's body, then shoved the weapon into her thigh.

Kathleen squealed and dropped to her knees as the electricity arched through her body for what seemed like an eternity while Hillary shocked her again and again with the weapon. Kathleen tasted blood where she'd bitten her tongue. She lay on the stained concrete behind the car unable to move, her muscles quivering like Jell-O.

"I told you I didn't want to have to hurt you again," Hillary said. "This was your fault."

If someone could do that again and again to another human being, killing them with one shot or one blow would be nothing.

Hillary was going to kill her before this was over.

TWO HOURS IN the close, claustrophobic room telling the same story over and over. Jesus Christ! What was wrong with these assholes? Cal had been as patient as he could force himself to be, but he had reached the end of it.

"Have you put out some kind of BOLO for Kathleen?"

"Yes, we have." Buckler answered. But he offered the information grudgingly. The two detectives, Buckler and Hart, had taken the place of the two police officers on the scene and had wasted no time in escorting him to the station and this interview room. Two hours had passed with no end in sight. "I'm done. I'm leaving. If you guys aren't going to get out there and look for her, I will."

"Sit down, Mr. Crowes." Detective rose from his seat.

"No." He fisted his hands, but curbed the need to punch something. "You either charge me with a crime or you cut me loose. I've given you my DNA, and my fingerprints, *and* I've told the same story ten different ways. I don't know what else you want. And I don't give a fuck if you believe me or not. I'm done. You charge me, or you let me go. And if you're charging me with something, I'm asking for a lawyer and I'll take my phone call *now*."

He whipped out his phone.

The two looked at each other. Detective Buckler sat back down. "I'll tell you what's holding us up. We believe that what happened to you last night is tied to this in some way. But we feel you haven't been completely forthcoming with everything you could tell us about it."

"You're still trying to imply that I had something to do with the theft of the welder, but I didn't. And why the fuck is that important when my girlfriend is missing. Isn't she the priority here? She's been missing for five hours."

"Just tell us how the welder got in your truck."

"How many times do I have to say it? Look through the paperwork. There has to be a paper trail for who loaded it and took it off-site. There was no theft. I think someone planted it in my truck, then called to report it stolen, hoping I'd be arrested for taking it. And because I was gone all day, the police never had a chance to pick me up. I didn't steal anything. Tom and I were trying to return it when we were attacked."

Cal straightened, glaring at the officers. "And I've already told you who I think might have been behind it. I've even told you everything Paul Warren said while sitting in my living room this morning. Have you picked him up?"

When they both remained silent, Cal shook his head. "You can't find him, can you?"

Hart ignored that and asked, "Where do you think you'll be able to find Kathleen?"

"I don't know. But I have someone in the media who owes me a favor, and she's the first person I'm going to for help getting Kathleen's picture out there. Someone had to have seen something. Someone knows where she is. And if I have to go door-to-door over the whole fucking state, I'm going to find her. Forget about all this fucking bullshit and do your fucking jobs."

Cal strode to the door and opened it. An armed police officer stood outside, blocking his exit. Cal shot a look over his shoulder at Buckler and Hart.

Hart's features twisted with disgust and frustration. "Let him go."

Cal rushed down the hall and into the main office of the Robbery-Homicide Division. They must have brought him to robbery because of the welder.

He hit the sidewalk outside like Buckler and Hart were in armed pursuit and paused to find the number to call a cab to take him back to Zach's house and his vehicle. A horn blew and caught his attention. Doc pulled up beside him in his SUV. "What the fuck took you so long?" he asked as soon as Cal opened the door.

"Tweedledee and Tweedledum were trying to pin the same bullshit on me as the cops last night. They're worrying about a welder instead of Kathleen. Goddamnit! They have fucking tunnel vision. And they can't find Paul Warren. They don't have a clue where he might be."

"And you do?"

"His sister lived in San Marcos. He was all broken up about his nephew Mitchell. And his sister committed suicide after Mitch was killed. How much you want to bet he still owns the house?"

CHAPTER 24

K ATHLEEN FOCUSED ON small things, small moments of time, to quell the constant fear. She decided out of all the things that hurt, her tongue bothered her the most. But it gave her a reason to remain silent and listen to Hillary's whispered phone conversation in the kitchen.

She might as well. With her hands and feet tied to a straight-backed chair in the middle of the living room, she had little else to do. She'd worn herself out trying to loosen the cotton clothesline Hillary used to bind her. Her wrists were raw from fighting it.

She analyzed the seventies décor, which leaned toward straight-lined furniture and stained shag carpet. The worst was right at her feet. It looked as though someone had dropped something there and scrubbed it until the nap was compressed. Where were the owners? Whose house was this?

And who had put Hillary up to this? She couldn't imagine the woman had gotten up one day and decided to kidnap someone she'd only known a few weeks.

"I know I messed up, but I'm trying to make up for it. No one will ever know you had anything to do with this."

So there was someone who'd put her up to this.

"He'll regret ever having hurt you. And he'll live the rest of his days knowing what it means to be responsible."

Who was she talking about? Cal? And what was he responsible for? And why was Hillary taking such a risk doing someone else's dirty work?

Hillary's voice dropped to just shy of a whisper. The first part of what she said Kathleen missed, but she did hear, "Last night meant so much to me. I love you, I've loved you since the first time we kissed. Last night proves you feel something too."

The only man Hillary had a thing for was Paul Warren. So Warren had to be involved.

"I'm going to take her to the place it first started between them. Don't you think that will be fitting?" There was a pause and Hillary said, "I knew you'd understand."

Hillary limped back into the living room. She had an injury, and the limp was getting worse. "It's time for us to go."

"Go where, Hillary?"

"You'll see when we get there." She unfastened Kathleen's feet, but left her hands tied behind her. She reached down the back of the chair, grabbed the clothesline binding her arms and jerked Kathleen to her feet, guiding her from behind toward the door leading into the garage.

"What have you done to your hip?"

"Your boyfriend hit me with a pipe last night."

Kathleen's mouth went dry. "It was you who attacked him and Tom Hill on the site?"

Hillary ignored the question.

Numb with shock, Kathleen didn't even try to argue when she opened the trunk, shoved her in, and closed the lid. She felt safer in the compartment than inside the car with a woman capable of attempted murder.

Hillary said she was going to take her where it all began. She and Cal had first met on the building site for the tower. A dropping sensation hit her stomach. Oh God, what did she intend to do?

WHILE ZACH DROVE, Cal called the television station and asked to speak to Nora Harper. He'd been such an asshole to her, he didn't know if she'd take his call, but it was worth a shot.

"Hello Mr. Crowes. How did you like your segment?"

"I didn't watch it."

Stunned silence filled the air between them.

"I have some breaking news, and I thought with your ambition you'd want to jump all over it."

"What is it?" Doubt tinged her tone.

"As of noon this afternoon my girlfriend Kathleen O'Connor was abducted from her home. She's been missing for five hours. I'm sending you her picture."

"How do you know she was abducted?"

"She had an appointment with a leasing agent at one. She never showed up. When I went to her apartment to check on her at two, and her purse, phone and car were there, but she wasn't, and there were signs of a struggle in the living room and blood on the carpet. The police have put out a BOLO on her, but nothing else."

He took a risk. "Now we both know what you did with the interview, how you manipulated it to get a rise in ratings, and to possibly pay me back a little for my bad attitude. This is your chance to do something truly helpful. Put Kathleen's picture out there, ask people to call San Diego Robbery-Homicide and ask for Detectives Buckler and Hart."

"Why Robbery-Homicide?"

"Beats the fuck out of me. That's who showed up when I dialed nine-one-one. Kathleen is alive. I'm going to find her with or without their help. You can call them and verify everything I've said."

"Okay. I will. And you can send a picture to my private phone number."

"Pen?" Cal asked.

"Glove box." Zach answered and whipped onto the I-15 North so fast Cal fell against the door. The man drove like he'd hit the last lap in the Indianapolis Five Hundred and was in the lead.

Cal wrote the number on his hand.

"And one other thing. Tell your viewers to quit calling me. If whoever has Kathleen is trying to get through, I'll miss the call because of their bullshit."

She fell silent again. "I'll tell them."

Was that a hint of regret he heard in her tone? "I appreciate your help, Miss Harper."

"We'll have this on the air as soon as you send the picture and I get confirmation from the police."

"Thanks."

When she said, "Good luck." It sounded like she meant it.

He rushed through the pictures he'd taken of Kathleen at Balboa Park on Saturday. Just looking at her smile, the way she'd mugged for the camera, caused a fresh wave of fear to crash over him to steal his breath, then cramp his stomach. He found a clear portrait of her he'd taken under the shade of one of the trees. She looked vibrant and beautiful, with her creamy skin and bright green eyes. He sent it to the number Harpy had given him.

"We're going to find her. She's going to be fine," Zach said from beside him. "She's tough. She's resourceful. She survived eight brothers, and can beat some of us at arm wrestling."

Cal wondered if he was trying to reassure him or himself.

It didn't matter. It wasn't working.

KATHLEEN WOKE, STARTLED and afraid, surrounded by the same darkness in which she'd fallen asleep. She'd been thinking of her family for hours, dreaming about them. How she'd slept at all was inexplicable. The confined space of the trunk left her little room to move, and her knees felt stiff and achy when she tried to straighten her legs.

The maneuver used by heroines in mystery novels, sliding their arms down the back of their body to get their hands in front was a lie perpetrated by writers. She tried, and it didn't work. Her arms were too short, her hips too wide. Or it could be her wrists were tied together too tightly. She'd moved her hands to keep the circulation going so often her wrists were raw from rope burns.

God, she was so thirsty. The two bottles of water she'd consumed all day only left her craving more. Her lips burned and were chapped and cracking with dehydration.

The silence in the cab of the car as well as the cooler temperatures inside the trunk slowly captured her attention. They were parked somewhere. Somewhere it was less bright and the temperature was actually bearable. Another garage, a parking garage, maybe.

She had to find a way out of this car and away from Hillary. She turned and wiggled until her back was where the locking mechanism might be. It took her several minutes and more rug burns on her elbow and her cheek to find it. Sometimes they had releases for just this instance. Blindly she searched around the lock and found—nothing. She could feel the lock but nothing around it suggested it would release.

She turned onto her knees and wiggled around in an attempted to raise her hands above her to find the loops dangling from above. She got rug burn on her forehead from carpet inside the trunk from scooting back and forth, feeling for the nylon strips. They had to be right there. Her fingers touched something and she gripped it and pulled. The seat released, and she saw a crack of dim light around the edge of the hard plastic seat backing. She pushed it forward.

The car was empty. Kathleen rushed to grab the other nylon handle. She wiggled over the hard seat back.

She didn't stop to check the door to see the childproof locks were still engaged, but turned on her side and wiggled and squirmed her way over the console between the front seats to the passenger door. Knowing Hillary might return at any moment spurred her on. Turning her back to the door, she strained every muscle to raise her hands high enough to hit the buttons on the door until the locks disengaged. The door release was higher up still. She shoved up onto her knees and her fingers scrambled over the surface looking for it. Oh my God, where the hell was it?

The driver's door opened and Hillary got in. "Are you going

somewhere, Kathleen?"

Defeat fell like a heavy bolder, crushing her every hope. Pain in every part of her body began to clamor. She had to have her hands free.

Letting her desperation show, she said, "I need to pee."

CAL USED HIS phone to find the address for Darleen Ellison. It was while he was doing that he noticed the text messages and voice mails had stopped. Harpy had come through.

Zach pulled in and parked one house up from the address. He and Zach observed the place for a few minutes for any activity. Other than a dull glow coming from the front window, nothing moved.

"I'll take the front, you take the back," Zach, said reaching up to turn off the cab light. "I'll knock and get their attention at the front door while you get in at the back."

Neither of them had a weapon. Zach had left his behind in his weapons locker on post. Their hands would have to be enough.

Halfway to the house, Zach motioned for him to break off. Cal followed the shade of the trees along the property line to the side yard. Zach continued on to the front of the house. Cal watched him long enough to see him saunter up the front walk as though he owned the place.

Cal double-timed it around to the backyard. He crowded in on the narrow stoop in front of a set of French doors leading out onto a patio. The kitchen was dark. The dull light of a back porch light next door touched on the metallic shape of a toaster, the face of the microwave. Cal narrowed his eyes to reduce the ambient glow and tried to look at shapes inside the darkness. A leg and foot took form.

He tapped on one of the windowpanes. Nothing. No movement. Oh God, had they come this far to find her dead in a strange house? His lungs seized and panicked desperation gripped him. He grabbed the doorknob and heaved against the door with his sore shoulder, and grunting at the pain. The flimsy lock gave way, and he stumbled into the kitchen and hit the light switch next to the door.

Paul Warren was leaning against the cabinets, his chin on his chest. A pool of congealed blood surrounded him, and a knife protruded from his chest.

KATHLEEN COULD BARELY keep her eyes open despite the fact that her heart beat like a metronome stuck on a fast tempo. She'd read somewhere that repeated shocks from a stun gun lowered blood sugar because it fired all the muscles and burned up reserves. Having had nothing to eat all day but half a bagel, she was feeling the effects. A clammy sweat beaded her skin, while a jittery nervousness made it hard for her to think or get a full breath. At least Hillary had untied her hands.

There wasn't a doubt in her mind Hillary intended to kill her. And she had questions. Questions she wanted answered before she had to face… "Did you delete my file that first week, Hillary?" she asked.

"No. I would never touch your work. But Paul thought it would be funny."

So Hillary had known who did it and where they were the whole time. What kind of relationship did she and Warren have?"

"I did puncture your tires. He was much too interested in you, and I hoped to scare you off."

Jesus! They were both certifiable.

"Did you send me an email trying to warn me away from Cal?"

"No." The woman's eyes narrowed. "What kind of email?"

Shit! She needed to get away from this subject. If she knew Warren had sent her an email she might get jealous again and go off. "Why are you doing this, Hillary? What have I done to you that I deserve to be hurt?"

"It isn't you, it's Cal Crowes who's going to pay. It's time to call him before we go over to the site."

"What has Cal done? He's a good man, Hillary."

"He's responsible for Paul's nephew's death, and Paul's sister's suicide. It was bad enough he was there when Mitchell died, but he had to visit his mother. It pushed her over the edge, and she killed herself."

Dear God. Did Cal know about the mother? That poor woman. It would be one more thing for Cal to feel guilty about. One more thing for him to punish himself for.

Hillary pulled a cell phone from her jacket pocket. "What's his number?"

"Please Hillary. Whatever you have planned…"

"What's his number?" The woman shrieked, so loudly Kathleen jerked away and covered her ears. For a moment the wild look in Hillary's eyes deepened into something else, and Kathleen thought she was about to attack her.

The woman was unbalanced. She should have seen it when she defended Paul Warren so adamantly a week earlier. How could he stand being the object of her obsession? How could he be a part of her plan?

Kathleen told her the number. Hillary dialed it, then brought out the Taser.

How much of a charge could it have left? She'd used it repeatedly. Surely it was almost dead.

Hillary turned the cell to speakerphone. Cal's phone went to voice mail, and a message came on. "If you're one of the female viewers from *Harping on the Truth*, and intend to leave your number looking for romance, I'm sorry. I met my perfect woman a few weeks ago, and I'm off the market. Her name is Kathleen, and I love her. I'm working to convince her she should love me, too. If you're not one of the viewers and are calling about anything else, leave your name and number, and I'll get back to you."

Hearing Cal's voice gave Kathleen an emotional boost. Hearing his message broke her heart. They weren't going to have time to explore their love. Hillary was going to make certain of it.

"How touching," Hillary sneered. "You'd better hope he answers the second time I call."

She redialed the number.

"Hello." Cal sounded breathless.

"Hello, Cal, I have someone here who wants to say something to you."

Hillary shoved the phone toward Kathleen. "It's me, Cal, Kathleen."

"Are you all right?"

"So far." She was so dehydrated her eyes wouldn't tear, but the need to cry burned them all the same. "Hillary and I heard your voice mail message. I love you, Callahan."

"Just hold on, honey."

Hillary jerked the phone away. "We'll be at the tower site in fifteen minutes. Meet us there, and we'll go up to the twentieth floor together."

"It's going to take me at least forty-five minutes to get there. I'm in San Marcos. We're here with Paul Warren."

Hillary's demeanor changed, her movements jerky and anxious. "Don't you hurt him. You've done enough damage. You let his nephew die and caused his sister to commit suicide. It's all your fault. Everything is your fault."

"I'm not going to hurt, Paul, Hillary. He's waiting for you here. Why don't you bring Kathleen here, and we'll all sit down and talk."

"No. We have to go back to where it all began. Kathleen and I will wait for you at the tower."

"Okay. I'm on my way. Don't go up without me, Hillary. I'll want to be with you both when we go up." Cal's soothing tone sent anxious prickles over Kathleen's skin. Something was horribly wrong.

"You'd better hurry." Hillary shut down her phone and rubbed her arms as if she was cold.

Straightening, she briskly holstered the Taser and reached under the driver's seat and to pull out a pistol. Kathleen recognized it as a nine millimeter Beretta. The weapon looked huge in the woman's hand as she turned and pointed it at Kathleen. "We're going now."

CHAPTER 25

CAL HELD ONTO the oh-shit handle above the passenger door as Zach wheeled onto I-15 South heading back to San Diego.

Zach found Warren's cell phone in the living room and used it to call the police. Then they'd wiped their fingerprints off it and the doorknobs and bugged out. They didn't have time to get caught up in a murder investigation when Kathleen's life hung in the balance.

"This Hillary, she's the one who had a thing for Warren?" Zach asked.

"Yeah. Kathleen said Hillary was half a step away from being a stalker. She always knew what Warren was up to. Kathleen suggested she move on to someone else and Hillary bit her head off."

Zach mulled that around for a second. "It looks like he may have rejected her one too many times."

Cal clenched his hands. "I think she's had some kind of psychotic break. She stayed quiet when I said I was with Warren. She asked me not to hurt him." Cal swallowed, though his throat was dry with fear. The woman was certifiably insane, and Kathleen had been with her all day. The things she might have done to her...

He couldn't think about that now. He'd go crazy himself. "He was dead. She killed the object of her obsession, but doesn't want to face it."

Zach glanced his way. "You know she's planning a last stand at the tower."

"Yeah. And she has Kathleen with her. There are security guards at the building site. But I don't know how well they're trained, or what they'll do when faced with a demented woman and her hostage."

Zach's features morphed into a heavy scowl. He pressed down on the gas, and the SUV surged forward even faster. "They fucking better not hurt my sister."

KATHLEEN'S SHOULDERS AND arms ached from having been in the same position all day. Her wrists, raw and bruised, had stiffened. She was no threat. She doubted she could lift her arms even to defend herself. With the muzzle of the Beretta jammed against her right kidney, it was hard for her to think of how to place one foot in front of the other. Her legs shook with a combination of weakness and icy fear. She knew what kind of damage one shot could do. She'd bleed to death before they could do a thing to save her.

She wanted to live. She wanted to spend a full night with Callahan and wake up with her head on his shoulder and feel his arms around her. Safe. Loved. She wanted to learn what they could have together, six months from now, a year.

She wanted the love she felt for him to have a chance to grow bigger, stronger.

His tone had remained level and calm, though underlying concern had tempered the way he spoke. He was coming, and he'd think of some way to end this. They were both going to come out of it alive. She wouldn't even consider any other outcome.

The twelve-foot-tall fence surrounding the site provided a barrier against any unauthorized foot traffic. They walked past the gate. "You say anything, shout out for help, or anything else, and I'll kill you first, then them."

Kathleen couldn't put anyone else's life at risk. She didn't want to put Cal's life in jeopardy, either. They turned back around as soon as they were certain the security guards weren't close by. Hillary produced a key and unlocked the huge padlock that held the gate closed with one hand while she held the gun on Kathleen with the other.

"How did you get a key?" Kathleen asked just past a whisper.

"Paul had it. He sometimes comes by after the day ends to check the work. This is one of his projects. He has to stay on top of quality control." She slid the lock free and shoved against Kathleen. "Get in there before they come out to make their rounds."

"How's Cal going to get in if the turnstile's locked?"

"I'm leaving it open for him." She slid the padlock back in place and positioned it so the security guards would have to touch it to realize it was unlocked.

And now they were inside the site Kathleen realized she didn't want Cal to come. She wanted him to stay away and just let whatever happened happen. She wanted him to live. He'd already paid enough with his leg and his PTSD. She wanted him to move on from it. He didn't need any more pain in his life. He deserved some peace.

"That way." Hillary pointed to a narrow patch of shade next to the foreman's trailer. "We're going to go around behind it and circle around. Stay close." She poked the gun into Kathleen's back for emphasis.

Too exhausted physically and emotionally to argue, Kathleen hugged the fence and stumbled around the trailer. They cut across to the steps leading onto platform.

When Hillary turned on the lights, the security guards would know they were here. They'd come and shoot them both and it would be over.

The light had gone soft and the temperature dropped. A chill permeated Kathleen's thin cotton clothes, and she shivered while they climbed onto the platform. Hillary unlocked the wire doors to the elevator and slid the inner door up.

"Get in." She used the gun to direct her.

Kathleen stepped inside the lift and wasn't surprised when Hillary pulled the wire doors shut and put the lock back on.

"I'll be back."

Kathleen slid down into the corner of the elevator and sat on the floor. She expected Hillary to walk around to the breaker, but instead she went back down the stairs and strode toward the guardhouse.

Kathleen struggled back to her feet and gripped the cage door. "Hillary don't. Please don't." The woman whirled around to face her and pointed the gun in her direction.

She was going to kill her anyway. If she did it now, there wouldn't be any reason for her to hurt the guards. "Leave them alone."

The guardhouse door flew open and two men dressed in drab brown uniforms ran out. Hillary whirled and fired. The man in the lead grabbed his side and fell to the ground. The other guard returned fire. One of the bullets ricocheted off of a metal support and Kathleen ducked into her corner. A couple more shots were fired and then silence reigned.

When steps crunched on the gritty ground outside, Kathleen curled against the side of the elevator. If it was Hillary, she was bound to kill her now. If it was the security guard, since he'd just been attacked, he might shoot first and ask questions later.

The lights flickered, then came on, casting a diamond pattern on the floor of the metal container. Kathleen cringed back into the corner. Hillary stepped up to the lift. Blood blotched her shirt and she held her arm against her side. She unlocked the gate, stepped onto the lift and shut the gates.

CAL STUDIED THE site from outside the gate in Zach's truck. Every light was on, but nothing moved. "She doesn't know you're with me. She thinks I'm alone. That could play to our advantage."

"If we can get past the security guards."

"I was here last night, so they'll know I'm part of the crew.

Maybe I can talk my way past them. With all the lights on, there should be movement." A niggling concern wormed its way into the pit of his stomach.

Zach shrugged a shoulder. "If you keep the guards busy, I'll find my own way in. I'll meet you at the lift."

"Okay." Adrenaline rushed through Cal's veins, fed by the blend of excitement and fear that had tinged every operation in the military. The weight of what this moment meant steadied him. Kathleen would be okay. He and Zach would make sure of it.

He removed his sling and tossed it on the seat before climbing out of the SUV and jogging to the gate where trucks came through to deliver supplies. Two bodies lay on the ground in front of the guardhouse. Cal braced a hand on the fence and reached for his phone. He pushed Zach's number.

"The guards are down."

"I'm on my way."

Cal moved on to the turnstile where the workmen entered and saw the lock was aligned but not closed. He jerked it free. Zach ran around the corner of the site straight toward him. They shoved their way through the turnstile and rushed to the guards. Both were still breathing, but bleeding badly. One had taken a round to the thigh. The other man had taken a round to the side.

"I'll see if I can find something to use for bandages." Zach ran into the guardhouse.

Cal whipped out his cell phone and dialed nine-one-one. He gave the dispatcher the address and situation, said, "We need an ambulance," then hung up. The guard with the thigh wound was already groggy from loss of blood. "She's crazy, man. I had to pretend to be dead to keep her from shooting me again."

Zach came back with a medical supply kit. He tossed Cal a roll of gauze. "Wrap that leg tight over his pants, while I deal with this other guy."

Cal slapped a thick pad of gauze over the thigh injury and wrapped it tight over top of the guard's pants.

A scream above them, high-pitched and panicked jerked their attention upward, the cry blended with the high-pitched wail of an approaching police car.

Two figures were perched on an extension of steel where a new floor was being structured, but no floor had yet been poured. The smaller of the two figures was sitting on the steel girder and clinging to it. The other stood above her.

"Sweet Jesus!" Zach exclaimed.

"I'm going. Hillary's made it clear I'm the one she wants. I'll do whatever it takes, get Kathleen clear."

Zach eyed him long and hard, his green gaze so much like Kathleen's it was hard for Cal to meet it. "Don't throw yourself on a sword until we've tried everything we can."

The word sword triggered an idea. "She doesn't believe Warren is dead. I have an idea."

Zach packed gauze over the other man's wound while Cal lifted him so Zach could wrap the dressing around him. Cal outlined the idea as they worked.

Cal dragged the other guard over to where his buddy lay and guided his hands over the dressing. "Keep pressure on his wound until EMS arrives."

He and Zach turned and ran toward the tower. It took precious time for the lift to come down and for them to go back up. "Stay in the lift until I'm out in front of them. Keep hidden behind the supports when you call to her."

"I understand where you're going with this. If it doesn't work…" Zach pressed a gun into his hand. "It's one of the guards'. There's eight rounds left."

Cal had thought his shooting days were behind him. He'd left all his guns behind in Texas. He slipped the weapon into the waistband of his jeans at the small of his back. He'd do what he had to do to protect Kathleen, Zach, or himself.

The lift stopped and Cal pulled the metal panel door up and pushed through the wire door. The floor on this level was partially poured, and he eased out of the lift and walked slow and easy over the forty-foot long section to where Hillary stood waiting.

His attention focused on Kathleen as she straddled the H beam and lay atop it holding on for dear life, her eyed clenched shut and her face sheet white. She had wide red splotches on her skin. One on her forehead, her knee and her elbows. Her clothes were wrinkled, her hair a tangled mess around her shoulders. She had never looked more beautiful to him. When she opened her eyes to look at him a second he nodded and tried to project comfort in his expression.

"It seems she has vertigo." Hillary said by way of greeting. "A commercial architect with a fear of heights. Don't you find that ironic?" Hillary's khaki pants were stained with blood running from her waist and down one leg. She held a 9-millimeter pistol at her side.

Cal shook his head. "But you're not afraid?"

"No. Heights have never been an issue for me." She raised her gaze to the deep purple sky streaked with red behind her. While she was distracted, Cal glanced toward the lift and caught a glimpse of Zach slipping behind one of the large vertical beams.

Several police cars and two ambulances pulled up below, their sirens a high soprano wail. Hillary seemed oblivious to them.

"Paul and I talked earlier today," Cal said.

"I know." Hillary's features twisted with anger. "How could he go to see you, talk to you like a human being? You killed his nephew. His sister died because of you."

Cal kept his tone even and reasonable. He was so sick of being blamed for something he'd had no control over. He'd done it to himself for too long. "His nephew died fighting for his country, Hillary. A terrorist's bomb killed him. It almost killed me, too. His sister had lost her only child. Maybe she wanted to be with Mitch, and that was the only way she could think to do it."

She shook her head and swayed on the beam. "No. Paul was angry with you. He wanted to kill you, but he couldn't."

"Well, he changed his mind. And he said he was going to leave Wiley Design."

"No." Panic shattered her face, and she grabbed at the lower part of her abdomen. "He'll never leave. He'll never leave me."

"You can discuss it with him, I brought him with me."

"Hillary?" Zach's voice carried from the right. "You're right. I won't ever leave you. I promise I won't."

She cocked her head as though confused. "Paul?"

Zach ad-libbed. "We have a lot of plans to make. If I decide to leave Wiley, you can come with me. Would you like that?"

"Yes. Of course I would." She blinked as though her eyes were growing heavy. "My life isn't anything without you." She shuffled forward on the beam toward Kathleen and for a moment it looked as though she might fall, but she regained her balance. Finding her way blocked, she raised the Berretta and pointed it at Kathleen. "Get out of my way, Kathleen. I have to go to Paul."

Cal reached for the pistol tucked into his waistband. His heart drummed in his ears. He hadn't shot a gun since leaving the military. He didn't want to now.

The sound of the lift going down reached him. He was torn between really needing some help and dreading that what they'd get would make the situation worse.

"Hillary. Kathleen's scared. If you'll let me help her, I'll get her out of your way."

He stepped forward and she swung the gun in his direction.

"No. You hurt Paul. He suffered so because of what you did. I'm going to end that for him. I'll do for him what he couldn't do." Her skin around her eyes, leached of color, had a bluish tinge in the dull light.

"You've already ended it for him, Hillary. You stabbed him. I found him at his sister's house. Why did you stab him?"

Kathleen's eyes opened wide at that.

Something shifted in Hillary's expression. "He won't leave me if I do this. He'll know how much I love him."

"He's dead, Hillary. He's already gone. You killed him. You buried a knife in his chest."

"No," she screamed the denial. "No." But realization was catching up with her. Her eyes shifted back and forth in a panicked dance. "He was going to leave me. He lied to me." She tottered, losing her balance, and threw an arm out to catch it. The gun flew out of her hand and over the side of the building. She staggered and fell toward Kathleen, her hand momentarily gripping Kathleen's shoulder, jostling them both.

Kathleen cried out. Hillary's eyes rolled up into her head and she fell away into space without a sound. Hillary's weight dragged Kathleen sideways over the side of the beam. With a terrified scream, she scrambled to maintain a hold.

Zach shouted, "Kathleen…" His feet pounding on the concrete as he ran toward them.

Cal dropped the gun and mounted the beam, his only thought to get to her. His feet somehow found the rail and stayed steady as he moved toward Kathleen.

He was there in an instant, straddling the beam and hooking his feet together beneath it. The metal dug into his thighs, his ankles. He grabbed the waistband of her crop pants and gripped the base beneath him to counterbalance her weight. He gritted his teeth against the pain, his injured shoulder bearing the brunt of it. "Get your knee up on the beam, Kathleen. I won't let you fall."

With the fear of a drowning person she threw her leg up on the steel and wiggled back in place, regaining her seat. "Get me down, please, get me down." The terror in her voice was painful to hear.

His body shook with the residual effects of fear-induced adrenaline. His vision blurred for a moment as tears of relief blinded him. "We will, Rose. I promise." He kept his hands resting over hers as she hugged the beam.

"Don't let go," she begged.

"I love you, Kathleen. Not a chance."

"You okay, Kathleen?" Zach asked, the strain of the last few minutes in every syllable of the words.

"I will be."

Her hands tightened on Cal's. "I love you, Cal. Once we get down I'm going to want you to hold me for a long, long time."

"I can do that."

The lift arrived.

"Here comes the cavalry, Callahan," Zach said from just behind him.

God, if it was SWAT… "Let's hope they're the right kind. I'd like it to be the fire department. I'm not having much luck with the police lately." He looked over his shoulder as the first wave of armed men swarmed out of the lift and spread out, their rifles at their shoulders in attack stance. For one extremely tense moment they converged on Zach, ordered him to his knees, and then searched him. Finding no weapons, he was still dragged aside for questioning.

Cal found himself looking into the barrel of an automatic rifle and the flinty eyes of the guy holding it. "Show me your hands."

Really? "It's okay, Kathleen." He released his hold on her with one hand, then the other.

The officer lowered his weapon. He scooped up the pistol Cal had dropped.

Five minutes later after the lift went back down then back up, and four guys from the fire department, dressed in their yellow turnout gear, trotted out carrying rope, tackle, and a medical kit.

"Finally!" Zach's voice was filled with relief. "You finally got your wish, Cal."

THE TWO DARK-HAIRED detectives stood beside the bed. Both were in their thirties, well built, tall, though the one who'd identified himself as Hart looked like he did some serious work with weights.

The one named Buckler said, "We'd like you to come down to the station at your earliest convenience and give us a statement, Ms. O'Connor."

Their subdued attitude tweaked her curiosity. "I could write up something at home and bring it down to you. Maybe tomorrow."

The one with the rounder face, Detective Hart, gave a nod. "That would be fine."

"Your boyfriend, Cal Crowes, wouldn't be around, would he?" Detective Buckler asked. He glanced around as though Cal might be under the bed and pop out at any moment.

"Yes, he and my brother have been here all night. I think he just stepped out to get something to drink. He should be back in a minute."

A quick tap on the door and it was pushed open. "I got you a Diet Pepsi downstairs since you don't drink coffee." Cal frowned when he noticed the detectives' presence. He set a cup of ice on the hospital table and the soft drink beside it.

He faced off with the two men, and Kathleen got an impression of three bristling dogs circling each other, deciding whether they were going to fight.

Whoa!

"It seems you had a really busy night, Mr. Crowes," Detective Hart said. "A one-man rescue mission."

"Actually there were two of us. Kathleen's brother Zach was with me."

Detective Buckler shot his partner a glance. "Thanks to both of you, the two security guards are going to be fine."

"Good, I'm glad."

Kathleen closed her eyes momentarily in relief. Had it been the sound of her voice that had drawn their attention and put them in harm's way, or had they seen Hillary? She'd never know. By pleading their case, she'd probably made things worse.

"Mr. Warren wasn't so lucky," Detective Buckler said, his dark brows practically becoming a unibrow, his frown was so intense.

Cal's expression grew solemn. "That's a real shame. He had enough tragedy in his family. He deserved better."

"If I were sitting on a jury, I wouldn't be so certain about that," Buckler said. "We've uncovered a whole history of emails between him and Ms. Bryant. It seems he discovered early on how obsessive she was about him. Instead of running for cover like any other guy, he actually encouraged it with an on-again, off-again thing. Just to keep her hooked."

"It was interesting how he manipulated the information about you to build her interest and her rage on his behalf. His last email placed all the blame for his leaving Wiley on you. He said he couldn't stand to work where he would see you all the time. When in fact he'd already submitted his resignation and left right after we started investigating the email Ms. O'Connor received."

"So you're saying he used her like a loaded gun and pointed her in my direction?"

"Something like that. She had a history of going off her meds now and then. Although she was a brilliant architect. Mr. Wiley said so himself."

"But she didn't come after me."

"No. But you got the girl. He also dated other women and threw it up to her before breaking it off and going back to Hillary." He shook his head. "I think she finally realized what he'd been doing all along and that he was really leaving to avoid prosecution and she lashed out at him."

Kathleen interrupted. "She spoke to him in the kitchen as though they were having a one-sided conversation. Was he already dead then?"

"Yes. She'd buried a knife in his chest."

Kathleen flinched.

"It happened that morning, right after he spoke to you, Mr. Crowes. You wouldn't know anything about a nine-one-one call from the residence reporting a murder, would you?" Hart eyed Cal, his expression hard.

"I never made any such call. I had enough on my plate looking for Kathleen without wanting to get involved in anything else."

Hart did everything but roll his eyes.

Overwhelmed suddenly by pity, Kathleen teared up. "She truly loved him. What he did to her was monstrous."

"Yeah. It was." Though Hart didn't say it, the implication was Warren had gotten what he deserved.

But had Hillary? She'd been ill, in need of medication and support. Not the attention of a manipulative asshole. Cal moved to take her hand and give it a comforting squeeze.

"Why did she go after Kathleen?"

"Warren planted the seed that he was interested in Kathleen to make her jealous. It was a game he played with her. Hillary had it all tangled up in her head."

Buckler took over for Hart, "She was the one who had the welder unloaded in your truck. We unscrambled the paperwork. And she did try to get you arrested."

Cal raised a brow. "Thanks for solving the mystery and clearing me."

"Thanks for siccing the whole viewing public of *Harping on the Truth* on us," he said sourly.

Quick amusement flitted across Cal's face then was gone. "Kathleen almost died while you were worrying about a stupid welder."

"We thought you'd stolen it, intending to sell it. Then got cold feet and returned it. We thought whoever you'd planned to sell it to had taken Kathleen."

"Are you shitting me? Kidnapping her over a four thousand dollar welder makes no sense."

Buckler grimaced. "You'd be surprised at what people will do."

Cal shook his head. "Guys, not everyone you look at is guilty until proven innocent. In fact, I think it's supposed to be the other way around."

"Most of the time they are guilty, Mr. Crowes," Hart said, his tone suddenly tired.

"That's very sad for you, Detective," Kathleen said, meaning it.

"Had I waited for you to catch up, Kathleen might not have made it," Cal pointed out.

The detectives looked at each other. Buckler said, "We'd appreciate that statement, Ms. O'Connor, whenever you feel up to making it."

And then the two hastily excused themselves and left.

Kathleen studied Cal's features. He looked exhausted. They'd both had a hideous day yesterday, and no sleep all night between police and medical staff checking on them. She folded back the sheet and thin blanket. "Come lie with me, Cal."

"Gladly." He toed off his tennis shoes and carefully wiggled in behind her. He slid his arm under her head and the injured one in its sling over her waist. His groan of pleasure made her laugh. "I think I could sleep a week with my nose right in the crook of your neck."

Finally, she felt safe and exactly where she needed to be. "Go to sleep. We both need to rest."

"Roger that." He wiggled closer, cupping her bottom with his thighs so they could spoon. His breathing leveled out in moments and he was fast asleep.

Zach slipped into the room. His gaze went to Cal, and then to her. He sauntered to the hospital bed to face her, and bracing an arm on the raised bed rail, leaned down to whisper, "Five-O cornered me in the hall. Don't those guys ever rest?"

"They're trying to tie up loose ends." She'd tell him about everything later. But right now she was too exhausted.

He tucked a stray strand of hair back behind her ear with a fingertip. "There's never been a time I felt more helpless or useless as I did watching you hug that fucking beam, Kathleen." Zach eyes glittered suspiciously and he looked away. "If anything had happened to you…"

She curled her fingers around his and brought them in against her cheek. "I've never been so terrified in my life. But knowing you and Callahan were there made it better. I knew you'd do something."

"I've never seen anyone dance across a beam like that. Cal could have won the Olympics with those moves. He saved you, Thorn."

The moment had been terrifying for her on two levels. She'd believed they were both going to die. Kathleen's eyes glazed with tears. "Does that mean you approve?"

He paused to study Callahan. "You don't need my approval. I think you have this covered." He leaned down to press a kiss to her tender, carpet-burned forehead. "But I'll still rip his head off if he does you wrong."

Her fingers tightened around his and her heart swelled. "That's what big brothers are for."

EPILOGUE

6 Weeks Later

KATHLEEN PACED BACK and forth around Cal's denim-clad legs. The upper part of his body was hidden inside the cabinet below her sink. "I called the owner," she fretted, "and he said he called a plumber two days ago."

Cal's voice sounded muffled. "They take at least a week to show up. I have this covered, Kathleen. And I need that bucket now."

Kathleen rushed to hand it to him. He slid out of the cabinet and maneuvered it under the curved pipe he'd been loosening. With one last turn, water drained from the sink into the bucket. He removed the elbow and wrinkled his nose at what he saw inside.

Kathleen didn't want to know what might be in there.

"Popsicle stick," he ordered, holding out his hand.

Kathleen handed it to him, and he dug inside the drain elbow and dumped what he found in the bucket.

"I think it was just clogged here, but I'm going to run the snake through a short distance just to be sure." He slipped on a pair of heavy work gloves.

Kathleen checked the time again. They'd be here within the hour. "Have I told you lately how handy you are, Callahan?"

"I seem to remember you saying something to that effect last night." His blue-green eyes held an amused gleam when he glanced up at her from feeding the long coiled metal snake into the pipe.

Kathleen smiled. "I don't think I mentioned your hands at all. I was too busy concentrating on other things."

"A week is going to seem like a long time without those other things," he said.

"Mom and Dad won't be here with me the entire time. We can sneak in a few conjugal visits."

He raised his brows. "Conjugal visits. Isn't that what they call it in jail?"

"I promise not to tell my father you're bopping his baby girl, so you won't be behind bars."

Cal cocked his head. "Kathleen, we can barely keep our hands off each other. They're going to take one look at the two of us and know we've been bopping each other's brains out, but they'll ignore it, because parents have a don't ask, don't tell policy when it comes to their children's sex lives."

Kathleen laughed. "Thank God."

Cal reversed the direction and started recoiling the snake. While he finished up with the sink, Kathleen checked the guest room for the third time. After Cal dealt with the bucket of waste, she went behind him to check the bathroom.

She paused in her own room to put on lipstick. She stood in front of the mirror and studied her expression. Meeting Cal had changed her. She was more… They both were more because they completed each other.

She chose the red lipstick because she knew he loved it on her, and because of the sexual charge it always gave him. Like last night when she'd fulfilled one of his fantasies. Or so he'd said.

She returned to the kitchen to find him scrubbing out the sink and washing his hands. She pressed in tight against his back and gave his trim waist a squeeze.

"You make me happy, Callahan. That's what my parents are going to see."

Cal dried his hands on a dishtowel and turned to face her. His gaze homed in on her lips and he raised a brow.

He looped his arms around her waist. "I remember thinking on our first date that being with you made me feel lighter. You took me out of my head and back into the world. You looked at me and saw a man. Not a wounded warrior or an amputee, but just a man. I wondered later if I could be half as good for you as you are for me." He bent his head to press a kiss into her palm.

"You are, Cal. You've made me see there are men out there who can be trusted to be faithful. I didn't doubt you even when your phone was going off with all those phone calls from Harpy's show." And she could have never dealt with the issues left behind after her eight-hour ordeal with Hillary without him. They'd tackled PTSD together, and it had brought them even closer.

"We've faced more together in two months than many couples do in years. My parents are going to be a piece of cake."

The doorbell rang, and Kathleen grabbed Cal's hand and tugged him toward the living room. Cal pulled her to a stop. "I'm not worried, Rose." He bent his head and swooped in for a kiss, leaving her breathless and tingling in all the right places. "I love you."

"I love you, too. They're going to see that, Callahan." She felt confident and happy. Nothing like the woman who'd left Boston nearly three months before. And Cal was stronger since the episode with Hillary. It was as though he'd come into his own. He'd quit rubbing his head when stressed. And never had a nightmare when she stayed over.

He waited as she brushed her fingertips over his lips to remove her lipstick, then bussed her cheek with a kiss. At the second tap on the door, he gave a decisive nod. "*We* got this."

THE END

Thank you for taking the time to read Breaking Boundaries. If you enjoyed it, please consider telling your friends or posting a short review. Word of mouth is an author's best friend, and much appreciated.

Thank you, Teresa J. Reasor

New York Times and USA Today bestselling author Teresa Reasor was born in Southeastern Kentucky, but grew up a Marine Corps brat. The love of reading instilled in her in kindergarten at Parris Island, South Carolina made books her friends during the many transfers her father's military career entailed. The transition from reading to writing came easily to her, and she penned her first book in second grade. But it wasn't until 2007 that her first published work was released.

After twenty-one years as an art teacher, and ten years as a part-time college instructor, she's now retired and living her dream as a full-time writer.

Her body of work includes both full-length novels and shorter pieces in many different genres, including Military Romantic Suspense, Paranormal Romance, Fantasy Romance, Historical Romance, Contemporary Romance, and Children's Books.

BOOKS BY TERESA REASOR

BREAKING FREE
(BOOK 1 of the SEAL TEAM HEARTBREAKERS)
BREAKING THROUGH
(BOOK 2 of the SEAL TEAM HEARTBREAKERS)
BREAKING AWAY
(BOOK 3 of the SEAL TEAM HEARTBREAKERS)
BUILDING TIES
(BOOK 4 of the SEAL TEAM HEARTBREAKERS)
TIMELESS
WHISPER IN MY EAR
HIGHLAND MOONLIGHT
CAPTIVE HEARTS

SHORT STORIES
AN AUTOMATED DEATH
TO CAPTURE A HIGHLANDER'S HEART: THE BEGINNING
CAUGHT IN THE ACT

NOVELLAS
BREAKING TIES
(A SEAL TEAM HEARTBREAKERS NOVELLA)
TO CAPTURE A HIGHLANDER'S HEART: THE COURTSHIP

CHILDREN'S BOOKS
WILLY C. SPARKS: THE DRAGON WHO LOST HIS FIRE

FOR NEW RELEASES

Website:

www.teresareasor.com

Blog:

mymusesmusings.blogspot.com

Facebook:

www.facebook.com/teresa.reasor

Facebook Author Page:

www.facebook.com/SEAL.Crazy

Twitter:

twitter.com/teresareasor

Substance-B:

substance-b.com/TeresaReasor.html

Goodreads:

www.goodreads.com/author/show/2308555.Teresa_J_Reasor

Pinterest:

www.pinterest.com/teresareasor

Authors Den:

www.authorsden.com/teresajreasor

Amazon Author Page:

www.amazon.com/Teresa-Reasor/e/B0056ZRB7E

Sign up for my Newsletter:
http://bit.ly/I7TtiC

Printed in Poland
by Amazon Fulfillment
Poland Sp. z o.o., Wrocław